Chester Himes was born in 1909 in Jefferson City, Missouri. After being expelled from university he was convicted of armed robbery at the age of nineteen and sentenced to twenty to twenty-five years' hard labour. It was while in jail (he was eventually released on parole after seven and a half years) that Himes started to write, publishing stories in a number of magazines, including *Esquire*. He then took a series of manual jobs while still writing. He published his first novel, *If He Hollers Let Him Go*, in 1945. A humiliating stint as a Hollywood scriptwriter ended in his being fired on racial grounds – as he wrote later, he felt he survived undamaged the earlier disasters in his life but it was 'under the mental corrosion of race prejudice in Los Angeles I became bitter and saturated with hate'.

Himes moved to Paris in 1953: a city that he – like many African-American writers of his generation – found sympathetic and stimulating. He lived much of the rest of his life first in France and then in Spain, where he moved in 1969. A meeting with Marcel Duhamel, the editor of Gallimard's crime list, 'La Série Noire', resulted in Himes being commissioned to write what became *La Reine des pommes*, published in English in 1957 as *For Love of Imabelle* or *A Rage in Harlem*, and which won the Grand Prix de la Littérature Policière. This was the first of the Harlem novels that were to make Himes famous and was followed by further titles, each translated first into French and then published in English, including *The Real Cool Killers*, *All Shot Up*, *The Heat's On* and *Cotton Comes to Harlem*. Himes was married twice. He died in Spain in 1984.

Will Self's most recent books are *The Butt*, *Liver: A Fictional Organ with a Surface Anatomy of Four Lobes* and *Psycho Too*.

CHESTER HIMES

Cotton Comes to Harlem

With an introduction by Will Self

PENGUIN BOOKS

PENGUIN CLASSICS

Published by the Penguin Group
Penguin Books Ltd, 80 Strand, London WC2R 0RL, England
Penguin Group (USA) Inc., 375 Hudson Street, New York, New York 10014, USA
Penguin Group (Canada), 90 Eglinton Avenue East, Suite 700, Toronto, Ontario, Canada M4P 2Y3
(a division of Pearson Penguin Canada Inc.)
Penguin Ireland, 25 St Stephen's Green, Dublin 2, Ireland (a division of Penguin Books Ltd)
Penguin Group (Australia), 250 Camberwell Road, Camberwell, Victoria 3124, Australia
(a division of Pearson Australia Group Pty Ltd)
Penguin Books India Pvt Ltd, 11 Community Centre, Panchsheel Park, New Delhi – 110 017, India
Penguin Group (NZ), 67 Apollo Drive, Rosedale, North Shore 0632, New Zealand
(a division of Pearson New Zealand Ltd)
Penguin Books (South Africa) (Pty) Ltd, 24 Sturdee Avenue, Rosebank, Johannesburg 2196, South Africa

Penguin Books Ltd, Registered Offices: 80 Strand, London WC2R 0RL, England

www.penguin.com

First published in France as *Retour en Afrique* in 1964 and in the USA as *Cotton Comes to Harlem* in 1965
Published in Penguin Classics 2011

1

Copyright © Chester Himes, 1965
Introduction Copyright © Will Self, 2011
All rights reserved

The moral right of the introducer has been asserted

Set in 11.25/14 pt Monotype Dante
Typeset by Ellipsis Digital Limited, Glasgow
Printed in England by Clays Ltd, St Ives plc

978-0-141-19645-9

www.greenpenguin.co.uk

Introduction

Somewhere in the strange and dusty melting pot of my family's book collection – my father was a Trollopian Englishman, my mother a Bellovian New Yorker – there were a number of Chester Himes's Harlem novels. I read them all, but the one I remember best you now hold in your hand. I suspect *Cotton Comes to Harlem* stayed with me partly because the copy we had was an old paperback edition with a lurid photographic cover showing a semi-naked mixed-race woman draping her long arms around the neck of a man whose head is incongruously sheathed in a brown paper bag – the kind used in American grocery stores. A nickel-plated automatic was somewhere in the frame as well – I like to think it was loaded.

There were also mouth- and eye-holes cut in the brown paper which were large enough to reveal the race of the bagged man; not that these were required, because he was also naked from the neck down – for, once the text was read, the bagged man was revealed to be none other than the hapless detective assigned to guard Iris O'Hara, the beautiful 'high-yellow' wife of Deke O'Hara (aka Reverend Deke O'Malley), the fraudster at the boiling eye of this cyclone of a thriller. The scene in which Iris strips naked to taunt her guard, then forces him to disrobe before donning a paper bag to hide his face if he wants to have sex with her, is written in Himes's characteristically phantasmagorical prose, and has the titillating elements any teenage boy – black, white or otherwise – would find compelling: a sexually knowing, lustful woman humiliating an ugly and incompetent male.

When I first read *Cotton Comes to Harlem* I thought, what? The sex scenes aroused me, the violence thrilled me, the jive-talk amused me – but I was decades away from appreciating the exact mapping of racial politics that Himes had threaded through the apparently haphazard labyrinth of its plot. True, I was already a precocious reader of American *noir*: the affectless psychopathy of Richard Stark and Jim Thomson, the maudlin *weltschmerz* of Raymond Chandler and the crypto-communist mysticism of Dashiell Hammett – but while I could see that Himes's Harlem had affinities with these other fictional landscapes, I lacked the elevation to grasp that the northernmost tip of Manhattan was no island cut off from the main, but rather integral to an understanding of twentieth-century America. Rereading the novel over thirty years later I am struck by the wild disjunction between its form and its function.

The parental paperback was probably published to coincide with the blaxploitation movie adaptation of *Cotton Comes to Harlem* released in 1972; certainly its cover graphic implied a certain joyful ease to interracial coupling; the woman's expression was happily seductive rather than manipulative, the paper bag could've been a kinky prop. Actually, the seven years that separated book from film had seen a convulsion in US race relations, and while it would be ridiculous to say that the US of the early seventies was an integrated society, African-American enfranchisement south of the Mason–Dixon Line and school integration countrywide were facts achieved on the ground.

But the America in which Deke O'Hara perpetrates his 'Back-to-Africa' scam, and Colonel Calhoun attempts to lure 'nigras' back to the cotton plantations of the Southland is recognizably the same place where Marcus Garvey was fitted up by the FBI for mail fraud and the trees along the Alabama turnpikes were hung with Billie Holiday's strange and putrescent fruit. When Himes chooses to humiliate a white man by stripping him naked and putting a paper bag on his head, the unmistakeable evocation is of Ralph Ellison's anti-antihero, the eponymous *Invisible Man* (1952). See how you like it? Himes seems to be saying, See how you like it when your race – upon which you rely for your specious sense of superiority – is taken from you and replaced by something as featureless as a brown paper bag.

Himes was undoubtedly an important writer when it came to crime – after all, he knew a great deal more about the sharp end of criminality than his peers (with the exception of Hammett, who had worked as a Pinkerton detective). Himes was the original prison writer; his first stories were published in *Esquire* in 1934 when he was serving a twenty to twenty-five year sentence for armed robbery, and appeared under his prison number – 59623 – but his was a curious kind of gutter love: he reverenced the street, but was by no means of it. The child of academic parents, Himes was being university educated until he dropped out into petty crime. He famously led his fellow students from a celebratory dinner for their – all-black – fraternity at the University of Ohio to a nearby brothel.

As a member of the very small African-American middle class of the early twentieth century, Himes was caught in the absurd position of looking down on the masses from a great height, while simultaneously being looked down on from an even greater one. He may have finished with crime after his arrest at the age of nineteen, but like many other black American intellectuals of the first half of the era – Richard Wright, James Baldwin – he remained an outsider, and after the frustrating war years in Los Angeles, where he was debarred from screenwriting by the endemic racism of the industry, he opted for geographical exile in France, and it was here that he spent much of the 1950s, and here too, aged forty-seven, that he began work on the Harlem series of novels that made his name.

Himes had already published five other books, but while some might argue that these conformed to what James Baldwin dismissively termed 'sociology' (when attacking Himes's mentor, Wright, in his essay 'Everybody's Protest Novel'), the elements of his mature Harlem style were already in evidence: the juxtapositions of kaleidoscopic, polychromatic fantasy and harshly monochrome reality; the wiseacre repartee and the dialectics of desperation. (Himes had been on the fringes of the Communist Party during his time in California.) However, it's only when Himes's ace detectives, Coffin Ed Johnson and Grave Digger Jones, came on stage that his ability to block out the *danse macabre* of racism took on a new and troubling vigour. As Himes said himself in the second of his two soul-searching memoirs, *My Life of Absurdity*, 'I thought I was writing realism. It never occurred to me that I was writing absurdity. Realism and absurdity are so similar in the lives of American blacks one cannot tell the difference.'

I think we should take Himes's Harlem novels at their author's own estimation: the brilliance of the books – and of *Cotton Comes to Harlem* in particular – lies in their pinpoint realism: the details of clothing, food and cars – the accuracy with which the characters move around the city, and the intensely evoked sensorium of impoverished urban life: 'The first thing that hit the detectives when they entered the dimly lit downstairs hallway was the smell of urine. "What American slums need is toilets," Coffin Ed said.' That this realism should take on the character of a nightmare is purely a function of the emotional landscape these physical objects and sensations occupy, one in which a few gradations of skin pigmentation either this way or that could determine a man or woman's entire fate. Coffin Ed and Grave Digger embody the starkness of this chromatic destiny: they are upholders of the law, and respected as such by the black Harlemites, but at the same time they are working for the Man – and so deeply suspect. Of course, this Janus-faced position (one chillingly emphasized by their actual physiognomies – Coffin Ed's acid-burned face, Grave Digger's scarred and lumpy head) is mirrored by the attitude of the white authorities who depend on them to keep order. Thus his protagonists' situation is a recapitulation of Himes's own – and this, too, gives the books an additional *vérité* bite; Raymond Chandler hymned the crime-fighting antiheroes of American *noir* as men who 'must walk these mean streets alone'; men whose ambiguous class position allowed them to reject a corrupt institutional morality – in *Cotton Comes to Harlem* Himes states his version of this job description with characteristic pith: 'Everyone has to believe in something; and the white people of America had left them nothing to believe in. But that didn't make a black man any less criminal than a white.'

But while Chandler never got much beyond a cod-anarchic griping at the plutocracy of Southern California, Himes's writing has acute political savvy. As I said, *Cotton Comes to Harlem* occupies recognizably the same milieu as Ellison's *Invisible Man* – or for that matter *Black Like Me* (1961), that bizarre exercise in reportage in which a white journalist, John Howard Griffin, disguised himself as a black man and travelled the byways of the American South in order to experience racism at first hand. But Himes's Harlem, while a microcosm of America, is also a city in its own right, with its own class gradations and political tendencies. The Reverend O'Malley's 'Back-to-Africa' movement may be model-led on Marcus Garvey's 'Black Star Line' of the 1900s, but a half-century on Himes seems to be saying that the fissiparous implications of Garveyite separatism have come to full fruition.

One of the most politically savvy moments in *Cotton Comes to Harlem* occurs when the two detectives face down a riot mounted by Black Muslim separatists against the racist Calhoun's Southland movement. Himes describes the banners lofted by the Muslims: 'WHITE PEOPLE EAT DOG . . . ALLAH IS GOD . . . BLACK MEN UNITE', and then beside a platform set up for speakers there was 'an open black coffin with a legend: *The Remains of Lumumba*. The coffin contained pictures of Lumumba in life and in death; a black suit said to have been worn by him when he was killed; and other mementoes said to have belonged to him in life. Bordering the sidewalk on removable flagstaffs were the flags of all the nations of black Africa.'

There is so much subtlety and ambiguity bound up in this one paragraph: like the nascent Nation of Islam, Garvey's separatism had more strategic common ground with the Ku Klux Klan (he personally met with the Grand Wizard on more than one occasion) than it did with the integrationist NAACP (National Association for the Advancement of Coloured People). Lumumba, the leader of independent Congo, had been assassinated by Congolese proxies of Belgium, the former colonial power – although this was not fully known at the time Himes was writing. Overall, there is a profound scepticism here: in the future of a decolonized Africa, in the comity of black people in general; all political aspiration – Himes seems to be saying – ends in base populism, while all political careers, no matter how principled, end in failure, corruption, or – which is possibly worse – martyrdom and its cheesy hagiographic afterlife.

And if Himes is politically astute, then he is equally sexually politicised – albeit not in a very correct fashion. The omnivorous and vain Iris O'Malley expresses both the rage and the self-hatred of African Americans whose 'othering' by whites consisted in large part in the equation of their sexuality with the animalistic. At one point in *Cotton Comes to Harlem* Iris expresses a desire to rape a violent hoodlum; at another juncture she experiences a spontaneous orgasm when held at gunpoint; then there's her humiliation of the nameless white detective who is left floundering, naked and bagged under the mocking eyes of his colleagues. Surely this is a considered inversion on Himes's part, a lustful man lynched by ridicule, just as Iris's overpowering sexuality and homicidal jealousy represent her absorption of all the calumnies heaped on her and her people then ejaculated back.

In the final shootout at the Star of Ham, Deke O'Malley's church on 121st Street, Grave Digger fires tracer bullets at black thugs setting the pulpits aflame – and this *Götterdämmerung* can serve as representative of Himes's fictional method whereby streaks of searing illumination lead unstoppably to satiric immolation. Himes may have denied the absurdism of his work, yet he belongs with those great demented realists – with Jonathan Swift, with Nathanael West, with Samuel Beckett – whose writing pitilessly exposes the ridiculousness of the human condition.

Wilf Self

The voice from the sound truck said:

'Each family, no matter how big it is, will be asked to put up one thousand dollars. You will get your transportation free, five acres of fertile land in Africa, a mule and a plow and all the seed you need, free. Cows, pigs and chickens cost extra, but at the minimum. No profit on this deal.'

A sea of dark faces wavered before the speaker's long table, rapturous and intent.

'Ain't it wonderful, honey?' said a big black woman with eyes like stars. 'We're going back to Africa.'

Her tall lean husband shook his head in awe. 'After all these four hundred years.'

'Here I is been cooking in white folk's kitchens for more than thirty years. Lord, can it be true?' A stooped old woman voiced a lingering doubt.

The smooth brown speaker with the honest eyes and earnest face heard her. 'It's true all right,' he said. 'Just step right up and give us the particulars and deposit your thousand dollars and you'll have a place on the first boat going over.'

A grumpy old man with a head of white hair shuffled forward to fill out a form and deposit his thousand dollars, muttering to himself, 'It sure took long enough.'

The two pretty black girls taking applications looked up with dazzling smiles.

'Look how long it took the Jews to get out of Egypt,' one said.

'The hand of God is slow but sure,' said the other.

It was a big night in the lives of all these assembled colored people. Now at last, after months of flaming denouncements of the injustice and hypocrisy of white people, hurled from the pulpit of his church; after months of eulogy heaped upon the holy land of Africa, young Reverend Deke O'Malley was at last putting words into action. Tonight he was signing up the people to go on his three ships back to Africa. Huge hand-drawings of the ships stood in prominent view behind the speaker's table, appearing to have the size and design of the *SS Queen Elizabeth*. Before them stood Reverend O'Malley, his tall lithe body clad in dark summer worsted, his fresh handsome face exuding benign authority and inspiring total confidence, flanked by his secretaries and the two young men most active in recruiting applicants.

A vacant lot in the 'Valley' of Harlem near the railroad tracks, where slum tenements had been razed for a new housing development, had been taken over for the occasion. More than a thousand people milled about the patches of old, uneven concrete amid the baked, cindery earth littered with stones, piles of rubbish, dog droppings, broken glass, scattered rags and clusters of stinkweed.

The hot summer night was lit by flashes of sheet lightning, threatening rain, and the air was oppressive with dust, density and motor fumes. Stink drifted from the surrounding slums, now more overcrowded than ever due to the relocation of families from the site of the new buildings to be erected to relieve the overcrowding. But nothing troubled the jubilance of these dark people filled with faith and hope.

The meeting was well organized. The speaker's table stood at

one end, draped with a banner reading: BACK TO AFRICA –
LAST CHANCE!!! Behind it, beside the drawings of the ships,
stood an armored truck, its back doors open, flanked by two
black guards wearing khaki uniforms and side arms. To the other
side stood the sound truck with amplifiers atop. Tee-shirted
young men in tight-fitting jeans roamed about with solemn,
unsmiling expressions, swelled with a sense of importance ready
to eject any doubters.

But for many of these true-believers it was also a picnic. Bottles
of wine, beer and whisky were passed about. Here and there a
soul-brother cut a dance step. White teeth flashed in black,
laughing faces. Eyes spoke. Bodies promised. They were all
charged with anticipation.

A pit had been dug in the center of the lot, housing a charcoal
fire covered with an iron grill. Rows of pork ribs were slowly
cooking on the grill, dripping fat into the hot coals with a sizzling
of pungent smoke, turned from time to time by four 'hook-men'
with long iron hooks. A white-uniformed chef with a long-
handled ladle basted the ribs with hot sauce as they cooked,
supervising the turning, his tall white chef's cap bobbing over
his sweating black face. Two matronly women clad in white
nurses' uniforms sat at a kitchen table, placing the cooked ribs
into paper plates, adding bread and potato salad, and selling them
for one dollar a serving.

The tempting, tantalizing smell of barbecued ribs rose in the
air above the stink. Shirt-sleeved men, thinly clad women and
half-naked children jostled each other good-naturedly, eating the
spicy meat and dropping the bones underfoot.

Above the din of transistor radios broadcasting the night's
baseball games, and the bursts of laughter, the sudden shrieks,
the other loud voices, came the blaring voice of Reverend Deke
O'Malley from the sound truck: 'Africa is our native land and we

are going back. No more picking cotton for the white folks and living on fatback and corn pone . . .'

'Yea, baby, yea.'

'See that sign,' Reverend O'Malley shouted, pointing to a large wooden sign against the wire fence which proclaimed that the low-rent housing development to be erected on that site would be completed within two and one half years, and listed the prices of the apartments, which no family among those assembled there could afford to pay. 'Two years you have to wait to move into some boxes – if you can get in, and if you can pay the high rent after you get in. By that time you will be harvesting your second crop in Africa, living in warm sunny houses where the only fire you'll ever need will be for cooking, where we'll have our own governments and our own rulers – *black*, like us –'

'I hear you, baby, I hear you.'

The thousand-dollar subscriptions poured in. The starry-eyed black people were putting their chips on hope. One after another they went forward solemnly and put down their thousand dollars and signed on the dotted line. The armed guards took the money and stacked it carefully into an open safe in the armored truck.

'How many?' Reverend O'Malley asked one of his secretaries in a whisper.

'Eighty-seven,' she whispered in reply.

'Tonight might be your last chance,' Reverend O'Malley said over the amplifiers. 'Next week I must go elsewhere and give all of our brothers a chance to return to our native land. God said the meek shall inherit the earth; we have been meek long enough; now we shall come into our inheritance.'

'Amen, Reverend! Amen!'

Sad-eyed Puerto Ricans from nearby Spanish Harlem and the lost and hungry black people from black Harlem who didn't have the thousand dollars to return to their native land congregated outside the high wire fence, smelling the tantalizing barbecue, dreaming of the day when they could also go back home in triumph and contentment.

'Who's that man?' one of them asked.

'Child, he's the young Communist Christian preacher who's going to take our folks back to Africa.'

A police cruiser was parked at the curb. Two white cops in the front seat cast sour looks over the assemblage.

'Where you think they got a permit for this meeting?'

'Search me. Lieutenant Anderson said leave them alone.'

'This country is being run by niggers.'

They lit cigarettes and smoked in sullen silence.

Inside the fence, three colored cops patrolled the assemblage, swapping jokes with their soul-brothers, exchanging grins, relaxed and friendly.

During a lull in the speaker's voice, two big colored men in dark rumpled suits approached the speaker's table. Bulges from pistols in shoulder slings showed beneath their coats. The guards of the armored truck became alert. The two young recruiting agents, flanking the table, pushed back their chairs.

But the two big men were polite and smiled easily.

'We're detectives from the D.A.'s office,' one said to O'Malley apologetically, as both presented their identifications. 'We have orders to bring you in for questioning.'

The two young recruiting agents came to their feet, tense and angry.

'These white mothers can't let us alone,' one said. 'Now they're using our brothers against us.'

Reverend O'Malley waved them down and spoke to the detectives, 'Have you got a warrant?'

'No, but it would save you a lot of trouble if you came peacefully.'

The second detective added, 'You can take your time and finish with your people, but I'd advise you to talk to the D.A.'

'All right,' Reverend O'Malley said calmly. 'Later.'

The detectives moved to one side. Everyone relaxed. One of the recruiting agents ordered a serving of barbecue.

For a moment attention was centered on a meat delivery truck which had entered the lot. It had been passed by the zealous volunteers guarding the gate.

'You're just in time, boy,' the black chef called to the white driver as the truck approached. 'We're running out of ribs.'

A flash of lightning spotlighted the grinning faces of the two white men on the front seat.

'Wait 'til we turn around, boss,' the driver's helper called in a southern voice.

The truck went forward towards the speaker's table. Eyes watched it indifferently. The truck turned, backed, gently plowing a path through the milling mob.

Ignoring the slight commotion, Reverend O'Malley continued speaking from the amplifiers: 'These damn southern white folks have worked us like dogs for four hundred years and when we ask them to pay off, they ship us up to the North . . .'

'Ain't it the truth!' a sister shouted.

'And these damn northern white folks don't want us –' But he never finished. He broke off in mid-sentence at the sight of two masked white men stepping from the back of the meat delivery truck with two black deadly-looking submachine guns in their hands. 'Unh!!!' he grunted as though someone had hit him in the stomach.

For the brief instant following, silence reigned. The scene became a tableau of suspended motion. Eyes were riveted on the black holes of death at the front ends of the machine guns. Muscles became paralysed. Brains stopped thinking.

Then a voice that sounded as though it had come from the backwoods of Mississippi said thickly: 'Everybody freeze an' nobody'll git hurt.'

The black men guarding the armored truck raised their hands in reflex action. Black faces broke out with a rash of white eyes. Reverend Deke O'Malley slid quickly beneath the table. The two big colored detectives froze as ordered.

But the young recruiting agent at the left end of the table, who was taking a bite of barbecue, saw his dream vanishing and reached towards his hip pocket for his pistol.

There was a burst from a machine gun. A mixture of teeth, barbecued pork ribs, and human brains flew through the air like macabre birds. A woman screamed. The young man, with half a head gone, sank down out of sight.

The Mississippi voice said furiously: 'Goddamn stupid mother-raper!'

The softer southern voice of the gunner said defensively, 'He was drawing.'

'Mother-rape it! Git the money, let's git going.' The big heavy white man with his black mask slowly moved the black-holed muzzle of his submachine gun over the crowd like the nozzle of a fire hose, saying, 'Doan git daid.'

Bodies remained rigid, eyes riveted, necks frozen, heads stationary, but there was a general movement away from the gun as though the earth itself were moving. Behind, among the people at the rear, panic began exploding like Chinese firecrackers.

The driver's helper got out from the front seat, waving another submachine gun, and the black people melted away.

The two sullen cops in the police cruiser jumped out and rushed to the fence, trying to see what was happening. But all they could see was a strange milling movement of black people.

The three colored cops inside, pistols drawn, were struggling forward against a tide of human flesh, but being slowly washed away.

The second machine-gunner, who had fired the burst, slung his gun over his shoulder, rushed towards the armored truck and began scooping money into a 'gunny-sack'.

'Merciful Jesus,' a woman wailed.

The black guards backed away, arms elevated, and let the white men take the money. Deke remained unseen beneath the table. All that was seen of the dead young man were some teeth still bleeding on the table, before the horrified eyes of the two young secretaries. The colored detectives hadn't breathed.

Outside the fence the cops rushed back to their cruiser. The motor caught, roared; the siren coughed, groaned, began screaming as the car went into a U-turn in the middle of the block heading back towards the gate.

The colored cops on the inside began shooting into the air, trying to clear a path, but only increased the pandemonium. A black tidal wave went over them as from a hurricane.

The white machine-gunner got all of the money – all $87,000 – and jumped into the back of the delivery truck. The motor roared. The other machine-gunner followed the first and slammed shut the back door. The driver's helper climbed in just as the car took off.

The police cruiser came in through the gate, siren screaming, as though black people were invisible. A fat black man flew through the air like an over-inflated football. A fender bumped a woman's bottom and started her spinning like a whirling dervish. People scattered, split, diving, jumping, running to get out of the cruiser's path, colliding and knocking one another down.

But a path was made for the rapidly accelerating meat delivery truck. The cops looked at the driver and his helper as they passed.

The two white men looked back, exchanging white looks. The cops went ahead, looking for colored criminals. The white machine-gunners got away.

The two black guards climbed into the front seat of the armored truck. The two colored detectives jumped on the running-boards, pistols in their hands. Deke came out from underneath the table and climbed into the back, beside the empty safe. The motor came instantly to life, sounding for all the world like a big Cadillac engine with four hundred horse-power. The armored truck backed, filled, pointed towards the gate, then hesitated.

'You want I should follow them?' the driver asked.

'Get 'em, goddammit. Run 'em down!' one of the colored detectives grated.

The driver hesitated a moment longer. 'They're armed for bear.'

'Bear ass!' the detective shouted. 'They're getting away, mother!'

There was a glimpse of gray paint as the meat delivery truck went past a taxi on Lexington Avenue, headed north.

The big engine of the armored truck roared; the truck jumped. The police cruiser wheeled to head it off. A woman wild with fright ran in front of it. The car slewed to miss her and ran head-on into the barbecue pit. Steam rose from the bursted radiator pouring on to the hot coals. A sudden flash of lightning lit the wild stampede of running people, seen through the cloud of steam.

'Great Godamighty, the earth's busted open,' a voice cried.

'An' let out all hell,' came the reply.

'Halt or I'll shoot,' a cop cried, climbing from the smoking ruins.

It was the same as talking to the lightning.

The armored truck bulldozed a path to the gate, urged on by a voice shouting, 'Go get 'em, go get 'em.'

It turned into Lexington on screaming tyres. The off-side detective fell off to the street, but they didn't stop for him. A roll of thunder blended with the motor sound as the big engine gathered speed, and another police cruiser fell in behind.

O'Malley tapped on the window separating the front seat from the rear compartment and passed an automatic rifle and a sawed-off shotgun to the guard. The remaining detective on the inside running-board was squatting low, holding on with his left hand and gripping a Colt .45 automatic in his right.

The armored truck was going faster than any armored truck ever seen before or since. The red light showed at 125th Street and a big diesel truck was coming from the west. The armored truck went through the red and passed in front of that big truck as close as a barber's shave.

A joker standing on the corner shouted jubilantly, 'Gawawwwed damn! Them mothers got it.'

The police cruiser stopped for the truck to pass.

'And gone!' the joker added.

The driver urged greater speed from the big laboring motor, 'Get your ass to moving.' But the meat delivery truck had got out of sight. The scream of the police siren was fading in the past.

The meat delivery truck turned left on 137th Street. In turning the back door was flung open and a bale of cotton slid slowly from the clutching hands of the two white machine-gunners and fell into the street. The truck dragged to a screaming sidewise stop and began backing up. But at that moment the armored truck came roaring around the corner like destiny coming on. The meat delivery truck reversed directions without a break in motion and took off again as though it had wings.

From inside the delivery truck came a red burst of machine-gun fire and the bullet-proof windshield of the armored truck was suddenly filled with stars, partly obscuring the driver's vision. He narrowly missed the bale of cotton, thinking he must have d.t.'s.

The guard was trying to get the muzzle of his rifle through a gun slot in the windshield when another burst of machine-gun fire came from the delivery truck and its back doors were slammed shut. No one noticed the detective on the running-board of the armored truck suddenly disappear. One moment he was there, the next he was gone.

The colored people on the tenement stoops, seeking relief from the hot night, began running over one another to get indoors. Some dove into the basement entrances beneath the stairs.

One loudmouthed comic shouted from the safety below the level of the sidewalk, 'Harlem Hospital straight ahead.'

From across the street another loudmouth shouted back, 'Morgue comes first.'

The meat delivery truck was gaining on the armored truck. It must have been powered to keep meat fresh from Texas.

From far behind came the faint sound of the scream of the siren from the police cruiser, seeming to cry, 'Wait for me!'

Lightning flashed. Before the sound of thunder was heard, rain came down in torrents.

2

'Well, kiss my foot if it isn't Jones,' Lieutenant Anderson exclaimed, rising from behind the captain's desk to extend his hand to his ace detectives. Slang sounded as phony as a copper's smile coming from his lips, but the warm smile lighting his thin pale face and the twinkle in his deep-set blue eyes squared it. 'Welcome home.'

Grave Digger Jones squeezed the small white hand in his own big, calloused paw and grinned. 'You need to get out in the sun, Lieutenant, 'fore someone takes you for a ghost,' he said as though continuing a conversation from the night before instead of a six months' interim.

The lieutenant eased back into his seat and stared at Grave Digger appraisingly. The upward glow from the green-shaded desk lamp gave his face a gangrenous hue.

'Same old Jones,' he said. 'We've been missing you, man.'

'Can't keep a good man down,' Coffin Ed Johnson said from behind.

It was Grave Digger's first night back on duty since he had been shot up by one of Benny Mason's hired guns in the caper resulting from the loss of a shipment of heroin. He had been in the hospital for three months fighting a running battle with death, and he had spent three months at home convalescing. Other than for the bullet scars hidden beneath his clothes and the finger-size scar obliterating the hairline at the base of his skull where the first bullet had burned off the hair, he looked much the same. Same dark brown lumpy face with the slowly smoldering reddish-brown eyes; same big, rugged, loosely knit frame of a day laborer in a steel mill; same dark, battered felt hat worn summer and winter perched on the back of his head; same rusty black alpaca suit showing the bulge of the long-barreled, nickel-plated, brass-lined .38 revolver on a .44 frame made to his own specifications resting in its left-side shoulder sling. As far back as Lieutenant Anderson could remember, both of them, his two ace detectives with their identical big hard-shooting, head-whipping pistols, had always looked like two hog farmers on a weekend in the Big Town.

'I just hope it hasn't left you on the quick side,' Lieutenant Anderson said softly.

Coffin Ed's acid-scarred face twitched slightly, the patches of grafted skin changing shape. 'I dig you, Lieutenant,' he said gruffly. 'You mean on the quick side like me.' His jaw knotted as he paused to swallow. 'Better to be quick than dead.'

The lieutenant turned to stare at him, but Grave Digger looked straight ahead. Four years previous a hoodlum had thrown a glass of acid into Coffin Ed's face. Afterwards he had earned the reputation of being quick on the trigger.

'You don't have to apologize,' Grave Digger said roughly. 'You're not getting paid to get killed.'

In the green light Lieutenant Anderson's face turned slightly purple. 'Well, hell,' he said defensively. 'I'm on your side. I know what you're up against here in Harlem. I know your beat. It's my beat too. But the commissioner feels you've killed too many people in this area –' He held up his hand to ward off an interruption. 'Hoodlums, I know – dangerous hoodlums – and you killed in self-defence. But you've been on the carpet a number of times and a short time ago you had three months' suspensions. Newspapers have been yapping about police brutality in Harlem and now various civic bodies have taken up the cry.'

'It's the white men on the force who commit the pointless brutality,' Coffin Ed grated. 'Digger and me ain't trying to play tough.'

'We are tough,' Grave Digger said.

Lieutenant Anderson shifted the papers on the desk and looked down at his hands. 'Yes, I know, but they're going to drop it on you two – if they can. You know that as well as I do. All I'm asking is to play it safe, from the police side. Don't take any chances, don't make any arrests until you have the evidence, don't use force unless in self-defence, and above all don't shoot anyone unless it's the last resort.'

'And let the criminals go,' Coffin Ed said.

'The commissioner feels there must be some other way to curtail crime besides brute force,' the lieutenant said, his blush deepening.

'Well, tell him to come up here and show us,' Coffin Ed said.

The arteries stood out in Grave Digger's swollen neck and his voice came out cotton dry. 'We got the highest crime rate on earth among the colored people in Harlem. And there ain't but three things to do about it: Make the criminals pay for it – you don't want to do that; pay the people enough to live decently – you ain't going to do that; so all that's left is let 'em eat one another up.'

A sudden blast of noise poured in from the booking room – shouts, curses, voices lifted in anger, women screaming, whines of protest, the scuffling of many feet – as a wagon emptied its haul from a raid on a whore-house where drugs were peddled.

The intercom on the desk spoke suddenly: 'Lieutenant, you're wanted out here on the desk; they've knocked over Big Liz's circus house.'

The lieutenant flicked the switch. 'In a few minutes, and for Christ's sake keep them quiet.'

He then looked from one detective to the other. 'What the hell's going on today? It's only ten o'clock in the evening and judging from the reports it's been going on like this since morning.' He leafed through the reports, reading charges: 'Man kills his wife with an axe for burning his breakfast pork chop . . . man shoots another man demonstrating a recent shooting he had witnessed . . . man stabs another man for spilling beer on his new suit . . . man kills self in a bar playing Russian roulette with a .32 revolver . . . woman stabs man in stomach fourteen times, no reason given . . . woman scalds neighboring woman with pot of boiling water for speaking to her husband . . . man arrested for threatening to blow up subway train because he entered wrong station and couldn't get his token back –'

'All colored citizens,' Coffin Ed interrupted.

Anderson ignored it. 'Man sees stranger wearing his own new suit, slashes him with a razor.' he read on. 'Man dressed as Cherokee Indian splits white bartender's skull with homemade tomahawk . . . man arrested on Seventh Avenue for hunting cats with hound dog and shotgun . . . twenty-five men arrested for trying to chase all the white people out of Harlem –'

'It's Independence Day,' Grave Digger interrupted.

'*Independence Day!*' Lieutenant Anderson echoed, taking a long, deep breath. He pushed away the reports and pulled a memo from the corner clip of the blotter. 'Well, here's your assignment – from the captain.'

Grave Digger perched a ham on the edge of the desk and cocked his head; but Coffin Ed backed against the wall into the shadow to hide his face, as was his habit when he expected the unexpected.

'You're to cover Deke O'Hara,' Anderson read.

The two colored detectives stared at him, alert but unquestioning, waiting for him to go on and give the handle to the joke.

'He was released ten months ago from the federal prison in Atlanta.'

'As who in Harlem doesn't know,' Grave Digger said drily.

'Many people don't know that ex-con Deke O'Hara is Reverend Deke O'Malley, leader of the new Back-to-Africa movement.'

'All right, omit the squares.'

'He's on the spot; the syndicate has voted to kill him,' Anderson said as if imparting information.

'Bullshit,' Grave Digger said bluntly. 'If the syndicate had wanted to kill him, he'd be decomposed by now.'

'Maybe.'

'What *maybe*? You could find a dozen punks in Harlem who'd kill him for a C-note.'

'O'Malley's not that easy to kill.'

'Anybody's easy to kill,' Coffin Ed stated. 'That's why we police wear pistols.'

'I don't dig this,' Grave Digger said, slapping his right thigh absentmindedly. 'Here's a rat who stooled on his former policy racketeer bosses, got thirteen indicted by the federal grand jury – even one of us, Lieutenant Brandon over in Brooklyn –'

'There's always one black bean,' Lieutenant Anderson said unwittingly.

Grave Digger stared at him. 'Damn right,' he said flatly.

Anderson blushed. 'I didn't mean it the way you're thinking.'

'I know how you meant it, but you don't know how I'm thinking.'

'Well, how are you thinking?'

'I'm thinking do you know why he did it?'

'For the reward,' Anderson said.

'Yeah, that's why. This world is full of people who will do anything for enough money. He thought he was going to get a half million bucks as the ten per cent reward for exposing tax cheats. He told how they'd swindled the government out of over five million in taxes. Seven out of thirteen went to prison; even the rat himself. He was doing so much squealing he confessed he hadn't paid any taxes either. So he got sent down too. He did thirty-one months and now he's out. I don't know how much Judas money he got.'

'About fifty grand,' Lieutenant Anderson said. 'He's put it all in his setup.'

'Digger and me could use fifty G's, but we're cops. If we squeal it all goes on the old pay cheque,' Coffin Ed said from the shadows.

'Let's not worry about that,' Lieutenant Anderson said impatiently. 'The point is to keep him alive.'

'Yeah, the syndicate's out to kill him, poor little rat,' Grave Digger said. 'I heard all about it. They were saying, "O'Malley may run but he can't hide." O'Malley didn't run and all the hiding he's been doing is behind the Bible. But he isn't dead. So what I would like to know is how all of a sudden he got important enough for a police cover when the syndicate had ten months to make the hit if they had wanted to.'

'Well, for one thing, the people here in Harlem, responsible people, the pastors and race leaders and politicians and such, believe he's doing a lot of good for the community. He paid off the mortgage on an old church and started this new Back-to-Africa movement –'

'The original Back-to-Africa movement denies him,' Coffin Ed interrupted.

'– and people have been pestering the commissioner to give him police protection because of his following. They've convinced the commissioner that there'll be a race riot if any white gunmen from downtown come up here and kill him.'

'Do you believe that, Lieutenant? Do you believe they've convinced the commissioner of that crap? That the syndicate's out to kill him after ten months?'

'Maybe it took these citizens that long to find out how useful he is to the community,' Anderson said.

'That's one thing,' Grave Digger conceded. 'What are some other things?'

'The commissioner didn't say. He doesn't always take me and the captain into his confidence,' the lieutenant said with slight sarcasm.

'Only when he's having nightmares about Digger and me shooting down all these innocent people,' Coffin Ed said.

'"*Ours not to reason why, ours but to do or die,*"' Anderson quoted.

'Those days are gone forever,' Grave Digger said. 'Wait until the next war and tell somebody that.'

'Well, let's get down to business,' Lieutenant Anderson said. 'O'Malley is co-operating with us.'

'Why shouldn't he? It's not costing him anything and it might save his life. O'Malley's a rat, but he's not a fool.'

'I'm going to feel downright ashamed nursemaiding that ex-con,' Coffin Ed said.

'Orders are orders,' Anderson said. 'And maybe it's not going to be like you think.'

'I just don't want anybody to tell me that crime doesn't pay,' Grave Digger said and stood up.

'You know the story about the prodigal son,' Anderson said.

'Yeah, I know it. But do you know the story about the fatted calf?'

'What about the fatted calf?'

'When the prodigal son returned, they couldn't find the fatted calf. They looked high and low and finally had to give up. So they went to the prodigal son to apologize, but when they saw how fat he'd gotten to be, they killed him and ate him in the place of the fatted calf.'

'Yes, but just don't let that happen to our prodigal son,' Anderson warned them unsmilingly.

At that instant the telephone rang. Lieutenant Anderson picked up the receiver.

A big happy voice said, '*Captain?*'

'*Lieutenant.*'

'Well, who ever you is, I just want to tell you that the earth has busted open and all hell's got loose over here,' and he gave the address where the Back-to-Africa rally had taken place.

3

'And then Jesus say, "John, the only thing worse than a two-timing woman is a two-timing man."'

'Jesus say that? Ain't it the truth?'

They were standing in the dim light directly in front of the huge brick front of the Abyssinian Baptist Church. The man was telling the woman about a dream he'd had the night before. In this dream he'd had a long conversation with Jesus Christ.

He was a nondescript-looking man with black and white striped suspenders draped over a blue sport shirt and buttoned to old-fashioned wide-legged dark brown pants. He looked like the born victim of a cheating wife.

But one could tell she was strictly a church sister by the prissy way she kept pursing up her mouth. One could tell right off that her soul was really saved. She was wearing a big black skirt and a lavender blouse and her lips pursed and her face shone with righteous indignation when he said:

'So I just out and asked Jesus who was the biggest sinner; my wife going with this man, or this man going with my wife, and Jesus say: "How come you ask me that, John? You ain't thinking 'bout doing nothing to them, is you?" I say, "No, Jesus, I ain't gonna bother 'em, but this man, he's married just like my wife, and I ain't going to be responsible for what might break out between him and his wife," and Jesus say, "Don't you worry, John, there's always going to be some left."'

Suddenly they were lit by a flash of lightning, which showed up a second man on his knees directly in back of the fascinated church sister. He held a safety razor blade between his right thumb and forefinger and he was cutting away the back of her skirt with such care and silence she didn't suspect a thing. First, holding the skirt firmly by the hem with his left hand, he split it in a straight line up to the point where it began to tighten over her buttocks. Then he split her slip in the same manner. After which, holding the right halves of both skirt and slip firmly but gently between the thumb and forefinger of his left hand, he cut out a wide half-circle down through the hem and carefully removed the cutout section and threw it carelessly against the wall of the church behind him. The operation revealed one black buttock encased in rose-colored rayon pants and the bare back of one thick black thigh showing above the rolled top of a beige rayon stocking. She hadn't felt a thing.

'"Anyone who commits adultery, makes no difference whether it be man or woman, breaks one of my Father's commandments," Jesus say: "Makes no difference how good it is,"' John said.

'Amen!' the church sister said. Her buttocks began to tremble as she contemplated this enormous sin.

Behind her, the kneeling man had begun to cut away the left side of her skirt, but the trembling of her buttocks forced him to exercise greater caution.

'I say to Jesus, "That's the trouble with Christianity, the good things is always sinful,"' John said.

'Lawd, ain't it the truth,' the church sister said, leaning forward to slap John on the shoulder in a spontaneous gesture of rising joy. The cutout left side section of the skirt and slip came off in the kneeling man's hand.

Now revealed was all the lower part of the big wide rose-encased buttocks and the backs of two thick black thighs above beige stockings. The black thighs bulged in all directions so that just below the crotch, where the torso began, there was a sort of pocket in which one could visualize the buttocks of some man gripped as in a vice. But now, in that pocket, hung a waterproof purse suspended from elastic bands passing up through the pants and encircling the waist.

With breathless delicacy but a sure touch and steady hand, as though performing a major operation on the brain, the kneeling man reached into the pocket and began cutting the elastic band which held the purse.

John leaned forward and touched her on the shoulder like a spontaneous caress. His voice thickened with suggestion. 'But Jesus say, "Commit all the 'dultry you want to, John. Just be prepared to roast in hell for it."'

'He-he-he,' laughed the church sister and slapped him again on the shoulder. 'He was just kidding you. He'd forgive us for just *one* time,' and she suddenly switched her trembling buttocks, no doubt to demonstrate Jesus's mercy.

In so doing she felt the hand easing the purse from between her legs. She slapped back automatically before she could begin to turn her body, and struck the kneeling man across the face.

'Mother-raper, you is trying to steal my money,' she screamed, turning on the thief.

Lightning flashed, revealing the thief leaping to one side and the big broad buttocks in rose-colored pants twitching in fury. And before the sound of thunder was heard, the rain came down.

The thief leapt blindly into the street. Before the church sister could follow, a meat delivery truck coming at blinding speed hit the thief head-on and knocked the body somersaulting ten yards down the street before running over it. The driver lost control as the truck went over the body. The truck jumped the curb and knocked down a telephone pole at the corner of Seventh Avenue; it slewed across the wet asphalt and crashed against the concrete barrier enclosing the park down the middle of the avenue.

The church sister ran toward the mangled body and snatched her purse still clutched in the dead man's hand, unmindful of the bright lights of the armored truck rushing towards her like twin comets out of the night, unmindful of the rain pouring down in torrents.

The driver of the armored car saw the rose-encased buttocks of a large black woman as she bent over to snatch something from what looked like a dead man lying in the middle of the street. He was convinced he had d.t.'s. But he tried desperately to avoid them at the speed he was going on that wet street, d.t.'s or not. The armored truck skidded, then began wobbling as though doing the shimmy. The brakes meant nothing on the wet asphalt of Seventh Avenue and the car skidded straight on across the avenue and was hit broadside by a big truck going south.

The church sister hurried down the street in the opposite direction, holding the purse clutched tightly in her hand. Near Lexington Avenue, men, women and children crowded about the body of another dead colored man lying in the street, being washed for the grave by the rain. It lay in a grotesque position on its stomach at a right angle to the curb, one arm outflung, the other beneath it. The side of the face turned up had been shot away. If there had been a pistol anywhere, now it was gone.

A police cruiser was parked nearby, crosswise to the street. One of the policemen was standing beside the body in the rain. The other one sat in the cruiser, phoning the precinct station.

The church sister was hurrying past on the opposite side of the street, trying to remain unnoticed. But a big colored laborer, wearing the overalls in which he had worked all day, saw her. His eyes popped and his mouth opened in his slack face.

'Lady,' he called tentatively. She didn't look around. 'Lady,' he called again. 'I just wanted to say, your ass is out.'

She turned on him furiously. 'Tend to your own mother-raping business.'

He backed away, touching his cap politely, 'I didn't mean no harm, lady. It's *your* ass.'

She hurried on down the street, worrying more about her hair in the rain than about her behind showing.

At the corner of Lexington Avenue, an old junk man of the kind who haunt the streets at night collecting old paper and discarded junk was struggling with a bale of cotton, trying to get it into his cart. Rain was pouring off his sloppy hat and wetting his ragged overalls to dark blue. His small dried face was framed with thick kinky white hair, giving him a benevolent look. No onc else was in sight; everybody who was out on the street in all that rain was looking at the body of the dead man. So when he saw this big strapping lady coming towards him he stopped struggling with the wet bale of cotton and asked politely, 'Ma'am, would you please help me get this bale of cotton into my cart, please, ma'am?'

He hadn't seen her from the rear so he was slightly surprised by her sudden hostility.

'What kind of trick is you playing?' she challenged, giving him an evil look.

'Ain't no trick, ma'am. I just tryna get this bale of cotton into my cart.'

'Cotton!' she shouted indignantly, looking at the bale of cotton with outright suspicion. 'Old and evil as you is you ought to be ashamed of yourself tryna trick me out my money with what you calls a bale of cotton. Does I look like that kinda fool?'

'No, ma'am, but if you was a Christian you wouldn't carry on like that just 'cause an old man asked you to help him lift a bale of cotton.'

'I is a Christian, you wicked bastard,' she shouted. 'That's why all you wicked bastards is tryna steal my money. But I ain't the kind of Christian fool enough not to know there ain't no bales of cotton lying in the street in New York City. If it weren't for my hair, I'd beat your ass, you old con-man.'

It had been a rough night for the old junk man. First he and a crony had found a half-filled whisky bottle with what they thought was whisky and had sat on a stoop to enjoy themselves, passing the bottle back and forth, when suddenly his crony had said, 'Man, dis ain't whisky; dis is piss.' Then after he'd spent his last money for a bottle of 'smoke' to settle his stomach, it had started to rain. And here was this evil bitch calling him a con-man, as broke as he was.

'You touch me and I'll mark you,' he threatened, reaching in his pocket.

She backed away from him and he turned his back to her, muttering to himself. He didn't see her wet red buttocks above her shining black legs when she hurried down the street and disappeared into a tenement.

Four minutes later, when the first of the police cruisers sent to bottle up the street screamed around the corner from Lexington Avenue, he was still struggling with the bale of cotton in the rain.

The cruiser stopped for the white cops to put the routine question to a colored man: 'Say, uncle, you didn't see any suspicious-looking person pass this way, did you?'

'Nawsuh, just an evil lady mad 'cause her hair got wet.'

The driver grinned, but the cop beside him looked at the bale of cotton curiously and asked, 'What you got there, uncle, a corpse bundled up?'

'Cotton, suh.'

Both cops straightened up and the driver leaned over to look at it too.

'*Cotton?*'

'Yassuh, this is cotton – a bale of cotton.'

'Where the hell did you get a bale of cotton in this city?'

'I found it, suh.'

'Found it? What the hell kind of double-talk is that? Found it where?'

'Right here, suh.'

'Right here?' the cop repeated incredulously. Slowly and deliberately he got out of the car. His attitude was threatening. He looked closely at the bale of cotton. He bent over and felt the cotton poking through the seams of the burlap wrapping. 'By God, it *is* cotton,' he said straightening up. 'A bale of cotton! What the hell's a bale of cotton doing here in the street?'

'I dunno, boss, I just found it here is all.'

'Probably fell from some truck,' the driver said from within the cruiser. 'Let somebody else take care of it, it ain't our business.'

The cop in the street said, 'Now, uncle, you take this cotton to the precinct station and turn it in. The owner will be looking for it.'

'Yassuh, boss, but I can't get it into my waggin.'

'Here, I'll help you,' the cop said, and together they got it onto the cart.

The junk man set off in the direction of the precinct station, pushing the cart in the rain, and the cop got back into the cruiser and they went on down the street in the direction of the dead man.

4

When Grave Digger and Coffin Ed arrived at the lot where the Back-to-Africa rally had taken place, they found it closed off by a police cordon and the desolate black people, surrounded by policemen, standing helpless in the rain. The police cruiser was still smoking in the barbecue pit and the white cops in their wet black slickers looked mean and dangerous. Coffin Ed's acid-burned face developed a tic and Grave Digger's neck began swelling with rage.

The dead body of the young recruiting agent lay face up in the rain, waiting for the medical examiner to come and pronounce it dead so the men from Homicide could begin their investigation. But the men from Homicide had not arrived, and nothing had been done.

Grave Digger and Coffin Ed stood over the body and looked down at all that was left of the young black face which a few short minutes ago had been so alive with hope. At that moment they felt the same as all the other helpless black people standing in the rain.

'Too bad O'Malley didn't get it instead of this young boy,' Grave Digger said, rain dripping from his black slouch hat over his wrinkled black suit.

'This is what happens when cops get soft on hoodlums,' Coffin Ed said.

'Yeah, we know O'Malley got him killed, but our job is to find out who pulled the trigger.'

They walked over to the herded people and Grave Digger asked, 'Who's in charge here?'

The other young recruiting agent came forward. He was hatless and his solemn black face was shining in the rain. 'I guess I am; the others have gone.'

They walked him over to one side and got the story of what had happened as he saw it. It wasn't much help.

'We were the whole organization,' the young man said. 'Reverend O'Malley, the two secretaries and me and John Hill who was killed. There were volunteers but we were the staff.'

'How about the guards?'

'The two guards with the armored truck? Why, they were sent with the truck from the bank.'

'What bank?'

'The African Bank in Washington, D.C.'

The detectives exchanged glances but didn't comment.

'What's your name, son?' Grave Digger asked.

'Bill Davis.'

'How far did you get in school?'

'I went to college, sir. In Greensboro, North Carolina.'

'And you still believe in the devil?' Coffin Ed asked.

'Let him alone,' Grave Digger said. 'He's telling us all he knows.' Turning to Bill he asked, 'And these two colored detectives from the D.A.'s office. Did you know them?'

'I never saw them before. I was supicious of them from the first. But Reverend O'Malley didn't seem perturbed and he made the decisions.'

'Didn't seem perturbed,' Grave Digger echoed. 'Did you suspect it might be a plant?'

'Sir?'

'Did it occur to you they might have been in cahoots with O'Malley to help him get away with the money?'

At first the young man didn't understand. Then he was shocked. 'How could you think that, sir? Reverend O'Malley is absolutely honest. He is very dedicated, sir.'

Coffin Ed sighed.

'Did you ever see the ships which were supposed to take you people back to Africa?' Grave Digger asked.

'No, but all of us have seen the correspondence with the steamship company – The Afro-Asian Line – verifying the year's lease he had negotiated.'

'How much did he pay?'

'It was on a per head basis; he was going to pay one hundred dollars per person. I don't believe they are really as large as they look in these pictures, but we were going to fill them to capacity.'

'How much money had you collected?'

'Eighty-seven thousand dollars from the . . . er . . . subscribers, but we had taken in quite a bit from other things, church socials and this barbecue deal, for instance.'

'And these four white men in the delivery truck got all of it?'

'Well, just the eighty-seven thousand dollars we had taken in tonight. But there were five of them. One stayed inside the truck behind a barricade all the time.'

The detectives became suddenly alert. 'What kind of barricade?' Grave Digger asked.

'I don't know exactly. I couldn't see inside the truck very well. But it looked like some kind of a box covered with burlap.'

'What provision company supplied your meat?' Coffin Ed asked.

'I don't know, sir. That wasn't part of my duties. You'll have to ask the chef.'

They sent for the chef and he came wet and bedraggled, his

white cap hanging over one ear like a rag. He was mad at every-thing – the bandits, the rain, and the police cruiser that had fallen into his barbecue pit. His eyes were bright red and he took it as a personal insult when they asked about the provision company.

'I don't know where the ribs come from after they left the hog,' he said angrily. 'I was just hired to superintend the cooking. I ain't had nothing to do with them white folks and I don't know how many they was – 'cept too many.'

'Leave this soul-brother go,' Coffin Ed said. 'Pretty soon he wouldn't have been here.'

Grave Digger wrote down O'Malley's official address, which he already knew, then as a last question asked, 'What was your connection with the original Back-to-Africa movement, the one headed by Mr Michaux?'

'None at all. Reverend O'Malley didn't have anything at all to do with Mr Michaux's group. In fact he didn't even like Lewis Michaux; I don't think he ever spoke to him.'

'Did it ever occur to you that Mr Michaux might not have had anything to do with Reverend O'Malley? Did you ever think that he might have known something about O'Malley that made him distrust O'Malley?'

'I don't think it was anything like that,' Bill contended. 'What reason could he have to distrust O'Malley? I just think he was envious, that's all. Reverend O'Malley thought he was too slow; he didn't see any reason for waiting any longer; we've waited long enough.'

'And you were intending to go back to Africa too?'

'Yes, sir, still intend to – as soon as we get the money back. You'll get the money back for us, won't you?'

'Son, if we don't, we're gonna raise so much hell they're gonna send us all back to Africa.'

'And for free, too,' Coffin Ed added grimly.

The young man thanked them and went back to stand with the others in the rain.

'Well, Ed, what do you think about it?' Grave Digger asked.

'One thing is for sure, it wasn't the syndicate pulled this caper – not the crime syndicate, anyway.'

'What other kinds of syndicates are there?'

'Don't ask me, I ain't the F.B.I.'

They were silent for a moment with the rain pouring over them, thinking of these eighty-seven families who had put down their thousand-dollar grubstakes on a dream. They knew that these families had come by their money the hard way. To many, it represented the savings of a lifetime. To most it represented long hours of hard work at menial jobs. None could afford to lose it.

They didn't consider these victims as squares or suckers. They understood them. These people were seeking a home – just the same as the Pilgrim Fathers. Harlem is a city of the homeless. These people had deserted the South because it could never be considered their home. Many had been sent north by the white southerners in revenge for the desegregation ruling. Others had fled, thinking the North was better. But they had not found a home in the North. They had not found a home in America. So they looked across the sea to Africa, where other black people were both the ruled and the rulers. Africa to them was a big free land which they could proudly call home, for there were buried the bones of their ancestors, there lay the roots of their families, and it was inhabited by the descendants of those same ancestors – which made them related by both blood and race. Everyone has to believe in something; and the white people of America had left them nothing to believe in. But that didn't make a black man any less criminal than a white; and they had to find the criminals who hijacked the money, black or white.

'Anyway, the first thing is to find Deke,' Grave Digger put voice to their thoughts. 'If he ain't responsible for this caper he'll sure as hell know who is.'

'He had better know,' Coffin Ed said grimly.

But Deke didn't know any more than they did. He had worked a long time to set up his movement and it had been expensive. At first he had turned to the church to hide from the syndicate. He had figured if he set himself up as a preacher and used his reward money for civil improvement, the syndicate would hesitate about rubbing him out.

But the syndicate hadn't shown any interest in him. That had worried him until he figured out that the syndicate simply didn't want to get involved in the race issue; he had already done all the harm he could do, so they left him to the soul-brothers.

Then he'd gotten the idea for his Back-to-Africa movement from reading a biography of Marcus Garvey, the Negro who had organized the first Back-to-Africa movement. It was said that Garvey had collected over a million dollars. He had been sent to prison, but most of his followers had contended that he was innocent and had still believed in him. Whether he had been innocent or not was not the question; what appealed to him was the fact his followers had still believed in him. That was the con-man's real genius, to keep the suckers always believing.

So he had started his own Back-to-Africa movement, the only difference being when he had got his million, he was going to cut out – he might go back to Africa, himself. He'd heard that people with money could live good in certain places there. The way he had planned it he would use two goons impersonating detectives to impound the money as he collected it; in that way he wouldn't have to bank it and could always keep it on hand.

He didn't know where these white hijackers fitted in. At the first glimpse he thought they were guns from the syndicate. That was why he had hidden beneath the table. But when he discovered they'd just come to grab the money, he had known it was something else again. So he had decided to chase them down and get the money back.

But when they had finally caught up with the meat delivery truck, the white men had disappeared. Perhaps it was just as well; by then he was outgunned anyway. Neither of his guards had been seriously hurt, but he'd lost one of his detectives. The wrecked truck hadn't told him anything and the driver of the truck that had run into them kept getting in the way.

He hadn't had much time so he had ordered them to split and assemble again every morning at 3 a.m. in the back room of a pool hall on Eighth Avenue and he would contact his other detective himself.

'I've got to see which way this mother-raping cat is jumping,' he said.

He had enough money on him to operate, over five hundred dollars. And he had a five-grand bank account under an alias in an all-night bank in midtown for his getaway money in case of an emergency. But he didn't know yet where to start looking for his eighty-seven grand. Some kind of lead would come. This was Harlem where all black folks were against the whites, and somebody would tell him something. What worried him most was how much information the police had. He knew that in any event they'd be rough on him because of his record; and he knew he'd better keep away from them if he wanted to get his money back.

First, however, he had to get into his house. He needed his pistol; and there were certain documents hidden there – the forged leases from the steamship line and the forged credentials of the Back-to-Africa movement – that would send him back to prison.

He walked down Seventh Avenue to Small's bar, on the pretense of going to call the police, and got into a taxi without attracting any attention. He had the driver take him over to Saint Mark's Church, paid the fare and walked up the stairs. The church door was closed and locked, as he had expected, but he could stand in the shadowed recess and watch the entrance to the Dorrence Brooks apartment house across the street where he lived.

He stood there for a long time casing the building. It was a V-shaped building at the corner of 138th Street and St Nicholas Avenue and he could see the entrance and the streets on both sides. He didn't see any strange cars parked nearby, no police cruisers, no gangster-type limousines. He didn't see any strange people, nothing and no one who looked suspicious. He could see through the glass doors into the front hall and there was not a soul about. The only thing was it was too damn empty.

He circled the church and entered the ark on the west side of St Nicholas Avenue and approached the building from across the street. He hid in the park beside a tool shed from which he had a full view of the windows of his fourth-floor apartment. Light showed in the windows of the living-room and dining-room. He watched for a long time. But not once did a shadow pass before one of the lighted windows. He got dripping wet in the rain.

His sixth sense told him to telephone, and from some phone booth in the street where the call couldn't be traced. So he walked up to 145th Street and phoned from the box on the corner.

'Hellooo,' she answered. He thought she sounded strange.

'Iris,' he whispered.

Standing beside her, Grave Digger's hand tightened warningly on her arm. He had already briefed her what to say when O'Malley called and the pressure meant he wasn't playing.

'Oh, Betty,' she cried. 'The police are here looking for –'

Grave Digger slapped her with such sudden violence she caromed off the center table and went sprawling on her hands and knees; her dress hiked up showing black lace pants above the creamy yellow skin of her thighs.

Coffin Ed came up and stood over her, the skin of his face jumping like a snake's belly over fire. 'You're so goddamn cute –'

Grave Digger was speaking urgently into the telephone: 'O'Malley, we just want some information, that's –' but the line had gone dead.

His neck swelled as he jiggled the hook to get the precinct station.

At the same moment Iris came up from the floor with the smooth vicious motion of a cat and slapped Coffin Ed across the face, thinking he was Grave Digger in her blinding fury.

She was a hard-bodied high-yellow woman with a perfect figure. She never wore a girdle and her jiggling buttocks gave all men amorous ideas. She had a heart-shaped face with the high cheekbones, big wide red painted mouth, and long-lashed speckled brown eyes of a sexpot and she was thirty-three years old, which gave her the experience. But she was strong as an ox and it was a solid pop she laid on Coffin Ed's cheek.

With pure reflex action he reached out and caught her around the throat with his two huge hands and bent her body backward.

'Easy, man, easy!' Grave Digger shouted, realizing instantly that Coffin Ed was sealed in such a fury he couldn't hear. He dropped the telephone and wheeled, hitting Coffin Ed across the back of the neck with the edge of his hand just a fraction of a second before he'd have crushed her windpipe.

Coffin Ed slumped forward, carrying Iris down with him, beneath him, and his hands slackened from her throat. Grave Digger picked him up by the armpits and propped him on the sofa, then he picked up Iris and dropped her into a chair. Her eyes were huge and limpid with fear and her throat was going black and blue.

Grave Digger stood looking down at them, listening to the phone click frantically, thinking, *Now we're in for it*; then thinking bitterly, *These half-white bitches*. Then he turned back to the telephone and answered the precinct station and asked for the telephone call to be traced. Before he could hang up, Lieutenant Anderson was on the wire.

'Jones, you and Johnson get over to 137th Street and Seventh Avenue. Both trucks are smashed up and everyone gone, but there are two bodies DOA and there might be a lead.' He paused for a moment, then asked, 'How's it going?'

Grave Digger looked from the slumped figure of Coffin Ed into the now blazing eyes of Iris and said, 'Cool, Lieutenant, everything's cool.'

'I'm sending over a man to keep her on ice. He ought to be there any moment.'

'Right.'

'And remember my warning – no force. We don't want anyone hurt if we can help it.'

'Don't worry, Lieutenant, we're like shepherds with new-born lambs.'

The lieutenant hung up.

Coffin Ed had come around and he looked at Grave Digger with a sheepish expression. No one spoke.

Then Iris said in a thick, throat-hurting voice, 'I'm going to get you coppers fired if it's the last thing I do.'

Coffin Ed looked as though he was going to reply, but Grave Digger spoke first: 'You weren't very smart, but neither were we. So we'd better call it quits and start all over.'

'Start over shit,' she flared. 'You break into my house without a search warrant, hold me prisoner, attack me physically, and say let's call it quits. You must think I'm a moron. Even if I'm guilty of a murder, you can't get away with that shit.'

'Eighty-seven colored families – like you and me –'

'Not like me!'

' – have lost their life's savings in this caper.'

'So what? You two are going to lose your mother-raping jobs.'

'So if you co-operate and help us get it back you'll get a ten-per cent reward – eight thousand, seven hundred dollars.'

'You chickenshit cop, what can I do with that chicken feed? Deke is worth ten times that much to me.'

'Not any more. His number's up and you'd better get on the winning side.'

She gave a short, harsh laugh. 'That ain't your side, big and ugly.'

Then she got up and went and stood directly in front of Coffin Ed where he sat on the sofa. Suddenly her fist flew out and hit him squarely on the nose. His eyes filled with tears as blood spurted from his nostrils. But he didn't move.

'That makes us even,' he said and reached for his handkerchief.

Someone rapped on the door and Grave Digger let in the white detective who had come to take over. Neither of them spoke; they kept the record straight.

'Come on, Ed,' Grave Digger said.

Coffin Ed stood up and the two of them walked to the door, Coffin Ed holding the bloodstained handkerchief to his nose. Just before they went out, Grave Digger turned and said, 'Chances go around, baby.'

5

The rain had stopped when they got outside and people were back on the wet sidewalks, strolling aimlessly and looking about as if to see what might have been washed from heaven. They walked up a couple of blocks where their little black battered sedan with the supercharged motor was parked. It had got much cleaner from the rain.

'You've got to take it easy, Ed man,' Grave Digger said. 'One more second and you'd have killed her.'

Coffin Ed took away the handkerchief and found that his nose had stopped bleeding. He got into the car without replying. He felt guilty for fear he might have gotten Digger into trouble, but for his part he didn't care.

Grave Digger understood. Ever since the hoodlum had thrown acid into his face, Coffin Ed had had no tolerance for crooks. He was too quick to blow up and too dangerous for safety in his sudden rages. But hell, Grave Digger thought, what can one expect? These colored hoodlums had no respect for colored cops unless you beat it into them or blew them away. He just hoped these slick boys wouldn't play it too cute.

The trucks were still where they had been wrecked, guarded by harness cops and surrounded by the usual morbid crowd; but they drove on down to where the bodies lay. They found Sergeant Wiley of Homicide beside the body of the bogus detective, talking to a precinct sergeant and looking bored. He was a quiet, gray-haired, scholarly-looking man dressed in a dark summer suit.

'Everything is wrapped up,' he said to them. 'We're just waiting for the wagon to take them away.' He pointed at the body. 'Know him?'

They looked him over carefully. 'He must be from out of town, eh, Ed?' Grave Digger said.

Coffin Ed nodded.

Sergeant Wiley gave them a rundown: No real identification of any kind, just a phoney ID card from the D.A.'s office and a bogus detective shield from headquarters. He had been a big man but now he looked small and forlorn on the wet street and very dead.

They went up and looked at the other body and exchanged looks.

Wiley noticed. 'Run over by the delivery truck,' he said. 'Mean anything?'

'No, he was just a sneak thief. Must have got in the way is all. True monicker was Early Gibson but he was called Early Riser. Worked with a partner most of the time. We'll try to find his partner. He might give us a lead.'

'Sure as hell ain't got no other,' Coffin Ed added.

'Do that,' Wiley said. 'And let me know what you find out.'

'We're going to take a look at the trucks.'

'Right-o, there's nothing more here. We took a statement from the driver of the truck that smashed the armored job and let him go. All he knew was what the three of them looked like and we know what they look like.'

'Any other witness?' Grave Digger asked.

'Hell, you know these people, Jones. All stone blind.'

'What you expect from people who're invisible themselves?' Coffin Ed said roughly.

Wiley let it pass. 'By the way,' he said, 'you'll find those heaps hopped up. The armored truck has an old Cadillac engine and the delivery truck the engine of a Chrysler 300. I've taken the numbers and put out tracers. You don't have to worry about that.'

They left Sergeant Wiley to wait for the wagon and went over to examine the trucks. The tonneau of the armored truck had been built on to the chassis of a 1957 Cadillac, but it didn't tell them anything. The Chrysler engine had been installed in the delivery truck, and it might be traced. They copied the licence and engine numbers on the off-chance of finding some garage that had serviced it, but they knew it was unlikely.

The curious crowd that had collected had begun to drift away. The harness cops guarding the wrecks until the police tow trucks carried them off looked extremely bored. The rain hadn't slackened the heat; it had only increased the density. The detectives could feel the sweat trickling down their bodies beneath their wet clothes.

It was getting late and they were impatient to get on to the trail of Deke, but they didn't want to overlook anything so they examined the truck inside and out with their hand torches.

The indistinct lettering: FREYBROS. INC. *Quality Meats*, 173 *West 116th Street*, showed faintly on the outside panels. They knew there wasn't any such thing as a meat provision firm at that address.

Then suddenly, as he was flashing his light inside, Coffin Ed said, 'Look at this.'

From the tone of his voice Grave Digger knew it was something curious before he looked. 'Cotton,' he said. He and Coffin Ed looked at each other, swapping thoughts.

Caught on a loose screw on the side panel were several strands of cotton. Both of them climbed into the truck and examined it carefully at close range.

'Unprocessed,' Grave Digger said. 'It's been a long time since I've seen any cotton like that.'

'Hush, man, you ain't never seen any cotton like that. You were born and raised in New York.'

Grave Digger chuckled. 'It was when I was in high school. We were studying the agricultural products of America.'

'Now what can a meat provision company use cotton for?'

'Hell, man, the way this car is powered, you'd think meat spoiled on the way to the store – if you want to think like that.'

'Cotton,' Coffin Ed ruminated. 'A mob of white bandits and cotton – in Harlem. Figure that one out.'

'Leave it to the fingerprinters and the other experts,' Grave Digger said, jumping down to the pavement. 'One thing is for sure, I ain't going to spend all night looking for a mother-raping sack of cotton – or a cotton picker either.'

'Let's go get Early Riser's buddy,' Coffin Ed said following him.

Grave Digger and Coffin Ed were realists. They knew they didn't have second sight. So they had stool pigeons from all walks of life: criminals, straight men and squares. They had their time and places for contacting their pigeons well organized; no pigeon knew another; and only a few of those who were really pigeons were known as pigeons. But without them most crimes would never be solved.

Now they began contacting their pigeons, but only those on the petty-larceny circuit. They knew they wouldn't find Deke through stool pigeons; not that night. But they might find a witness who saw the white men leave.

First they stopped in Big Wilt's Small's Paradise Inn at 135th Street and Seventh Avenue and stood for a moment at the front of the circular bar. They drank two whiskies each and talked to each other about the caper.

The barstools and surrounding tables were filled with the flashily dressed people of many colors and occupations who could afford the price for air-conditioned atmosphere and the professional smiles of the light-bright chicks tending bar. The fat black manager waived the bill on the house and they accepted; they could afford to drink freebies at Small's, it was a straight joint.

Afterwards they sauntered towards the back and stood beside the bandstand, watching the white and black couples dancing the twist in the cabaret. The horns were talking and the saxes talking back.

'Listen to that,' Grave Digger said when the horn took eight on a frenetic solo. 'Talking under their clothes, ain't it?'

Then the two saxes started swapping fours with the rhythm always in the back. 'Somewhere in that jungle is the solution to the world,' Coffin Ed said. 'If we could only find it.'

'Yeah, it's like the sidewalks trying to speak in a language never heard. But they can't spell it either.'

'Naw,' Coffin Ed said. 'Unless there's an alphabet for emotion.'

'The emotion that comes out of experience. If we could read that language, man, we would solve all the crimes in the world.'

'Let's split,' Coffin Ed said. 'Jazz talks too much to me.'

'It ain't so much what it says,' Grave Digger agreed. 'It's what you can't do about it.'

They left the white and black couples in their frenetic embrace, guided by the talking of the jazz, and went back to their car.

'Life could be great but there are hoodlums abroad,' Grave Digger said, climbing beneath the wheel.

'You just ain't saying it, Digger; hoodlums high, and hoodlums low.'

They turned off on 132nd Street beside the new housing development and parked in the darkest spot in the block, cut the motor and doused the lights and waited.

The stool pigeon came in about ten minutes. He was the shiny-haired pimp wearing a white silk shirt and green silk pants who had sat beside them at the bar, with his back turned, talking to a tan-skinned blonde. He opened the door quickly and got into the back seat in the dark.

Coffin Ed turned around to face him. 'You know Early Riser?'

'Yeah. He's a snatcher but I don't know no sting he's made recently.'

'Who does he work with?'

'Work with? I never heard of him working no way but alone.'

'Think hard,' Grave Digger said harshly without turning around.

'I dunno, boss. That's the honest truth. I swear 'fore God.'

'You know about the rumble on '37th Street?' Coffin Ed continued.

'I heard about it but I didn't go see it. I heard the syndicate robbed Deke O'Hara out of a hundred grand he'd just collected from his Back-to-Africa pitch.'

That sounded straight enough so Coffin Ed just said, 'Okay. Do some dreaming about Early Riser,' and let him go.

'Let's try lower Eighth,' Grave Digger said. 'Early was on shit.'

'Yeah, I saw the marks,' Coffin Ed agreed.

Their next stop was a dingy bar on Eighth Avenue near the corner of 112th Street. This was the neighborhood of the cheap addicts, whisky-heads, stumblebums, the flotsam of Harlem; the end of the line for the whores, the hard squeeze for the poor honest laborers and a breeding ground for crime. Blank-eyed whores stood on the street corners swapping obscenities with twitching junkies. Muggers and thieves slouched in dark doorways waiting for someone to rob; but there wasn't anyone but each other. Children ran down the street, the dirty street littered with rotting vegetables, uncollected garbage, bartered garbage cans, broken glass, dog offal – always running, ducking and dodging. God help them if they got caught. Listless mothers stood in the dark entrances of tenements and swapped talk about their men, their jobs, their poverty, their hunger, their debts, their Gods, their religions, their preachers, their children, their aches and pains, their bad luck with the numbers and the evilness of white people. Workingmen staggered down the sidewalks filled with aimless resentment, muttering curses, hating to go to their hotbox hovels but having nowhere else to go.

'All I wish is that I was God for just one mother-raping second,' Grave Digger said, his voice cotton-dry with rage.

'I know,' Coffin Ed said. 'You'd concrete the face of the mother-raping earth and turn white folks into hogs.'

'But I ain't God,' Grave Digger said, pushing into the bar.

The bar stools were filled with drunken relics, shabby men, ancient whores draped over tired laborers drinking ruckus juice to get their courage up. The tables were filled with the already drunk sleeping on folded arms.

No one recognized the two detectives. They looked prosperous and sober. A wave of vague alertness ran through the joint; everyone thought fresh money was coming in. This sudden greed was indefinably communicated to the sleeping drunks. They stirred in their sleep and awakened, waiting for the moment to get up and cadge another drink.

Grave Digger and Coffin Ed leaned against the bar at the front and waited for one of the two husky bartenders to serve them.

Coffin Ed nodded to a sign over the bar. 'Do you believe that?'

Grave Digger looked up and read: NO JUNKIES SERVED HERE! He said, 'Why not? Poor and raggedy as these junkies are, they ain't got no money for whisky.'

The fat bald-headed bartender with shoulders like a wood-chopper came up. 'What's yours, gentlemen?'

Coffin Ed said sourly, 'Hell, man, you expecting any gentlemen in here?'

The bartender didn't have a sense of humor. 'All my customers is gentlemen,' he said.

'Two bourbons on the rocks,' Grave Digger said.

'Doubles,' Coffin Ed added.

The bartender served them with the elaborate courtesy he reserved for all well-paying customers. He rang up the bill and slapped down the change. His eyes flickered at the fifty-cent tip. 'Thank you, gentlemen,' he said, and strolled casually down the bar, winking at a buxom yellow whore at the other end clad in a tight red dress.

Casually she detached herself from the asbestos joker she was trying to kindle and strolled to the head of the bar. Without preamble she squeezed in between Grave Digger and Coffin Ed and draped a big bare yellow arm about the shoulders of each. She smelled like unwashed armpits bathed in dime-store perfume and overpowering bed odor. 'You wanna see a girl?' she asked, sharing her stale whisky breath between them.

'Where's any girl?' Coffin Ed said.

She snatched her arm from about his shoulder and gave her full attention to Grave Digger. Everyone in the joint had seen the obvious play and were waiting eagerly for the result.

'Later,' Grave Digger said. 'I got a word first for Early Riser's gunsel.'

Her eyes flashed. 'Loboy! He ain't no gunsel, he the boss.'

'Gunsel or boss, I got word for him.'

'See me first, honey. I'll pass him the word.'

'No, business first.'

'Don't be like that, honey,' she said, touching his leg. 'There's no time like bedtime.' She fingered his ribs, promising pleasure. Her fingers touched something hard; they stiffened, paused, and then she plainly felt the big .38 revolver in the shoulder sling. Her hand came off as though it had touched something red hot; her whole body stiffened; her eyes widened and her flaccid face looked twenty years older. 'You from the syndicate?' she asked in a strained whisper.

Grave Digger fished out a leather folder from his right coat pocket, opened it. His shield flashed in the light. 'No, I'm the man.'

Coffin Ed stared at the two bartenders.

Every eye in the room watched tensely. She backed further away; her mouth came open like a scar. 'Git away from me,' she almost screamed. 'I'm a respectable lady.'

All eyes looked down into shot glasses as though reading the answers to all the problems in the world; ears closed up like safe doors, hands froze.

'I'll believe it if you tell me where he's at,' Grave Digger said.

A bartender moved and Coffin Ed's pistol came into his hand. The bartender didn't move again.

'Where who at?' the whore screamed. 'I don't know where nobody at. I'm in here, tending to my own business, ain't bothering nobody, and here you come in here and start messing with me. I ain't no criminal, I'm a church lady –' she was becoming hysterical from her load of junk.

'Let's go,' Coffin Ed said. One of the sleeping drunks staggered out a few minutes later. He found the detectives parked in the black dark in the middle of the slum block on 113th Street. He got quickly into the back and sat in the dark as had the other pigeon.

'I thought you were drunk, Cousin,' Coffin Ed said.

Cousin was an old man with unkempt, dirty, gray-streaked,

kinky hair, washed-out brown eyes slowly fading to blue, and skin the color and texture of a dried prune. His wrinkled old thrown-away summer suit smelled of urine, vomit and offal. He was strictly a wino. He looked harmless. But he was one of their ace stool pigeons because no one thought he had the sense for it.

'Nawsah, boss, jes' waitin',' he said in a whining, cowardly-sounding voice.

'Just waiting to get drunk.'

'Thass it, boss, thass jes' what.'

'You know Loboy?' Grave Digger said.

'Yassah, boss, knows him when I sees him.'

'Know who he works with?'

'Early Riser mostly, boss. Leasewise they's together likes as if they's working.'

'Stealing,' Grave Digger said harshly. 'Snatching purses. Robbing women.'

'Yassah, boss, that's what they calls working.'

'What's their pitch? Snatching and running or just mugging?'

'All I knows is what I hears, boss. Folks say they works the *holy dream*.'

'*Holy dream*! What's that?'

'Folks say they worked it out themselves. They gits a church sister what carries her money twixt her legs. Loboy charms her lak a snake do a bird telling her this holy dream whilst Early Riser kneel behind her and cut out the back of her skirt and nip off de money sack. Must work, they's always flush.'

'Live and learn,' Coffin Ed said and Grave Digger asked: 'You seen either one of them tonight?'

'Jes' Loboy. I seen him 'bout an hour ago looking wild and scairt going into Hijenks to get a shot and when he come out he stop in the bar for a glass of sweet wine and then he cut out in a hurry. Looked worried and movin' fast.'

'Where does Loboy live?'

'I dunno, boss, 'round here sommers. Hijenks oughta know.'

'How 'bout that whore who makes like he's hers?'

'She just big-gatin', boss, tryna run up de price. Loboy got a fat chick sommers.'

'All right, where can we find Hijenks?'

'Back there on the corner, boss. Go through the bar an' you come to a door say "Toilet". Keep on an' you see a door say "Closet". Go in an' you see a nail with a cloth hangin' on it. Push the nail twice, then once, then three times an' a invisible door open in the back of the closet. Then you go up some stairs an' you come to 'nother door. Knock three times, then once, then twice.'

'All that? He must be a connection.'

'Got a shooting gallery's all I knows.'

'All right, Cousin, take this five dollars and get drunk and forget what we asked you,' Coffin Ed said, passing him a bill.

'Bless you, boss, bless you.' Cousin shuffled about in the darkness, hiding the bill in his clothes, then he said in his whining cowardly voice, 'Be careful, boss, be careful.'

'Either that or dead,' Grave Digger said.

Cousin chuckled and got out and melted in the dark.

'This is going to be a lot of trouble.' Grave Digger said. 'I hope it ain't for nothing.'

6

Reverend Deke O'Malley didn't know it was Grave Digger's voice over the telephone, but he knew it was the voice of a cop. He got out of the booth as though it had caught on fire. It was still raining but he was already wet and it just obscured his vision. Just the same he saw the light of the taxi coming down the hill on St Nicholas Avenue and hailed it. He climbed in and leaned forward and said, 'Penn Station and goose it.'

He straightened up to wipe the rain out of his eyes and his back hit the seat with a thud. The broad-shouldered young black driver had taken off as though he were powering a rocket ship to heaven.

Deke didn't mind. Speed was what he needed. He had got so far behind everyone the speed gave him a sense of catching up. He figured he could trust Iris. Anyway, he didn't have any choice. As long as she kept his documents hidden, he was relatively safe. But he knew the police would keep her under surveillance and there'd be no way to reach her for a time. He didn't know what the police had on him and that worried him as much as the loss of the money.

He had to admit the robbery had been a cute caper, well organized, bold, even risky. Perhaps it had succeeded just because it was risky. But it had been too well organized for a crime of that dimension, for $87,000, or so it seemed to him; it couldn't have been any better organized for a million dollars. But there seemed a lot of easier ways to get $87,000. One interpretation, of course, was that the syndicate had staged it not only to break him but to frame him. But if it had been the syndicate, why hadn't they just hit him?

Penn Station came before he had finished thinking.

He found a long line of telephone booths and telephoned Mrs John Hill, the wife of the young recruiting agent who had been killed. He didn't remember her but he knew she was a member of his church.

'Are you alone, Mrs Hill?' he asked in a disguised voice.

'Yes,' she replied tentatively, fearfully. 'That is – who's speaking, please?'

'This is Reverend O'Malley,' he announced in his natural voice.

He heard the relief in hers. 'Oh, Reverend O'Malley, I'm so glad you called.'

'I want to offer my sympathy and condolences. I cannot find the words to express my infinite sorrow for this unfortunate accident which has deprived you of your husband –' He knew he sounded like an ass but she'd understand that kind of proper talk.

'Oh, Reverend O'Malley, you are so kind.'

He could tell that she was crying. *Good!* he thought. 'May I be of help to you in any way whatsoever?'

'I just want you to preach his funeral.'

'Of course I shall, Mrs Hill, of course. You may set your mind at peace on that score. But, well, if you will forgive my asking, are you in need of money?'

'Oh, Reverend O'Malley, thank you, but he had life insurance and we have a little saved up – and, well, we haven't any children.'

'Well, if you have any need you must let me know. Tell me, have the police been bothering you?'

'Oh, they were here but they just asked questions about our

life – where we worked and that kind of thing – and they asked about our Back-to-Africa movement. I was proud to tell them all I knew . . .' Thank God that was nothing, he thought. 'Then, well, they left. They were – well, they were white and I knew they were unsympathetic – I could just feel it – and I was glad when they left.'

'Yes, my dear, we must be prepared for their attitude, that is why our movement was born. And I must confess I have no idea who the vicious white bandits are who murdered your fine . . . er . . . upstanding husband. But I am going to find them and God will punish them. But I have to do it alone. I can't depend on the white police.'

'Oh, don't I know it.'

'In fact, they will do everything to stop me.'

'What makes white folks like that?'

'We must not think *why* they are like that. We must accept it as a fact and go ahead and outwit them and beat them at their own game. And I might need your help, Mrs Hill.'

'Oh, Reverend O'Malley, I'm so glad to hear you say that. I understand just what you mean and I'll do everything in my power to help you track down those foul murderers and get our money back.'

Thank God for squares, O'Malley thought as he said, 'I have utmost confidence in you, Mrs Hill. We both have the same aim in view.'

'Oh, Reverend O'Malley, your confidence is not misplaced.'

He smiled at her stilted speech but he knew she meant it.

'The main thing is for me to stay free of the police while we conduct our own investigation. The police must not know of my whereabouts or that we are working together to bring these foul murderers to justice. They must not know that I have communicated with you or that I will see you.'

'I won't mention your name,' she promised solemnly.

'Do you expect them to return tonight?'

'I'm sure they're not coming back.'

'In that case I will come to your house in an hour and we will make that our headquarters to launch our investigation. Will that be all right?'

'Oh, Reverend O'Malley, I'm thrilled to be doing something to get revenge – I mean to see those white murderers punished – instead of just sitting here grieving.'

'Yes, Mrs Hill, we shall hunt down the killers for God to punish and perhaps you will draw your shades before I come.'

'And I'll turn out the lights too so you won't have to worry about anyone seeing you.'

'Turn out the lights?' For a moment he was startled. He envisioned himself walking into a pitch-dark ambush and being seized by the cops. Then he realized he had nothing to fear from Mrs Hill. 'Yes, very good,' he said. 'That will be fine. I will telephone you shortly before arriving and if the police are there you must say, "Come on up," but if you are alone, say, "Reverend O'Malley, it's all right."'

'I'll do just that,' she promised. He could hear the excitement in her voice. 'But I'm sure they won't be here.'

'Nothing in life is certain,' he said. 'Just remember what to say when I telephone – in about an hour.'

'I will remember; and good-bye now, until then.'

He hung up. Sweat was streaming down his face. He hadn't realized until then it was so hot in the booth.

He found the big men's room and ordered a shower. Then he undressed and gave his suit to the black attendant to be pressed while he was taking his shower. He luxuriated in the warm needles of water washing away the fear and panic, then he turned on cold and felt a new life and exhilaration replace the fatigue . . . *The indestructible Deke O'Hara,* he thought gloatingly. *What do I care about eighty-seven grand as long as there are squares?*

'Your suit's ready, daddy,' the attendant called, breaking off his reverie.

'Right-o, my man.'

Deke dried, dressed, paid and tipped the attendant and sat on the stand for a shoeshine, reading about the robbery and himself in the morning *Daily News.* The clock on the wall read 2.21 a.m.

Mrs Hill lived uptown in the Riverton Apartments near the Harlem River north of 135th Street. He knew she would be waiting impatiently. He was very familiar with her type: young, thought herself good-looking with the defensive conceit with which they convinced themselves they were more beautiful than all white women; ambitious to get ahead and subconsciously desired white men, hating them at the same time because they frustrated her attempts to get ahead and refused to recognize her innate superiority over white women. More than anything she wanted to escape her drab existence; if she couldn't be middle class and live in a big house in the suburbs she wanted to leave it all and go back to Africa, where she just *knew* she would be important. He didn't care for the type, but he knew for these reasons he could trust her.

He went out to the ramp to get a taxi. Two empty taxis with white drivers passed him; then a colored driver, seeing his predicament, passed some white people to pick him up. The white policeman supervising the loading saw nothing.

'You know ain't no white cabby gonna take you to Harlem, man,' the colored driver said.

'Hell, they're just losing money and ain't making me mad at all,' Deke said.

The colored driver chuckled.

Deke had him wait at the 125th Street Station while he phoned.

The coast was clear. She buzzed the downstairs door the moment he touched the bell and he went up to the seventh floor and found her waiting in her half-open doorway. Behind her the apartment was pitch dark.

'Oh, Reverend O'Malley, I was worried,' she greeted him. 'I thought the police had got you.'

He smiled warmly and patted her hand as he passed to go inside. She closed the door and followed him and for a moment they stood in the pitch dark of the small front hall, their bodies slightly touching.

'We can have some light,' he said. 'I'm sure it's safe enough.'

She clicked switches and the rooms sprang into view. The shades were drawn and the curtains closed and the apartment was just as he had imagined it. A living-room opening through a wide archway to a small dining-room with the closed door of the kitchen beyond. On the other side a door opening to the bedroom and bath. The furniture was the polished oak veneer featured in the credit stores that tried to look expensive, and to one side of the living-room was a long sofa that could be let out into a bed. It had already been let out and the bed made up.

She saw him looking and said apologetically, 'I thought you might want to sleep first.'

'That was very thoughtful of you,' he said. 'But first we must talk.'

'Oh, yesss,' she agreed jubilantly.

The only surprise was herself. She was a really beautiful woman with a smooth brown oval face topped by black curly hair that came in natural ringlets. She had sloe eyes and a petite turned-up nose with very faint black down on her upper lip. Her mouth was wide, generous, with rose-tinted lips and a sudden smile showing even white teeth. Wrapped in a bright blue silk negligee which showed all her curves, her body looked adorable.

He sat at the small round table which had been pushed to one side when the bed was made and indicated her to sit opposite. Then he began speaking to her with pontifical solemnity and seriousness.

'Have you prepared for John's funeral?'

'No, the morgue still has his body but I'm hoping to get Mr Clay for the undertaker and have the funeral in your – our church – and for you to preach the funeral sermon.'

'Of course, Mrs Hill, and I hope by then to have our money back and turn an occasion of deep sorrow also into one of thanksgiving.'

'You can call me Mabel, that's my name,' she said.

'Yes, Mabel, and tomorrow I want you to go to the police and find out what they know so we can use it for our own investigation.' He smiled winningly. 'You're going to be my Mata Hari, Mabel – but one on the side of God.'

Her face lit up with her own brilliant, trusting smile. 'Yes, Reverend O'Malley, oh, I'm so thrilled,' she said delightedly, involuntarily leaning towards him.

Her whole attitude portrayed such devotion he blinked. My God, he thought, this bitch has already forgotten her dead husband and he isn't even in his coffin.

'I'm so glad, Mabel.' He reached across the table and took one of her hands and held it while he looked deeply into her eyes. 'You don't know how much I depend on you.'

'Oh, Reverend O'Malley, I'll do anything for you,' she vowed.

He had to exercise great restraint. 'Now we will kneel and pray to God for the salvation of the soul of your poor dead husband.'

She suddenly sobered and knelt beside him on the floor.

'O Lord, our Saviour and our Master, receive the soul of our dear departed brother, John Hill, who gave his life in support of our humble aspiration to return to our home in Africa.'

'Amen,' she said. 'He was a good husband.'

'You hear, O Lord, a good husband and a good, upright and honest man. Take him and keep him, O Lord, and have mercy and kindness to his poor wife who must remain longer in this vale of tears without the benefit of a husband to fulfil her desires and quench the flames of her body.'

'Amen,' she whispered.

'And grant her a new lease on life, and yes, O Lord, a new man, for life must go on even out of the depths of death, for life is everlasting, O Lord, and we are but human, all of us.'

'Yes,' she cried. 'Yes.'

He figured it was time to cut that shit out before he found himself in bed with her and he didn't want to confuse the issue – he just wanted his money back. So he said, 'Amen.'

'Amen,' she repeated, disappointedly.

They arose and she asked him if she could fix him anything to eat. He said he wouldn't mind some scrambled eggs, toast and coffee, so she took him into the kitchen and made him sit on one of the padded tubular chairs to the spotless masonite tubular table while she went about preparing his snack. It was a kitchen that went along with the rest of the apartment – electric stove, refrigerator, coffee maker, eggbeater, potato whipper and the like; all electric – compactly arranged, brightly painted and superbly hygienic. But he was entranced by the curves of her body beneath the blue silk negligee as she moved about, bent over to get cream and eggs from the refrigerator, turned quickly here and there to do several things at once; and the swinging of her hips when she moved from stove to table.

But when she sat down opposite him she was too self-conscious to talk. A slow blush rose beneath her smooth brown skin, giving her a sun-kissed look. The snack was excellent, crisp bacon, soft scrambled eggs, firm brown toast with a veneer of butter. English marmalade and strong black espresso coffee with thick cream.

He kept the conversation going on the merits of her late husband and how much he would be missed by the Back-to-Africa movement; but he was slowly getting impatient for her to go to bed. It was a relief when she stacked the dishes in the sink and retired to her bedroom with a shy good-night and a wish that he sleep well.

He waited until he felt she was asleep and cracked her door soundlessly. He listened to the even murmur of her breathing. Then he turned on the light in the living-room so he could see her better. If she had awakened he would have pretended to be searching for the bathroom, but she was sleeping soundly with her left hand tight between her legs and her right flung across her exposed breasts. He closed the door and went to the telephone and dialed a number.

'Let me speak to Barry Waterfield, please,' he said when he got an answer.

A sleepy male voice said evilly, 'It's too damn late to be calling roomers. Call in the morning.'

'I just got in town,' Deke said. 'Just passing through – I'm leaving on the 5.45 for Atlanta. I got an important message for him that won't keep.'

'Jussa minute,' the voice said.

Finally another voice came on the line, harsh and heavy with suspicion. 'Who's there?'

'Deke.'

'Oh!'

'Just listen and say nothing. The police are after me. I'm holed up with the wife of our boy, John Hill, who got croaked.' He gave the telephone number and address. 'Nobody knows I'm here but you. And don't call me unless you have to. If she answers tell her your name is James. I'll brief her. Stay out of sight today. Now hang up.'

He listened to the click as the phone was hung up, then waited to see if the line was still open and someone was eavesdropping. Satisfied, he hung up and went back to bed. He turned out the light and lay on his back. A thousand thoughts ran through his mind. He banished them all and finally went to sleep.

He dreamed he was running through a pitch-dark forest and he was terrified and suddenly he saw the moon through the trees and the trees had the shapes of women with breasts hanging like coconuts and suddenly he fell into a pit and it was warm and engulfed him in a warm wet embrace and he felt the most exquisite ecstasy –

'Oh, Reverend O'Malley!' she cried. Light from the bedroom shone across her body, clad only in a frilly nightgown, one ripe brown breast hanging out. She was trembling violently and her face was streaked with tears.

He was so shocked seeing her like this after his dream he leapt from bed and put his arm about her trembling body, wondering if he had attacked her in his sleep. He could feel the warm firm flesh move beneath his hand as she sobbed hysterically.

'Oh, Reverend O'Malley, I've had the most terrible dream.'

'There, there,' he soothed, pulling her body to his. 'Dreams don't mean anything.'

She drew away from him and sat on his bed with her face cupped in her hands, muffling her voice. 'Oh, Reverend O'Malley, I dreamed that you were hurt terribly and when I came to your rescue you looked at me as though you thought I had betrayed you.'

He sat down beside her and began gently stroking her arm. 'I would never think you had betrayed me,' he said soothingly, counting the soft gentle strokes of his hand on the smooth bare flesh of her arm, thinking, any woman will surrender within a hundred strokes. 'I believe in you utterly. You would never be the cause of hurt to me. You will always bring me joy and happiness.'

'Oh, Reverend O'Malley, I feel so inadequate,' she said.

Gently, still counting the strokes of his hand on her arm, he pushed her back and said, 'Now lie down and try not to blame yourself for a silly dream. If I get hurt it will be God's will. We must all bow to God's will. Now repeat after me: If Reverend O'Malley gets hurt, it will be God's will.'

'If Reverend O'Malley gets hurt, it will be God's will,' she repeated dutifully in a low voice.

'We must all bow to God's will.'

'We must all bow to God's will.'

With his free hand he opened her legs.

'God's will must be served,' he said.

'God's will must be served,' she repeated.

'This is God's will,' he said hypnotically.

'This is God's will,' she repeated trance-like.

When he penetrated her she believed it was God's will and she cried, 'Oh-oh! I think you're wonderful!'

7

Grave Digger drove east on 113th Street to Seventh Avenue and Harlem showed another face. A few blocks south was the north end of Central Park and the big kidney-shaped lagoon; north of 116th Street was the 'Avenue' – the lush bars and night clubs, Shalimar, Sugar Ray's, Dickie Well's, Count Basie's, Small's, The Red Rooster; the Hotel Theresa, the National Memorial Book Store (*World History Book Outlet on 600,000,000 Colored People*); the beauty parlors (hairdressers); the hash joints (home cooking); the undertakers and the churches. But here, at 113th Street, Seventh Avenue was deserted at this late hour of the night and the old well-kept stone apartment buildings were dark.

Coffin Ed telephoned the station from the car and got Lieutenant Anderson. 'Anything new?'

'Homicide got a colored taxi driver who picked up three white men and a colored woman outside of Small's and drove them to an address far out on Bedford Avenue in Brooklyn. He said the men didn't look like people who go to Small's and the woman was just a common prostitute.'

'Give me his address and the firm he works for.'

Anderson gave him the information but said, 'That's Homicide's baby. We got nothing on O'Hara. What's your score?'

'We're going to Hijenks' shooting gallery looking for a junkie called Loboy who might know something.'

'Hijenks. That's up on Edgecombe at the Roger Morris, isn't it?'

'He's moved down on Eight. Why don't the Feds knock him off? Who's he paying?'

'Don't ask me; I'm a precinct lieutenant.'

'Well, look for us when we get there.'

They drove down to 110th Street and turned back to Eighth Avenue and filled in the square. Near 112th Street they passed an old junk man pushing his cart piled high with the night's load.

'Old Uncle Bud,' said Coffin Ed. 'Shall we dig him a little?'

'What for? He won't co-operate; he wants to keep on living.'

They parked the car and walked to the bar on the corner of 113th Street. A man and a woman stood at the head of the bar, drinking beer and swapping chatter with the bartender. Grave Digger kept on through to the door marked 'Toilet' and went inside. Coffin Ed stopped at the middle of the bar. The bartender looked quickly towards the toilet door and hastened towards Coffin Ed and began wiping the spotless bar with his damp towel.

'What's yours, sir?' he asked. He was a thin tall, stooped-shouldered, light-complexioned man with a narrow moustache and thinning straight hair. He looked neat in a white jacket and black tie; far too neat for that neck of the woods, Coffin Ed thought.

'Bourbon on the rocks.' The bartender hesitated for an instant and Coffin Ed added, 'Two.' The bartender looked relieved.

Grave Digger came back from the toilet as the bartender was serving the drinks.

'You gentlemen are new around here, aren't you?' the bartender asked conversationally.

'We aren't, but you are,' Grave Digger said.

The bartender smiled noncommittally.

'You see that mark down there on the bar?' Grave Digger said. 'I made it ten years ago.'

The bartender looked down the bar. The wooden bar was covered with marks – names, drawings, signatures. 'What mark?'

'Come here, I'll show you,' Grave Digger said, going down to the end of the bar.

The bartender followed slowly, curiosity overcoming caution. Coffin Ed followed him. Grave Digger pointed at the only unmarked spot on the entire bar. The bartender looked. The couple at the front of the bar had stopped talking and stared curiously.

'I don't see nothing,' the bartender said.

'Look closer,' Grave Digger said, reaching inside his coat.

The bartender bent over to look more closely. 'I still don't see nothing.'

'Look up then,' Grave Digger said.

The bartender looked up into the muzzle of Grave Digger's long-barreled, nickel-plated .38. His eyes popped from their sockets and he turned yellow-green.

'Keep looking,' Grave Digger said.

The bartender gulped but couldn't find his voice. The couple at the head of the bar, thinking it was a stickup, melted into the night. It was like magic, one instant they were there the next instant they were gone.

Chuckling, Coffin Ed went through the 'Toilet' and opened the 'Closet' and gave the signal on the nail holding a dirty rag. The nail was a switch and a light flashed in the entrance hallway upstairs where the lookout sat, reading a comic book. The lookout glanced at the red bulb which should flash the bartender's signal that strangers were downstairs. It didn't flash. He pushed a button and the back door in the closet opened with a soft buzzing sound. Coffin Ed opened the door to the bar and beckoned to Grave

Digger, then jumped back to the door upstairs to keep it from closing.

'Good night,' Grave Digger said to the bartender.

The bartender was about to reply but lights went on in his head and briefly he saw the Milky Way before the sky turned black. A junkie was coming from outside when he saw Grave Digger hit the bartender alongside the head and without putting down his foot turned on his heel and started to run. The bartender slumped down behind the bar, unconscious. Grave Digger had only hit him hard enough to knock him out. Without another look, he leapt towards the 'Toilet' and followed Coffin Ed through the concealed door in the 'Closet' up the narrow stairs.

There was no landing at the top of the stairs and the door was the width of the stairway. There was no place to hide.

Halfway up, Grave Digger took Coffin Ed by the arm. 'This is too dangerous for guns; let's play it straight,' he whispered.

Coffin Ed nodded.

They walked up the stairs and Grave Digger knocked out the signal and stood in front of the peephole so he could be seen.

Inside was a small front hallway furnished with a table littered with comic books; above hung a rack containing numerous pigeonholes where weapons were placed before the addicts were allowed into the shooting gallery. A padded chair was drawn up to the table where the lookouts spent their days. On the left side of the door there were several loose nails in the doorframe. The top nail was the switch that blinked the lights in the shooting gallery in case of a raid. The lookout peered at Grave Digger with a finger poised over the blinker. He didn't recognize him.

'Who're you?' he asked.

Grave Digger flashed his shield and said, 'Detectives Jones and Johnson from the precinct.'

'What you want?'

'We want to talk to Hijenks.'

'Beat it, coppers, there ain't nobody here by that name.'

'You want me to shoot this door open?' Coffin Ed flared.

'Don't make me laugh,' the lookout said. 'This door is bullet-proof and you can't butt it down.'

'Easy, Ed,' Grave Digger cautioned, then to the lookout: 'All right, son, we'll wait.'

'We're just having a little prayer meeting, with the Lord's consent,' the lookout said, but he sounded a little worried.

'Who's the Lord in this case?' Coffin Ed asked harshly.

'Ain't you,' the lookout said.

After that there was silence. Then they heard him moving around inside. Finally they heard another voice ask, 'What is it, Joe?'

'Some nigger cops out there from the precinct.'

'I'll see you sometime, Joe; see who's the niggermost,' Coffin Ed grated.

'You can see me now –' Joe began to bluster, grown brave in the presence of his boss.

'Shut up, Joe,' the voice said. Then they heard the slight sound of the peephole being opened.

'It's Jones and Johnson, Hijenks,' Grave Digger said. 'We just want some information.'

'There's no one here by that name,' Hijenks said.

'By whatever name,' Grave Digger conceded. 'We're looking for Loboy.'

'For what?'

'He might have seen something on that caper where Deke O'Hara's Back-to-Africa group got hijacked.'

'You don't think he was involved?'

'No, he's not involved,' Grave Digger stated flatly. 'But he was in the vicinity of 137th Street and Seventh Avenue when the trucks were wrecked.'

'How do you know that?'

'His sidekick was run over and killed by the hijackers' truck.'

'Well –' Hijenks began, but the lookout cut him off.

'Don't tell those coppers nothing, boss.'

'Shut up, Joe; when I want your advice I'll ask it.'

'We're going to find him anyway, even if we have to get the Feds to break in here to look for him. So if he's here, you'd be doing yourself a favor as well as us if you send him out.'

'At this hour of the night you might find him in Sarah's crib on 105th Street in Spanish Harlem. Do you know where it is?'

'Sarah is an old friend of ours.'

'I'll bet,' Hijenks said. 'Anyway, I don't know where he lives.'

That ended the conversation. No one expected any gratitude for the information; it was strictly business.

They drove across town on 110th Street, past the well-kept old apartment houses overlooking the north end of Central Park and the lagoon where the more affluent colored people lived. It was a quiet street, renamed Cathedral Parkway in honor of the Cathedral of St John the Divine, New York's most beautiful church, which fronted on it – a street of change. The west end, in the vicinity of the cathedral, was still inhabited by whites; but the colored people had taken over that section of Morningside which fronts on the park.

At Fifth Avenue they came to the circle where Spanish Harlem begins. Suddenly the street goes squalid, dirty, teeming with the many colors of Puerto Ricans – so many packed into the incredible slums it seems as though the rotten walls are bursting wtih human flesh. The English language gives way to Spanish, colored Americans give way to colored Puerto Ricans. By the time they reached Madison Avenue, they were in a Puerto Rican city with Puerto Rican customs, Puerto Rican food; with all stores, restaurants, professional offices, business establishments and such bearing signs and notices in Spanish, offering Puerto Rican services and Puerto Rican goods.

'People talk about Harlem,' Grave Digger said. 'These slums are many times worse.'

'Yeah, but when a Puerto Rican becomes white enough he's accepted as white, but no matter how white a spook might become he's still a nigger,' Coffin Ed replied.

'Hell, man, leave that for the anthropologists,' Grave Digger said, turning south on Lexington towards 105th Street.

Sarah had the top flat in an old-fashioned brick apartment building that had seen better days. Directly beneath her top-floor crib lived a Puerto Rican clan of so many families the apartments on the floor could not hold them all; therefore eating, sleeping, cooking and making love was done in turns while the others stayed outside in the street until those inside were finished. Radios blared at top volume all day and night. Combined with the natural sounds of Spanish speech, laughter and quarreling, the din drowned all sounds that might come from Sarah's above. How the families below fared was of no concern.

Grave Digger and Coffin Ed parked down the street and walked. No one gave them a second look. They were men and that's all that interested Sarah: white men, black men, yellow men, brown men, straight men, crooked men and squares. Sarah said she only barred women; she didn't run a joint for 'freaks'. She paid for protection. Everyone knew she was a stool pigeon; but she pigeoned on the police too.

The first thing that hit the detectives when they entered the dimly lit downstairs hallway was the smell of urine.

'What American slums need is toilets,' Coffin Ed said.

Smelling odors of cooking, loving, hair frying, dogs farting, cats pissing, boys masturbating and the stale fumes of stale wine and black tobacco, Grave Digger said, 'That wouldn't help much.'

Next they noticed the graffiti on the walls.

'Hell, no wonder they make so many babies; that's all they think about,' Coffin Ed concluded.

'If you lived here, what else would you think about?'

They ascended in silence. The stink lessened as they climbed the six flights, the walls became less tattooed. The whorehouse floor was practically clean.

They knocked at a red-painted door at the front. It was opened by a grinning Puerto Rican girl who didn't bother to look through the peephole. 'Welcome, señors,' she said. 'You're at the right place.'

They entered a vestibule and looked at the hooks on the walls.

'We want to talk to Sarah,' Grave Digger said.

The girl waved towards a door. 'Come on in. You don't have to see her.'

'We want to see her. You go in like a good little girl and send her out.'

The girl stopped grinning. 'Who're you?'

Both detectives flashed their shields. 'We're the law.'

The girl sneered and turned quickly into the big front room, leaving the door ajar. They could see into what Sarah called her 'reception room'. The floor was covered with polished red linoleum. Chairs lined the walls: overstuffed chairs for the Johns, straight-backed chairs for the girls; but most of the time the girls were either sitting in the laps of the Johns or bringing them food and drink.

The girls were all dressed alike in one-piece shifts showing their shapes, and high-heeled shoes of different colors. They were all light-complexioned Puerto Rican girls with hair shades ranging from blonde to black; all were young. They looked gay and natural and picturesque flitting about the room, peddling their bodies.

Against the back wall a brilliantly lighted jukebox was playing Spanish music and two couples were dancing. The others were sitting, drinking whisky highballs and eating, saving their energy for the real thing.

Alongside the jukebox was a long dimly lit hallway, flanked by the small bedrooms for business. The bathroom and the kitchen were at the rear. A dark brown motherly-type woman fried the chicken, dished out the potato salad and mixed the drinks, keeping a sharp eye on the money.

Two apartments had been put together to make Sarah's crib and the back apartment was her private residence.

Grave Digger said, 'If our people were ever let loose they'd be a sensation in the business world, with the flair they got for crooked organizing.'

'That's what the white folks is scared of,' Coffin Ed said.

They watched Sarah come from the back and cross the big room. The girls treated her as though she were the queen. She was a buxom black woman with snow-white hair done in curls as tight as springs. She had a round face, broad flat nose, thick, dark, unpainted lips and a dazzling white-toothed smile. She wore a black satin gown with long sleeves and a high décolleté; on one wrist was a small platinum watch with a diamond-studded band; on the ring finger a wedding ring set with a diamond the size of an acorn. Several keys dangled on a gold chain about her neck.

She came towards them smiling only with her teeth; her dark eyes were stone cold behind rimless lenses. She closed the door behind her.

'Hello, boys,' she said, shaking hands in turn. 'How are you?'

'Fine, Sarah, business is booming; how's your business?' Grave Digger said.

'Booming too, Digger. Only the criminals got money, and all they do with it is buy pussy. You know how it is, runs hand in hand; girls sell when cotton and corn are a drag on the market. What do you boys want?'

'We want Loboy, Sarah,' Grave Digger said harshly, souring at this landprop's philosophy.

Her smiled went out. 'What's he done, Digger?' she asked in a toneless voice.

'None of your mother-raping business,' Coffin Ed flared.

She looked at him. 'Be careful, Edward,' she warned.

'It's not what he's done this time, Sarah,' Grave Digger said soothingly. 'We're curious about what he's seen. We just want to talk to him.'

'I know what that means. But he's kinda nervous and upset now –'

'High, you mean,' Coffin Ed said.

She looked at him again. 'Don't get tough with me, Edward. I'll have you thrown out here on your ass.'

'Look, Sarah, let's level,' Grave Digger said. 'It's not like you think. You know Deke O'Hara got hijacked tonight.'

'I heard it on the radio. But you ain't stupid enough to think Loboy was on that caper.'

'Not that stupid, Sarah. And we don't give a damn about Deke either. But eighty-seven grand of colored people's hard-earned money got lost in the caper; and we want to get it back.'

'How's Loboy fit that act?'

'Chances are he saw the hijackers. He was working in the neighborhood when their getaway truck crashed and they had to split.'

She studied his face impassively; finally she said, 'I dig.'

Suddenly her smile came on again. 'I'll do anything to help our poor colored people.'

'I believe you,' Coffin Ed said.

She turned back into the reception room without another word and closed the door behind her. A few minutes later she brought out Loboy.

They took him to 137th Street and told him to reconstruct his activities and tell everything he saw before he got out of the vicinity.

At first Loboy protested, 'I ain't done nothing and I ain't seen nothing and you ain't got nothing against me. I been sick all day, at home and in bed.' He was so high his speech was blurred and he kept dozing off in the middle of each sentence.

Coffin Ed slapped him with his open palm a half-dozen times. Tears came to his eyes.

'You ain't got no right to hit me like that. I'm gonna tell Sarah. You ain't got nothing against me.'

'I'm just trying to get your attention is all,' Coffin Ed said.

He got Loboy's attention, but that was all. Loboy admitted getting a glimpse of the driver of the delivery truck that hit Early Riser, but he didn't remember what he looked like. 'He was white is all I remember. All white folks look alike to me,' he said.

He hadn't seen the white men when they had got out from the wrecked truck. He hadn't seen the armored truck at all. By the time it had passed he had jumped the iron fence beside the church and was running down the passageway to 136th Street, headed towards Lenox.

'Which way did the woman go?' Grave Digger asked.

'I didn't stop to see,' Loboy confessed.

'What did she look like?'

'I don't remember; big and strong is all.'

They let him go. By then it was past four in the morning. They drove to the precinct station to check out. They were frustrated and dead beat, and no nearer the solution than at the start. Lieutenant Anderson said nothing new had come in; he had put a tap on Deke's private telephone line but no one had called.

'We should have talked to the driver who took those three white men to Brooklyn, instead of wasting time on Loboy,' Grave Digger said.

'There's no point in second-guessing,' Anderson said. 'Go home and get some sleep.'

He looked white about the gills himself. It had been a hot, raw night – Independence night, he thought – filled with big and little crime. He was sick of crime and criminals; sick of both cops and robbers; sick of Harlem and colored people. He liked colored people all right; they couldn't help it because they were colored. He was quite attached to his two ace colored detectives; in fact he depended on them. They probably kept his job for him. He was second in command to the precinct captain, and had charge of the night shift. His was the sole responsibility when the captain went home, and without his two aces he might not have been able to carry it. Harlem was a mean rough city and you had to be meaner and rougher to keep any kind of order. He understood why colored people were mean and rough; he'd be mean and rough himself if he was colored. He understood all the evils of segregation. He sympathized with the colored people in his precinct, and with colored people in general. But right now he was good and god-damned sick of them. All he wanted was to go home to his quiet house in Queens in a quiet white neighborhood and kiss his white wife and look in on his two sleeping white children and crawl into bed between two white sheets and go to hell to sleep.

So when the telephone rang and a big happy colored voice sang, '. . . O where de cotton and de corn grow . . .' he turned purple with anger.

'Go on the stage, clown!' he shouted and banged down the receiver.

The detectives grinned sympathetically. They hadn't heard the voice but they knew it had been some lunatic talking in jive.

'You'll get used to it if you live long enough,' Grave Digger said.

'I doubt it,' Anderson muttered.

Grave Digger and Coffin Ed started home. They both lived on the same street in Astoria, Long Island, and they only used one of their private cars to travel back and forth to work. They kept their official car, the little battered black sedan with the hopped-up engine, in the precinct garage.

But tonight when they went to put it away, they found it had been stolen.

'Well, that's the bitter end,' Coffin Ed said.

'One thing is for sure,' Grave Digger said. 'I ain't going in and report it.'

'Damn right,' Coffin Ed agreed.

8

The next morning, at eight o'clock, an open bed truck pulled up before a store on Seventh Avenue that was being remodeled. Formerly, there had been a notion goods store with a shoeshine parlor serving as a numbers drop on the site. But it had been taken over by a new tenant and a high board wall covering the entire front had been erected during the remodeling.

There had been much speculation in the neighborhood concerning the new business. Some said it would be a bar, others a night club. But Small's Paradise Inn was only a short distance away, and the cognoscenti ruled those out. Others said it was an ideal spot for a barbershop or a hairdresser, or even a bowling alley; some half-wits opted for another funeral parlor, as though colored folks weren't dying fast enough as it is. Those in the know claimed they had seen office furnishings moved in during the night and they had it at first hand that it was going to be the headquarters for the Harlem political committee of the Republican Party. But those with the last word said that Big Wilt Chamberlain, the professional basketball player who had bought Small's Cabaret, was going to open a bank to store all the money he was making hand over fist.

By the time the workmen began taking down the wall, a small crowd had collected. But when they had finished, the crowd overflowed into the street. Harlemites, big and little, old and young, strong and feeble, the halt and the blind, male and female, boys and girls, stared in pop-eyed amazement.

'Great leaping Jesus!' said the fat black barber from down the street, expressing the opinion of all.

Plate-glass windows, trimmed with stainless steel, formed a glass front above a strip of shining steel along the sidewalk. Across the top, above the glass, was a big wooden sign glistening with spotless white paint upon which big, bold, black letters announced:

HEADQUARTERS OF
B.T.S. BACK-TO-THE-SOUTHLAND
MOVEMENT B.T.S.
Sign Up Now!!! Be a 'FIRST NEGRO!'
$1,000 Bonus to First Families Signing!

The entire glass front was plastered with bright-colored paintings of conk-haired black cotton-pickers, clad in overalls that resembled Italian-tailored suits, delicately lifting enormous snow-white balls of cotton from rose-colored cotton bolls that looked for all the world like great cones of ice cream, and grinning happily with even whiter teeth; others showed darkies, clad in the same Italian fashion, hoeing corn as though doing the cakewalk, their heads lifted in song that must surely be spirituals. One scene showed these happy darkies at the end of the day celebrating in a clearing in front of ranch-type cabins, dancing the twist, their teeth gleaming in the setting sun, their hips rolling in the playful shadows to the music of a banjo player in a candy-striped suit; while the elders looked on with approval, bobbing their nappy white heads and clapping their manicured hands. Another showed a tall white man with a white mane of hair, a white moustache and white goatee, wearing a black frock coat and shoestring tie, his pink face bubbling with brotherly love, passing out fantastic bundles of bank notes to a row of grinning darkies, above the caption: *Paid by the week*. Lodged between the larger scenes were smaller paintings identified as ALL GOOD THINGS TO EAT: grotesquely oversized animals and edibles with the accompanying captions: *Big-legged Chickens . . . Chitterling Bred Shoats . . . Yams! What Am . . . O! Possum! . . . Lasses In The Jug . . . Grits and Gravy . . . Pappy's Bar-B-Q and Mammy's Hog Maw Stew . . . Corn Whisky . . . Buttermilk . . . Hoppin John*.

In the center of all this jubilation of good food, good times and good pay, were a blown-up photomontage beside a similarly sized drawing: one showing pictures of famine in the Congo, tribal wars, mutilations, depravities, hunger and disease, above the caption, *Unhappy Africa*; the other depicting fat, grinning colored people sitting at tables laden with food, driving about in cars as big as Pullman coaches, black children entering modernistic schools equipped with stadiums and swimming-pools, elderly people clad in Brooks Brothers suits and Saks Fifth Avenue dresses filing into a church that looked astonishingly like Saint Peter's Cathedral in Rome, with its caption: *The Happy South*.

At the bottom was another big white-painted, black-lettered banner reading:

FARE PAID . . . HIGH WAGES . . .
ACCOMMODATIONS FOR COTTON PICKERS
$1,000 Bonus for Each Family of Five Able-Bodied Persons

The small notice in one lower corner which read, *Wanted, a bale of cotton*, went unnoticed.

On the inside, the walls were decorated with more slogans and pictures of the same papier-mâché cotton plants and bamboo corn stalks were scattered about the floor, in the center of which was an artificial bale of cotton bearing the etched brass legend: *Our Front Line of Defense*.

At the front to one side was a large flat-topped desk with a nameplate stating: Colonel Robert L. Calhoun. Colonel Calhoun in the flesh sat behind the desk, smoking a long, thin cheroot and looking out the window at the crowd of Harlemites with a benign expression. He looked like the model who had posed for the portrait of the colonel in the window, paying off the happy darkies. He had the same narrow, hawklike face crowned by the same mane of snow-white hair, the same wide, drooping white moustache, the same white goatee. There the resemblance stopped. His narrow-set eyes were ice-cold blue and his back was ramrod straight. But he was clad in a similar black frock coat and black shoestring tie, and on the ring finger of his long pale hand was a solid gold signet ring with the letters CSA.

A young blond white man in a seersucker suit, who looked as though he might be an alumnus of Ole Miss, sat on the edge of the Colonel's desk, swinging his leg.

'Are you going to talk to them?' he asked in a college-trained voice with a slight southern accent.

The Colonel removed his cheroot and studied the ash on the tip. His actions were deliberate; his expression impassive. He spoke in a voice that was slow and calculated, with a southern accent as thick as molasses in the winter.

'Not yet, son, let's let it simmer a bit. You can't rush these darkies; they'll come around in their own good time.'

The young man peered through a clear crack in the plastered window. He looked anxious. 'We haven't got all the time in the world,' he said.

The Colonel looked up at him, smiling with perfect white dentures, but his eyes remained cold. 'What's your hurry, son, you got a gal waiting?'

The young man blushed and looked down sullenly. 'All these niggers make me nervous,' he confessed.

'Now don't start feeling guilty, son,' the Colonel said. 'Remember it's for their own good. You got to learn to think of niggers with love and charity.'

The young man smiled sardonically and remained silent.

At the back of the room were two desks side by side, bearing the legends: *Applications*. They were presided over by two neat young colored men who shuffled application forms to look occupied. From time to time the Colonel looked at them approvingly, as though to say, 'See how far you've come.' But they had the expressions of guilty fathers who've been caught robbing their babies' banks.

Outside, on the sidewalk and in the street, black people were expressing righteous indignation.

'Ain't it a scandal, Lord, right up here in Harlem?'

'God ought to strike 'em daid, that's whut.'

'These peckerwoods don't know what they want. One day they's sending us north to get rid of us, and the next they's up here tryna con us into going back.'

'Man, trust white folks and go from Cadillacs to cotton sacks.'

'Ain't it the truth! I'd sooner trust a white-mouthed moccasin sucking at my tiddy.'

'Man, I ought to go in there and say to that ol' colonel, "You wants me to go back south, eh?" and he says, "That's right, boy," and I says, "You gonna let me vote?" and he says, "That's right, boy, vote all you want, just so long you don't cast no ballots," and I says, "You gonna let me marry yo' daughter –"'

His audience fell out laughing. But one joker didn't think it was funny; he said, 'There he is, what's stopping you?'

Everyone stopped laughing.

The comedian said shamefacedly, 'Hell, man, I don't do everything I oughta do, you knows that.'

A big matronly woman said, 'Just you wait 'til Reverend
O'Malley hears 'bout all this, and then you'll see some action.'

Reverend O'Malley had already heard. Barry Waterfield, the
phoney detective in his employ, had telephoned him and given
him the lowdown. Reverend O'Malley had sent him to see the
Colonel with implicit instructions.

Barry was a big, clean-shaven man with hair cropped short
and a nose flattened in the ring. His dark brown face bore other
lumps it had taken during his career as bodyguard, bouncer,
mugger and finally killer. He had small brown eyes partly obscured by scar tissue, and two gold teeth in front. He was easily
identifiable, which limited his usefulness, but Deke didn't have
any other choice.

Barry shaved, carefully brushed his hair, dressed in a dark
business suit, but couldn't resist the hand-painted tie depicting
an orange sunset on a green background.

When he pushed through the crowd and entered the office of
the Back-to-the-Southland movement, talk stopped momentarily
and people stared at him. No one knew him, but no one would
forget him.

He walked straight to the colonel's desk and said, 'Colonel
Calhoun, I'm Mr Waterfield from the Back-to-Africa movement.'

Colonel Calhoun looked up through cold blue eyes and
appraised him from head to foot. Colonel Calhoun dug him
instantly. The Colonel removed the cheroot from his white
moustache and his dentures gleamed whitely.

'What can I do for you . . . er . . . what did you say your name
was?'

'Barry Waterfield.'

'Barry. What can I do for you, boy?'

'Well, you see, we have a group of good people we're going to send back to Africa.'

'Back to Africa!' the Colonel exclaimed in horror. 'My boy, you must be raving mad. Uprooting these people from their native land. Don't do it, boy, don't do it.'

'Well, sir, you see, it's going to cost a lot –' He remained standing, as the Colonel had not invited him to be seated.

'A fortune, my boy, a veritable fortune,' the Colonel agreed, rearing back in his chair. 'And who's going to pay for this costly nonsense?'

'Well, sir, you see, that's the trouble. You see, last night we were having a big rally to sign up the families who were going to leave first, and then some bandits robbed us of their money. Eighty-seven thousand dollars.'

The Colonel whistled softly.

'You must have heard about it, sir.'

'No, I can't say that I have, my boy; but I've been pretty busy with this philanthropy of ours. But I'm sorry for those misguided people, even though their misfortune might turn out to be a blessing in disguise. I'm ashamed of you, my boy, an honest-looking American nigra like you, leading your people astray. If you knew what we know, you wouldn't dream of sending your poor people to Africa. Only pestilence and starvation await them there, in those foreign lands. The South is the place for them, the good old reliable Southland. We love and take care of our darkies.'

'Well, you see, sir, that's what I want to talk to you about. These poor people have got ready to go somewhere, and now since they can't go back to Africa it might be best they go back south.'

'Right you are, my boy. You just send them to me and we'll do right by them. The Happy Southland is the only home of your people.'

The two young colored clerks who had been eavesdropping on the conversation were downright shocked to hear Barry say, 'Well, sir, I'm inclined to agree with you, sir.'

The blond young man was standing at the front window, peering out at the milling black mob which he now began to see in a different light. They didn't look dangerous any longer; now they appeared innocent and gullible and he could barely suppress a smile as he thought of how easy it was going to be. Then he frowned at a sudden memory and turned back to stare at Barry with searching suspicion. This nigger sounded too good to be true, he thought.

But the Colonel didn't seem to entertain a doubt. 'You just trust me, my boy,' he went on, 'and we'll take care of your people.'

'Well, you see, sir, I trust you,' Barry said. 'I know you'll do the right thing by us. But our leader, Reverend O'Malley, won't like it, my giving you my confidence. You see, sir, he's a dangerous man.'

A line of white dentures peeped from beneath the Colonel's white moustache, and Barry had a fleeting thought that this mother-raping white man looked too mother-raping white. But the Colonel continued unsuspectingly, 'Don't worry about that nigra, my boy, we're going to take care of him and put an end to his un-American activities.'

Barry leaned a little forward and lowered his voice. 'You see, sir, the point is we have the eighty-seven families of able-bodied people all packed and ready to go; and I've got to tell them if you're ready to pay them their bonuses.'

'My boy, their bonuses is as good as in the bank. You tell them that,' the Colonel said and rolled the cheroot between his lips only to find it had gone out.

He tossed it carelessly on the floor and carefully selected

another from a silver case in his breast pocket. Then he clipped the end with a cigar cutter from his vest pocket, stuck the clipped cheroot between his lips and rolled it over and over until the outer leaves of the lip-end were agreeably wet. Both Barry and the blond young man snapped their lighters to offer a light, but the Colonel preferred Barry's flame.

Barry said, 'Well, that is fine of you, sir, that's all I want to know. We got more than a thousand families recruited and I'll sell you the whole list.'

For an instant both the Colonel and the blond young man became immobile. Then the Colonel's dentures showed. 'If I heard you correctly, my boy,' he said smoothly, 'you said *sell*.'

'Well, sir, you see, sir, it's like this,' Barry began, his voice pitched low and grown husky. 'Naturally I would want a little something for myself, taking all this risk. You see, sir, the list is highly confidential and it has taken us months to select and recruit all these able-bodied people. And if they knew I was turning this list over to you, they might make trouble, sir – even though it is for their own good. And I'd want to be able to get away for a while, sir. You understand, sir.'

'My boy, nothing could be plainer,' the Colonel said and puffed his cheroot. 'Plain talk suits me fine. Now how much do you want for your list?'

'Well, sir. I was thinking fifty dollars a family would be about fair, sir.'

'You're a boy after my own heart, even though you do belong to the nigra race,' the Colonel said. The blond young man frowned and opened his mouth as though to speak, but the Colonel ignored him. 'Now, my boy, I understand your predicament and I don't want to jeopardize your position and usefulness by permitting you to come back here and be seen and suspected by all your people. So I'm going to tell you what I want you to do. You bring the list to me at midnight. I'll be waiting down by the Harlem River underneath the subway extension to the Polo Grounds in my cah, and I'll pay you right then and there. It will be dark and deserted at that time of night and nobody'll see you.'

Barry hesitated, looking torn between fear and greed. 'Well, frankly, sir, that's a good sound idea, but I'm scared of the dark, sir,' he confessed.

The Colonel chuckled. 'There's nothing about the dark to fear, my boy. That's just nigra superstition. The dark never hurt anyone. You'll be as safe as in the arms of Jesus. I give you my word.'

Barry looked relieved at this. 'Well, sir, if you give me your word I know can't nothing happen to me. I'll be there at midnight sharp.'

Without further ado, the Colonel waved a hand, dismissing him.

'Are you going to trust that –' the blond young man began.

For the first time the Colonel showed displeasure in a frown. The blond young man shut up.

As he was leaving, Barry noticed the small sign in the window through the corners of his eyes: *Wanted, a bale of cotton*. What for? he wondered.

9

No one knew where Uncle Bud slept. He could be found any night somewhere on the streets of Harlem, pushing his cart, his eyes searching the darkness for anything valuable enough to sell. He had an exceptional divination of anything of value, because in Harlem no one ever threw anything away valuable enough to sell, if they knew it. But he managed to collect enough saleable junk to exist, and when day broke he was to be seen at one of those run-down junkyards where scrawny-necked, beady-eyed white men paid a few cents for the rags, paper, glass and iron he had collected. Actually he slept in his cart during the summer. He would wheel it to some shady spot on some slum street where no one thought it strange to find a junk man sleeping in his cart, and curl up on the burlap rags covering his load and sleep, undisturbed by the sounds of motor-cars and trucks, children screaming, men cursing and fighting, women gossiping, police sirens wailing, or even by the dead awakening. Nothing troubled his sleep.

On this night, because his cart was filled with the bale of cotton, he wheeled it towards a street beneath the 125th Street approach to the Triborough Bridge, where he would be near Mr Goodman's junkyard when he woke up.

A police cruiser containing two white cops pulled up beside him. 'What you got there, boy?' the one on the inside asked.

Uncle Bud stopped and scratched his head and ruminated. 'Wal, boss, I'se got some cahdbo'd and papuh an' I'se got some bedsprings an' some bottles an' some rags an' –'

'You ain't got no money, have you?' the cop cracked. 'You ain't got no eighty-seven thousand dollars?'

'Nawsuh, wish I did.'

'What would you do with eighty-seven grand?'

Uncle Bud scratched his head again. 'Wal, suh, I'd buy me a brand new waggin. An' then I reckon I'd go to Africa,' he said, adding underneath his breath: 'Where wouldn't any white mother-rapers like you be fucking with me all the time.'

Naturally the cops didn't hear the last, but they laughed at the first and drove on.

Uncle Bud found a spot beside an abandoned truck down by the river and went to sleep. When he awakened the sun was high. At about the same time Barry Waterfield was approaching Colonel Calhoun on Seventh Avenue, he was approaching the junkyard alongside the river south of the bridge.

It was a fenced-in enclosure about piles of scrap iron and dilapidated wooden sheds housing other kinds of junk. Uncle Bud stopped before a small gate at one side of the main office building, a one-storey wooden box fronting on the street. A big black hairless dog the size of a Great Dane came silently to the gate and stared at him through yellow eyes.

'Nice doggie,' Uncle Bud said through the wire gate.

The dog didn't blink.

A shabbily dressed, unshaven white man came from the office and led the dog away and chained it up. Then he returned and said, 'All right, Uncle Bud, what you got there?'

Uncle Bud looked at the white man through the corners of his eyes. 'A bale of cotton, Mr Goodman.'

Mr Goodman was startled. 'A bale of cotton?'

'Yassuh,' Uncle Bud said proudly as he uncovered the bale. 'Genuwine Mississippi cotton.'

Mr Goodman unlocked the gate and came outside to look at it. Most of the cotton was obscured by the burlap covering. But he pulled out a few shreds from the seams and smelled it. 'How do you know it's *Mississippi* cotton?'

'I'd know Mississippi cotton anywhere I seed it,' Uncle Bud stated flatly. 'Much as I has picked.'

'Ain't much of this to be seen,' Mr Goodman observed.

'I can smell it,' Uncle Bud said. 'It smell like nigger-sweat.'

Mr Goodman sniffed at the cotton again. 'Anything special about that?'

'Yassuh, makes it stronger.'

Two colored workmen in overalls came up. 'Cotton!' one exclaimed. 'Lord, lord.'

'Makes you homesick, don't it?' the other one said.

'Homesick for your mama,' the first one said, looking at him sidewise.

'Watch out, man, I don't play the dozzens,' the second one said.

Mr Goodman knew they were just kidding. 'All right, get it on the scales,' he ordered.

The bale weighed four hundred and eighty-seven pounds.

'I'll give you five dollars for it,' Mr Goodman said.

'Five bones!' Uncle Bud exclaimed indignantly. 'Why, dis cotton is worth thirty-nine cents a pound.'

'You're thinking about the First World War,' Mr Goodman said. 'Nowadays they're giving cotton away.'

The two workmen exchanged glances silently.

'I ain't giving dis away,' Uncle Bud said.

'Where can I sell a bale of cotton?' Mr Goodman said. 'Who wants unprocessed cotton? Not even good for bullets no more.

Nowadays they shoot atoms. It ain't like as if it was drugstore cotton.'

Uncle Bud was silent.

'All right, ten dollars then,' Mr Goodman said.

'Fifty dollars,' Uncle Bud countered.

'*Mein Gott*, he wants fifty dollars yet!' Mr Goodman appealed to his colored workmen. 'That's more than I'd pay for brass.'

The colored workmen stood with their hands in their pockets, blank-faced and silent. Uncle Bud kept a stubborn silence. All three colored men were against Mr Goodman. He felt trapped and guilty, as though he'd been caught taking advantage of Uncle Bud.

'Since it's you, I'll give you fifteen dollars.'

'Forty,' Uncle Bud muttered.

Mr Goodman gestured eloquently. 'What am I, your father, to give you money for nothing?' The three colored men stared at him accusingly. 'You think I am Abraham Lincoln instead of Abraham Goodman?' The colored men didn't think he was funny. 'Twenty,' Mr Goodman said desperately and turned towards the office.

'Thirty,' Uncle Bud said.

The colored workmen shifted the bale of cotton as though asking whether to take it in or put it back.

'Twenty-five,' Mr Goodman said angrily. 'And I should have my head examined.'

'Sold,' Uncle Bud said.

About that time the Colonel had finished his interview with Barry and was having his breakfast. It had been sent from a 'home-cooking' restaurant down the street. The Colonel seemed to be demonstrating to the colored people outside, many of whom were now peeking through the cracks between the posters covering most of the window, what they could be eating for breakfast if they signed up with him and went back south.

He had a bowl of grits, swimming with butter; four fried eggs sunny side up; six fried home-made sausages; six down-home biscuits, each an inch thick, with big slabs of butter stuck between the halves; and a pitcher of sorghum molasses. The Colonel had brought his own food with him and merely paid the restaurant to cook it. Alongside his heaping plate stood a tall bourbon whisky highball.

The colored people, watching the Colonel shovel grits, eggs and sausage into his mouth and chomp off a hunk of biscuit, felt nostalgic. But when they saw him cover all his food with a thick layer of sorghum molasses, many felt absolutely homesick.

'I wouldn't mind going down home for dinner ever day,' one joker said. 'But I wouldn't want to stay overnight.'

'Baby, seeing that scoff makes my stomach feel lak my throat is cut,' another replied.

Bill Davis, the clean-cut young man who was Reverend O'Malley's recruiting agent, entered the Back-to-the-Southland office as Colonel Calhoun was taking an oversize mouthful of grits, eggs and sausage mixed with molasses. He paused before the Colonel's desk, erect and purposeful.

'Colonel Calhoun, I am Mister Davis,' he said. 'I represent the Back-to-Africa movement of Reverend O'Malley's. I want a word with you.'

The Colonel looked up at Bill Davis through cold blue eyes, continuing to chew slowly and deliberately like a camel chewing its cud. But he took much longer in his appraisal than he had done with Barry Waterfield. When he had finished chewing, he washed his mouth with a sip from his bourbon highball, cleared his throat and said, 'Come back in half an hour, after I've et my breakfast.'

'What I have to say to you I'm going to say now,' Bill Davis said.

The Colonel looked up at him again. The blond young man who had been standing in the background moved closer. The young colored men at their desks in the rear became nervous.

'Well, what can I do for you . . . er . . . what did you say your name was?' the Colonel said.

'My name is *Mister* Davis, and I'll make it short and sweet. *Get out of town!*'

The blond young man started around the desk and Bill Davis got set to hit him, but the Colonel waved him back.

'Is that all you got to say, my boy?'

'That's all, and I'm not your boy,' Bill Davis said.

'Then you've said it,' the Colonel said and deliberately began eating again.

When Bill emerged, the black people parted to let him pass. They didn't know what he had said to the Colonel, but whatever it was they were for him. He had stood right up to that ol' white man and tol' him something to his teeth. They respected him.

A half-hour later the pickets moved in. They marched up and down Seventh Avenue, holding aloft a Back-to-Africa banner and carrying placards reading: *Goddamn White Man GO! GO! GO! Black Man STAY! STAY! STAY!* There were twenty-five in the picket line and two or three hundred followers. The pickets formed a circle in front of the Back-to-the-Southland office and chanted as they marched, 'Go, white man, go while you can . . . Go, white man, go while you can . . .' Bill Davis stood to one side between two elderly colored men.

Colored people poured into the vicinity from far and wide, overflowed the sidewalks and spilled into the street. Traffic was stopped. The atmosphere grew tense, pregnant with premonition. A black youth ran forward with a brick to hurl through the plate-glass window. A Back-to-Africa follower grabbed him and took it away. 'None of that, son, we're peaceful,' he said.

'What for?' the youth asked.

The man couldn't answer.

Suddenly the air was filled with the distant wailing of the sirens, sounding at first like the faint wailing of banshees, growing ever louder as the police cruisers roared nearer, like souls escaped from hell.

The first cruiser ploughed through the mob and shrieked to a stop on the wrong side of the street. Two uniformed white cops hit the pavement with pistols drawn, shouting, 'Get back! Get off the street! Clear the street!' Then another cruiser plowed through the mob and shrieked to a stop . . . Then a third . . . Then a fourth . . . Then a fifth. Out came the white cops, brandishing their pistols, like trained performers in a macabre ballet entitled 'If You're Black Get Back'.

The mood of the mob became dangerous. A cop pushed a black man. The black man got set to hit the cop. Another cop quickly intervened.

A woman fell down and was trampled. 'Help! Murder!' she screamed.

The mob moved in her direction, taking the cops with it.

'Goddamned mother-raping shit! Here it is!' a young black man shouted, whipping out his switch-blade knife.

Then the precinct captain arrived in a sound truck. 'All officers back to your cars,' he ordered, his voice loud and clear from the amplifiers. 'Back to your cars. And, folks, let's have some order.'

The cops retreated to their cars. The danger passed. Some people cheered. Slowly the people returned to the sidewalks. Passenger cars that had been lined up for more than ten blocks began to move along, curious faces peering out at the black people crowding the sidewalks.

The captain went over and talked to Bill Davis and the two men with him. 'Only nine persons are permitted on a picket line by New York law,' he said. 'Will you thin these pickets down to nine?'

Bill looked at the elderly men. They nodded. He said, 'All right,' to the captain and thinned out the picket line.

Then the captain went inside the office and approached Colonel Calhoun; he asked to see his licence. The Colonel's papers were in order; he had a New York City permit to recruit farm labor as the agent of the Back-to-the-Southland movement, which was registered in Birmingham, Alabama.

The captain returned to the street and stationed ten policemen in front of the office to keep order, and two police cruisers to keep the street clear. Then he shook hands with Bill Davis and got back into the sound truck and left.

The mob began to disperse.

'I knew we'd get some action from Reverend O'Malley, soon as he heard about all this,' the church sister said.

Her companion looked bewildered. 'What I wants to know,' she asked, 'is we won or lost?'

Inside, the blond young man asked Colonel Calhoun, 'Aren't we pretty well finished now?'

Colonel Calhoun lit a fresh cheroot and took a puff. 'It's just good publicity, son,' he said.

By then it was noon, and the two young colored clerks slipped out the back door to go to lunch.

Later that afternoon one of Mr Goodman's workmen stood in the crowd surrounding the Back-to-Africa pickets, admiring the poster art on the windows of the Back-to-the-Southland office. He had bathed and shaved and dressed up for a big Saturday night and he was just killing time until his date. Suddenly his gaze fell on the small sign in the corner reading: *Wanted, a bale of cotton*. He started inside. A Back-to-Africa sympathizer grabbed his arm.

'Don't go in there, friend. You don't believe that crap, do you?'

'Baby, I ain't thinking 'bout going south. I ain't never been south. I just wanna talk to the man.'

''Bout what?'

'I just wanna ask the man if them chicken really got legs that big,' he said, pointing to the picture of the chicken.

The man bent over laughing. 'You go 'head and ast him, man, and you tell me what he say.'

The workman went inside and walked up to Colonel Calhoun's desk and took off his cap. 'Colonel,' he said, 'I'm just the man you wanna see. My name is Josh.'

The Colonel gave him the customary cold-eyed appraisal, sitting reared back in his chair as though he hadn't moved. The blond young man stood beside him.

'Well, Josh, what can you do for me?' the Colonel asked, showing his dentures in a smile.

'I can get you a bale of cotton,' Josh said.

The tableau froze. The Colonel was caught in the act of returning the cheroot to his lips. The blond young man was caught in the act of turning to look out towards the street. Then, deliberately, without a change of expression, the Colonel put the cheroot between his lips and puffed. The blond young man turned back to stare wordlessly at Josh, leaning slightly forward.

'You want a bale of cotton, don't you?' Josh asked.

'Where would you get a bale of cotton, my boy?' the Colonel asked casually.

'We got one in the junkyard where I work.'

The blond young man let out his breath in a disappointed sigh.

'A junk man sold it to us just this morning,' Josh went on, hoping to get an offer.

The blond young man tensed again.

But the Colonel continued to appear relaxed and amiable. 'He didn't steal it, did he? We don't want to buy any stolen goods.'

'Oh, Uncle Bud didn't steal it, I'm sure,' Josh said. 'He must of found it somewheres.'

'Found a bale of cotton?' The Colonel sounded sceptical.

'Must have,' Josh contended. 'He spends every night traveling 'bout the streets, picking up junk what's been lost or thrown away. Where could he steal a bale of cotton?'

'And he sold it to you this morning?'

'Yassuh, to Mr Goodman, that is; he owns the junkyard, I just work there. But I can get it for you.'

'When?'

'Well, ain't nobody there now. We close at noon on Sat'day and Mr Goodman go home; but I can get it for you tonight if you wants it right away.'

'How?'

'Well, suh, I got a key, and we don't have to bother Mr Goodman; I can just sell it to you myself.'

'Well,' the Colonel said and puffed his cheroot. 'We'll pick you up in my cah at the 125th Street railroad station at ten o'clock tonight. Can you be there?'

'Oh, yassuh, I can be there!' Josh declared, then hesitated. 'That's all right, but how much you going to pay me?'

'Name your own price,' the Colonel said.

'A hundred dollars,' Josh said, holding his breath.

'Right,' the Colonel said.

IO

Iris lay on her sofa in the sitting-room reading *Ebony* magazine and eating chocolate candy. She had been under twenty-four-hour surveillance since the hijacking. A police matron had spent the night in her bedroom while a detective had sat up in the sitting-room. Now there was another detective there alone. He had orders not to let her out of his sight. He had followed her from room to room, even keeping the bathroom door in view after having removed the razor blades and all other instruments by which she might injure herself.

He sat facing her in an overstuffed chair, leafing through a book called *Sex and Race* by W. G. Rogers. The only others books in the house were the Bible and *The Life of Marcus Garvey. Sex and Race* didn't interest him. Garvey didn't interest him either. He had read the Bible, at least all he needed to read.

He was bored. He didn't like his assignment. But the captain thought that sooner or later Deke was going to try to contact her, or she him, and he was taking every precaution. The telephone was bugged and the operators alerted to trace all incoming calls; and there was a police cruiser with a radio-telephone parked within thirty seconds' distance down the street, manned by four detectives.

The captain wanted Deke as bad as people in hell want ice water.

Iris threw down the magazine and sat up. She was wearing a silk print dress and the skirt hiked up, showing smooth yellow thighs above tan nylon stockings.

The book fell from the detective's hands.

'Why the hell don't you just arrest me and have it done with?' she flared in her vulgar husky voice.

Her voice grated on the detective's nerves. And her vulgar sensuality bothered him. He was a home-loving man with a wife and three children, and her perfumed voluptuous body with its effluvium of sex outraged his sensibilities. His puritanical soul felt affronted by this aura of sex and his perverse imagination filled him with a sense of guilt. But he had himself well under control.

'I just take orders, ma'am,' he said mildly. 'Any time you want to go to the station of your own accord I'll take you.'

'Shit,' she said, looking at him with disgust.

He was a tall, balding, redheaded, middle-aged man with a slight stoop. A small dried face between huge red ears gave him a monkeyish look and his white skin was blotched with large brown freckles. He was a plain-clothes precinct detective and he looked underpaid.

Iris examined him appraisingly. 'If you weren't such an ugly mother-raper at least we could pass time making love,' she said.

He was beginning to suspect that was the reason the captain had chosen him for the assignment and he felt slightly piqued. But he just grinned and said, jokingly, 'I'll put a sack over my head.'

She started to grin and then looked suddenly caught. Her face mirrored her thoughts. 'All right,' she said, getting up.

He looked alarmed. 'I was just joking,' he said foolishly.

'I'll go undress and you come in with nothing showing but your eyes and mouth.'

He grinned shamefacedly. 'You know I couldn't do that.'

'Why not?' she said. 'You ain't never had nobody like me.'

Red came out in his face as though it had caught fire. He looked like a small boy caught in a guilty act. 'Now, ma'am, you got to be sensible; this surveillance ain't going to last for ever –'

She turned quickly on her high heels and started towards the kitchen. Her walk was exaggerated, like that of a prostitute soliciting trade. But he had to follow her, cursing his instincts which kept defying his will.

She searched in the pantry, paying him no attention. He felt a slight trace of trepidation, fearing she might come out with a gun. But she found what she wanted, a brown paper sack. She turned and tried to put it over his head, but he jumped back and warded her off as though she held a live rattlesnake.

'I just wanted to try it for size,' she said, trying it on her own head instead. 'What are you anyway, a pansy?'

He was incensed by her allusion to his masculinity, but he consoled himself with the thought that in different circumstances he'd ride that yellow bitch until she yelled quits.

She switched past him, looking at him through the corners of her eyes and brushing him lightly with her hips. Then she deliberately shook her buttocks and waved the sack over her head like a dare and went into the bedroom.

He debated whether to follow her. This bitch was getting on his nerves, he told himself. She wasn't the only one who could make love, hell, his wife – He stopped that thought; that wasn't going to get him anywhere. Finally he gave in and followed her. Orders were orders, he told himself.

He found her with a pair of nail scissors in her hand, cutting eyeholes in the paper sack. He felt his ears burning. He looked about the room for a telephone extension, but didn't see any. Against his will he watched her cut out a place for his mouth.

Unconsciously his vision strayed to her wide luscious mouth. She licked her lips and stuck out the tip of her tongue.

'Now, ma'am, this has gone far enough,' he protested.

She acted as though she hadn't heard, measuring his head with her eyes. Then she cut out a place for his ears, saying, 'Big ears, big you-know-what.' His ears burned as though on fire. For a moment she stood looking at her handiwork. He looked too.

'You've got to breathe, haven't you, baby?' she cooed and cut out a place for his nose.

'Now you come out of here and sit down and behave yourself,' he said, trying to sound stern, but his voice was thick with tongue.

She went over to the small record player against the wall and put on a slow sexy blues number and stood for a moment weaving her body tantalizingly, snapping her fingers.

'I'll have to use force,' he warned.

She swung around and threw open her arms and advanced on him. 'Come on and force me, daddy,' she said.

He turned his back and stood in the doorway. She stood before the mirror and took off her ear-rings and necklace and ran her fingers through her hair, whistling a low accompaniment to the music, seemingly paying him no attention. Then she took off her dress.

He turned around to see what she was doing and damn near jumped out of his skin. 'Don't do that!' he shouted.

'You can't stop me from undressing in my own bedroom,' she said.

He went over and snatched up the dressing-table chair and planted it in the doorway and plopped himself down with an air of determination. 'All right, go ahead,' he said, turning his profile towards her so he could watch her for mischief through the corners of his eyes.

She tilted the dressing-table mirror so he could see her re-flection, then pulled up her slip over her head. Now her creamy yellow body was clad only in a thin black strapless bra and tiny black pants trimmed with lace, over a garter belt.

'If you're scared, go home,' she taunted.

He gritted his teeth and continued to look away.

She took off her bra and pants and stood facing the mirror cupping her breasts in her hands and gently caressing her teaties. With only the garter belt and nylon stockings and high-heeled shoes, she looked more nude than were she stark-naked. She saw him peeping at her reflection in the mirror, and began doing things with her stomach and hips.

He swallowed. From the neck up he was blindly furious; but from the neck down he was on a live wire edge. His insides were a battleground for his will and his lust, with his organs suffering the consequences. Whole areas of his body seemed on fire. The fire seemed breaking through his skin. Centipedes were crawling over his testicles and ants were attacking his phallus. He squirmed in his seat as it became more and more unbearable; his pants were too tight; his coat was too small; his head was too hot; his mouth was too dry.

With a flourish like a stripteaser removing her G-string, she took off one shoe and tossed it into his lap. He knocked it violently aside. She took off the other shoe and tossed it into his lap. He caught himself just in time to keep from grabbing it and biting it. She stripped off her stockings and garter belt and approached him to drape them about his neck.

He came to his feet like a Jack-in-the-box, saying in a squeaky voice, 'This has gone far enough.'

'No, it hasn't,' she said and moved into him.

He tried to push her away but she clung to him with all strength, pushing her stomach into him and wrapping her legs about his body. The odor of hot-bodied woman, wet cunt and perfume came up from her and drowned him.

'Goddamned whore!' he grated, and backed her to the bed. He tore off his coat, mouthing, 'I'll show you who's a pansy, you hot-ass slut.'

But at the last moment he regained enough composure to go hang his holstered pistol on the outside doorknob out of her reach, then he turned back towards her.

'Come and get it, pansy,' she taunted, lying on the bed with her legs open and her brown-nippled teats pointing at him like the vision of the great whore who lives in the minds of all puritanical men.

He stripped the zipper of his pants getting them off; popped the buttons from his shirt. When he was nude he tried to dive into her like into the sea, but she fought him off.

'You got to put on your sack first,' she said, snatching it up from the floor and pulling it down over his head backwards by mistake. 'Oop!' she cried.

Blinded momentarily, his hands flew up to tear it off, but she snatched it off first and slipped it on him the right way, so that only his eyes, mouth, nose and ears were showing.

'Now, baby, now,' she cried.

At that moment the telephone rang.

He jumped out of bed as though the furies had attacked him, his lust going out like a light. In his haste he knocked over the chair in the doorway, bruising his shins, and slammed into the doorjamb. Curses spewed from his gasping mouth like geysers of profanity. His lank white body with stooped shoulders and reddish hair moved awkwardly and looked as though it had just come from the grave.

With a quick lithe motion she opened a secret compartment

in the bed-table, snatched up the receiver of the telephone extension, and cried, 'Help!' then quickly hung up.

In his haste he didn't hear her. He reached the telephone in the sitting-room and said breathlessly, 'Henderson speaking,' but the connection had been broken. She could hear him jiggling the receiver as she slipped on a sport coat and snatched up a pair of shoes. 'Hello, hello,' he was still shouting when she went barefooted from the bedroom, locking the door behind her and taking the key, on back to the kitchen and went barefooted out of the house by the service door.

'Your party has hung up,' came the cool voice of the telephone operator.

He realized instantly the call had come from the police cruiser parked down the street. Panic exploded in his head as he realized he didn't even have his pistol. He ran naked back to the bedroom, snatched his pistol from the doorknob and tried to open the door. He found it locked. He became frantic. He couldn't risk shooting off the lock, he might hit her. The detectives from the cruiser would be there any instant and he'd catch hell. He had to get into the goddamned room. He tried breaking in, but it was a strong door with a good lock and his shoulder was taking a beating. He had forgotten the paper sack over his head.

The detectives from the cruiser had rushed there post-haste and had let themselves in with a pass-key. Over the telephone they had heard a woman cry for help. God only knew what was going on in there, but they were ready for it. They went into the apartment and spread out, their pistols in their hands. The sitting-room was empty.

They started through towards the rear. They drew up as though they had run into an invisible wall.

Down the hall was a buck-naked white man with a paper sack

over his head and a holstered pistol in his hand, trying to break down the bedroom door with his bare shoulder.

No one ever knew who was the first one to explode with laughter.

Iris went down the service stairway barefooted. The sport coat was a belted wraparound of tan gaberdine and no one could tell she was naked underneath it. At the service exit on St Nicholas Avenue, she slipped into her shoes and peeped out into the street.

A car stood at the kerb in front of the apartment next door with the motor idling. A smartly dressed woman got out and ran towards the entrance. Iris cased her as an afternoon prostitute or a cheating wife. The man behind the wheel called softly, 'Bye now, baby,' and the woman fluttered her fingers and ducked out of sight.

Iris walked rapidly to the car, opened the door and got into the seat the other woman had just vacated. The man looked at her and said, ''Lo, baby,' as though she was the same woman he'd just told good-bye. He was a nice-looking chocolate-brown man dressed in a beautiful gray silk suit, but Iris just glanced at him.

'Drive on, daddy,' she said.

He steered from the curb and climbed St Nicholas Avenue. 'Running *to* or *from*?' he asked.

'Neither,' she said and when they came to the church at 142nd Street she said: 'Turn left here up to Convent.'

He left-turned up the steep hill past Hamilton Terrace to the quiet stretch of Convent Avenue north of City College.

'Right here,' she directed.

He right-turned north on Convent and when he came opposite the big apartment house she said, 'This is good, daddy.'

'Could be better,' he said.

'Later,' she said and got out.

'Coming back?' he called but she didn't hear him.

She was already running across the street, up the steps and into the foyer of a big well-kept apartment house with two automatic elevators. One was waiting and she took it to the fourth floor and turned towards the apartment at the back of the hall. A serious-looking man wearing black suspenders, a white collarless shirt, and sagging black pants opened the door. He took himself as seriously as a deacon in a solvent church.

'And what can I do for you, young lady?'

'I want to see Barry Waterfield.'

'He don't want to see you, he's already got company,' he leered. 'How 'bout me?'

'Stand aside, buster,' she said, pushing past him. 'And quit peeping through keyholes.'

She went straight to Barry's room but the door was locked and she had to knock.

'Who is it?' asked a woman's voice.

'Iris. Tell Barry to let me in.'

The door was unlocked and Barry stood to one side wearing only a purple silk dressing gown. He closed the door behind her. A naked high-yellow woman lay in the bed with the sheet drawn up to her neck.

Clothes were draped over the only chair so Iris sat on the bed and ignored the naked woman. 'Where's Deke?' she asked Barry.

He hesitated before replying, 'He's all right, he's holed up safe.'

'If you're scared of talking then write it,' she said,

He looked uncomfortable. 'How'd you get away?'

'None of your business,' she snapped.

'You're sure you weren't tailed?'

'Don't make me laugh. If the cops wanted you they'd have had you long ago, stupid as you are. Just tell me where Deke is and let others do the thinking.'

'I'll call him,' he said, going towards the door.

She started to go with him but pressure on her hip stopped her, and she said only, 'Tell him I'm coming to see him.'

He went out and locked the door from the outside without answering.

The woman in the bed whispered quickly, 'He's with Mabel Hill in the Riverton Apartments,' and gave the street, number and telephone. 'I heard Barry talking.'

Iris looked blank. 'Mabel Hill. The only Mabel Hill I know vaguely is the Mabel Hill who was married to the John Hill who got croaked.'

'That's the cutie,' the woman whispered.

Iris couldn't control the rage that distorted her face.

Barry came in at that moment and looked at her, 'What's the matter with you?'

'Did you get Deke?' she countered.

He wasn't clever enough to dissemble and she knew he was lying when he said, 'Deke's cut out but he left word he would call me. He's changing his hideout.'

'Thanks for nothing,' Iris said, getting up to go.

The naked woman underneath the sheet said, 'Wait a minute and I'll give you a lift. I got my car downstairs.'

'No, you ain't,' Barry said roughly, pushing her down.

Iris unlocked the door and opened it, then turned and said, 'Go to hell, you big mother-raping square,' and slammed the door behind her.

II

Deke hadn't left Mabel's apartment but he'd had some close shaves. Two Homicide detectives had shown up at ten o'clock to question her again. He had hid in the closet, feeling defenceless and stark-naked without a gun, listening to every word with his heart in his mouth for fear he might have left something incriminating in the room, sweating blood from fear they might decide to search the house, and literally sweating in the close dusty heat. The dust had tickled his nose and he'd had to bite his lip to keep from sneezing.

Later, Mr Clay, the undertaker, had come and caught him in the bedroom and he'd had to hide under the bed. They had talked so interminably about money he had begun to wonder whether they intended to bury John Hill or hold his body for ransom.

Then Mabel had again turned into the weeping widow and bemoaned her fate with buckets of tears and enough hysterics for a revival meeting and nothing turned them off but to console her in bed. He had consoled her in bed so many times he'd concluded that if John Hill hadn't been shot she'd have loved him to death. Or was she like that because her mother-raping husband was dead? he asked himself. Was this some kind of freakishness that came out in her? Whore complex or something? But if she had to wait for her mother-raping husband to get killed before she could get her nuts off, hadn't he better take care himself? Or was he the exception being her minister; a minister is supposed to minister. Or was it that she thought if she sinned with her minister, God would forgive her; and the more she sinned, the greater would be God's forgiveness? Or did this bitch just have a hot ass? Anyway, he was goddamned tired of her everlasting urge and he was mentally damning John Hill to hell for getting himself killed.

But finally just before he'd had to holler calf-rope she'd calmed down enough to keep her appointment with the undertaker to go get John's body from the morgue.

It gave him a chance to contact Barry and his other two guns and arrange the caper with the Colonel for that night. So when she came home hysterical again he was ready for her.

Afterwards he was just lounging around in his shorts, drinking bourbon highballs, and she was in the kitchen doing he didn't know what – probably taking an aphrodisiac – when the telephone rang.

It was Barry, telling him that Iris had got loose and was looking for him. He didn't want to see Iris and he didn't want her to find him for fear she might be tailed. So he had given Barry his answer. He figured if the police picked her up it was better she didn't know where he was, then they couldn't get it out of her. Furthermore, she was too damn jealous, and one hitch at a time was enough.

To his annoyance he saw that Mabel had been listening to his conversation. She made herself a lemon coke with ice and sat down beside him on the sofa.

'I'm glad she's not coming here,' she said.

'Jealousy is one of the seven cardinal sins,' he said.

For a moment he thought she was going to become hysterical again, but she just looked at him possessively and said, 'Oh, Reverend O'Malley, pray with me.'

'Later,' he snapped and got up to get a refill.

He was in the kitchen getting ice from the tray when the doorbell rang. Ice cubes flew into the air like startled birds. He didn't have time to retrieve them. He shoved the tray back, slammed the door shut and dumped his drink into the sink. Then he rushed into the closet in the back hall opposite the bathroom where his clothes were hung, waving a signal to Mabel as he passed through the sitting-room. He had found an old .32 revolver of John Hill's and he snatched it from the shelf where he had hidden it and held it in his shaking hand.

Mabel was flustered. She didn't know whether he had meant she should answer the door or not answer it.

The bell rang again, long and insistently, as though whoever it was must know she was at home. She decided to answer it. There was a chain on the door; and anyway, even if the police did catch Reverend O'Malley there, he hadn't done anything really wrong, she thought. He was just trying to get their money back.

She unlocked the door and someone tried to push it open but the chain caught it. Then through the crack she saw the face of Iris, distorted with rage.

'Open this mother-raping door,' Iris grated in her throaty voice, her lips popping wetly.

'He's not here,' Mabel said smugly from behind the chained door. 'Reverend O'Malley, I mean.'

'I'll start screaming and get the police here and then you tell them that,' Iris threatened.

'If that's all he means to you . . .' Mabel began and flung wide the door. 'Come in.' And she chained and locked the door after her.

Iris went through the house like a gun dog looking for a game bird.

'He heard what you said,' Mabel called after her.

'These mother-raping bitches!' Deke muttered to himself and came out of the closet, covered with a film of sweat, still holding the pistol in his hand. 'Why don't you have some sense?' He said to Iris's back as she was looking into the bathroom.

She wheeled, and her eyes widened and went pitch-black when she saw him in his shorts. Her face convulsed with uncontrollable jealousy. All she thought of then was him in bed with this other woman.

'You chickenshit cheat,' she mouthed, spittle flying from her popping lips. 'You sneaking pimp. You get me out of the way and shack up with some chippy whore.'

'Shut up,' he said dangerously. 'I had to hide out.'

'Hide out? Between this slut's legs!'

From the doorway into the sitting-room Mabel said, 'Reverend O'Malley is just trying to get our money back; he doesn't want it all bungled by the police.'

Iris turned on her. 'I suppose you call him Reverend O'Malley in bed,' she stormed. 'If your mouth isn't too full.'

'I'm not like you,' Mabel said angrily. 'I do it the way God intended.'

Iris rushed at her and tried to scratch her face. Her coat flew open, showing her naked body. Mabel grabbed her by the wrists and shouted tauntingly, 'I'm going to have his baby.' Iris couldn't have a baby and it was the worst thing Mabel could have said. Iris went berserk; she spat in Mabel's face and kicked her shins and struggled to break free. But Mabel was the stronger and she spat back in Iris's face and let go her hands to grab her hair. Iris scratched her on the neck and shoulders and tore her negligee, but Mabel was pulling her hair out by the roots and pain filled her eyes with tears, blinding her.

Deke grabbed Iris by the coat collar with his left hand, still holding the revolver in his right. He hadn't had time to put it away and he was afraid to drop it on the floor. Iris's coat came off in his hand and she was naked except for shoes and there was nothing else to clutch. So he tried to break Mabel's grip on her hair. But Mabel was so infuriated she wouldn't turn loose.

'Break loose, you mother-raping whores!' Deke grated and hit at Mabel's hands with his pistol.

He mashed her fingers against Iris's skull. Iris screamed and scratched eight red lines across his ribs. He hit her in the stomach with his free left hand, then grabbed Mabel's negligee to pull her away. The negligee came off in his hand and she was naked too. Iris clawed her like a cat, streaking her body, and the blood began to flow. Mabel couldn't use her hands but she bent Iris's head down with her arms and bit her in the shoulder. Screaming in pain, with her head bent down, Iris saw the pistol in Deke's hand. She snatched it and shot Mabel in the body until it was empty.

It happened so fast it didn't register on Deke's brain. He heard the thunder of shots; he saw the surprised look of anguish on Mabel's face as she loosened her grip on Iris's head and slowly began to crumble. But it was like a horrifying nightmare before the horror comes.

Then awareness hit him like a time bomb exploding in his head. His body erupted into action as his brain went rattled with panic. He hit Iris in the breast with his left fist, rocking her back, and crossed a right to her neck, knocking her off-balance. He kicked her in the stomach with his bare foot and, when she doubled over, hit her on the back of the head with the side of his fist, knocking her face downward to the floor.

Suddenly the panic started going off in his head like a chain of explosions, each one bigger than the ones before. He leapt over Iris's prostrate figure, started towards the closet to get his clothes, then wheeled and snatched up the pistol from the floor where Iris had dropped it. He didn't look at Mabel; his mind knew she was dead but he tried not to think of it. Somewhere in his head he knew he didn't have any more bullets for the pistol which wasn't his. He dropped it to the floor as though it was burning his hand.

Wheeling, he leapt into the hall, rushed to the closet. The knob slipped in his hand and one half of his brain began cursing, the other half praying.

In the front of all other thoughts was the sure knowledge that in a few minutes the police would come. Before the shooting, there had been enough screaming to raise the dead; and he knew in this nigger-proper house someone would have called the police. He knew his only hope was flight. To get away before the police got there. It was his life. And these mother-raping seconds were running out. But he knew he'd never get away looking half-dressed. Some meddling mother-raper in this nigger-heaven house would stop him on suspicion and he didn't have a gun.

He tried to dress fast. Quick-quick-quick, urged his brain. But his mother-raping fingers had turned to thumbs. It seemed as though it took him seven hundred mother-raping years to button up his shirt; and some more mother-raping centuries to lace his shoes.

He leapt to the mirror to tie his tie and search for tell-tale scratches. His dark face was powder gray, his stretched eyes like black eight-balls, but there were no scratches showing. He was trying to decide whether to take the elevator down five floors and walk the remaining two, or take the fire-escape and try the roof. He didn't know how these buildings were made, whether the roofs were on the same level and he could get from one to another. In the back of his head he kept thinking there was something he was leaving. Then he realized it was Iris's life. Fear urged him to go back and take the pistol and beat her to death; stop her from talking forever.

He turned from the bathroom, turned towards the sitting-room, and was caught in midstep by the hammering on the door. He ran on his toes to the back window in the bedroom that let onto the outside fire-escape. He opened it quickly, went out and down without hesitation. He didn't have time to decide; he was committed. His feet felt nothing as they touched the iron steps of the steep ladder. His eyes searched the windows he passed.

The fire-escape was on one of the private streets of the housing development. He could only be seen by people across the street or in the windows he passed. Halfway down he saw the hem of a curtain fluttering from a half-open bedroom window. He didn't hesitate. He stopped at the window, opened it and went in. The apartment was arranged the same as the one he had just quit. There was no one in the bedroom. He went through on his toes, praying the house was empty, but with no intention of stopping if it was filled with wedding guests. He came out into the back hall. He could hear a woman singing in the kitchen at the front of the sitting-room. He got to the front door, found it locked and chained. He tried to open it silently; he held his breath as he turned the lock and took off the chain. Time was drowning him in a whirlpool of flying seconds. He got the door unlocked, the chain off. He heard the singing stop. He closed the door quickly behind him and ran down the hall towards the service stairway. He got onto the landing and closed the door just before he heard a faint woman's voice call, 'Henry, where are you, Henry?'

He went down the stairway like a dive-bomber, didn't stop until he was in the basement. He heard footsteps coming his way. He froze behind the closed door, assembling his face, making up his story. But the footsteps went on past him into silence. Cautiously he looked out into the basement. No one was in sight. He went in the direction opposite the one the footsteps had taken and found a door. It opened onto a short flight of stairs. He went up the stairs and found a heavy iron door locked with a Yale snap lock. He unlocked it and pushed the door open a crack and looked out.

He saw 135th Street. Colored people were out in numbers, walking about in their summertime rags. Two men were eating watermelon from a wagon. In the wagon the melons were kept on ice to keep them cool. Children were gathered around a small pushcart, eating cones of shaved ice flavored with colored syrups from bottles. Others were playing stickball in the street. Women were conversing in loud voices; a drunken man weaved down the sidewalk, cursing the world; a blind beggar tapped a path with his white stick, rattling a penny in his tin cup; a dog was messing on the sidewalk; a line of men was sitting in the shade on the steps of a church, talking about the white folks and the Negro problem.

He stepped from the doorway and crossed the street, and soon he was lost in that big turbulent sea of black humanity which is Harlem.

12

When Grave Digger and Coffin Ed came on duty at 8 p.m., Lieutenant Anderson said, 'Your car was found abandoned up at 163rd Street and Edgecombe Drive. Does that tell you anything?'

Coffin Ed backed against the wall in the shadows where Anderson couldn't see his expression, but Anderson heard him make some kind of sound that sounded like a snort. Grave Digger perched a ham on the edge of the desk and massaged his chin. The curve of his back concealed the bulge of the .38 revolver over his heart but made his shoulders look wider. He thought about it and chuckled.

'Tell me it was stolen,' he said finally. 'What you think, Ed?'

'Either that or it drove itself.'

Anderson looked quizzically from one to the other. 'Well, was it stolen?'

Grave Digger chuckled again. 'Think we're going to admit it if it was?'

'It was them chickens, boss?' Coffin Ed said.

Lieutenant Anderson reddened slightly and shook his head. He didn't always dig the private humor of his two ace detectives and sometimes it made him feel uncomfortable. But he realized they attached no significance to the fact their car had been stolen. Whenever they got a clue of importance the air around them became electric.

It became electric now when he said, 'We're holding Deke O'Hara's woman Iris on a homicide rap.'

Both detectives froze in that immobility which denotes full attention. But neither spoke; they knew a story went with it. They waited.

'She was arrested in the apartment of the man killed in the Back-to-Africa hijack, John Hill. John Hill's wife Mabel had been shot five times; she was dead when the police arrived. Both women were nude and badly mauled – scratched and beaten as though they'd had a furious go with each other. Tenants had called the police before the shooting to report what sounded like a woman fight in the apartment. A gun was found on the floor – a .32 revolver. It had been recently fired and there's no doubt it is the murder gun; but it has gone to ballistics. Her fingerprints were on the stock and smeared on the trigger but are partly obliterated by a clear set of prints by a man. Homicide figures a man handled the gun afterwards; maybe Deke. They're checking against his Bertillon card and we'll soon know.'

Grave Digger and Coffin Ed exchanged looks but said nothing.

'Iris contends Deke wasn't there. An hour earlier she had escaped from her own apartment. She admits going there looking for him but swears he hadn't been there. She had escaped on a ruse – you'll hear all about it. She admits that she and the Hill woman had a fight and she says she took the gun away from the Hill woman and it went off accidentally. She says it was a private fight and had nothing to do with the Back-to-Africa hijacking, but she won't give any reason for it.'

Both detectives turned and looked at him as though guided by the same impulse.

'Do you want to talk to her?' Anderson asked.

The detectives exchanged looks.

'How long after the shooting before the car crew arrived?'
Grave Digger asked.

'About two and a half minutes.'

'What floor?'

'Seventh, but there's a fast elevator and he would have had
time to get down and away before the police arrived,' he said,
reading their thoughts.

'Not if they were naked,' Coffin Ed said.

Anderson blushed. He hadn't gotten to be a lieutenant by
being a square but he was always slightly embarrassed by their
bald way of stating the facts of life.

'And he'd have to dress well in that neighborhood,' Grave
Digger added.

'And completely,' Coffin Ed concluded.

'There was an open window on the fire-escape at the back,'
Anderson said. 'But no one has been found who saw him leave.'
He looked through the reports on his desk. 'A woman on the
fourth floor directly below telephoned to report that she thought
she heard her front door being opened and when she went to
look found the chain off. But nothing was missing from the
house. Homicide found the window open onto the fire-escape
but she said she had left it open. Any prints that might have been
left on the doorknob were smeared by her son coming and going
afterwards, and she wiped whatever prints there may have been
from the windowsill when dusting.'

'They believe in keeping spick and span in those apartments,'
Grave Digger said.

'So clean that even Deke gets away clean,' Coffin Ed said.

'Who knows?' Grave Digger said. 'Let's go talk to her.'

They had her taken from the cell where she was held, await-
ing magistrate's court Monday morning, to the interrogation
room in the basement known to the Harlem underworld as the

'Pigeons' Nest'. It was claimed that more pigeons were hatched there than beneath all the eaves in Harlem.

It was a soundproof, windowless room with a stool in the center bolted to the floor and surrounded by floodlights bright enough to make the blackest man transparent.

But only the overhead light was on when the jailer brought her in. She saw Grave Digger standing beside the stool, waiting for her. The door was closed and locked behind her. She had a sudden feeling of being taken from the earth. Then she saw the vague outline of Coffin Ed backed against the wall in the shadows. His acid-burned face looked like a Mardi Gras masque to scare little children. She shuddered.

Grave Digger said, 'Sit down, baby, and tell us how you are.'

She stood defiantly. 'I'm not talking in this hole. You've got it bugged.'

'What for? Ed and me are going to remember anything you say.'

Coffin Ed stepped forward. He looked like the dead killer in the play *Winterset*, coming up out of East River. 'Sit down anyway,' he said.

She sat down. He stepped towards her. Grave Digger switched on the floodlights. She blinked. Coffin Ed had intended to slap her. But now he saw her. He caught his hand. 'Well, well, well,' he said. 'Ain't you beautiful.'

Her smooth, yellow, creamed and perfumed flesh of the day before now ran through all the colors of the spectrum, from black to bright orange; her neck was swollen, one breast was twice the size of the other; red, raw scratches ran down her face, over her neck and shoulders, to disappear beneath her dress; and her hair looked like it had been doused in the river Styx.

'It could have been worse,' Grave Digger said.

'How?' she asked, squinting at the bright lights. The bruises and scratches looked painted on her transparent skin.

'You could be dead.'

She shrugged faintly. 'You call that worse?'

'Well, hell, you're still alive,' Coffin Ed said. 'And you can get eight thousand and seven hundred dollars' reward money if you help us.'

'How about this chickenshit rap they're holding me on?' she bargained.

'That's your baby,' Grave Digger said.

She winced at the word *baby*; that was what had started it all.

'And it ain't chickenshit,' Coffin Ed added.

'It's a rap,' she said.

'Where's Deke?' Grave Digger asked.

'If I knew where the mother-raper was, I'd sure tell you.'

'But you went there to see him.'

She sat thinking for a time, then seemingly she made up her mind. 'He was there,' she admitted. 'In his drawers. Why else would I be mad enough to shoot the chippy whore. But I don't remember him getting away. He had knocked me unconscious.' After a moment she added, 'I wonder why he didn't kill me.'

'How did you get away from the detective guarding you?' he asked.

She laughed suddenly and her marks formed another pattern like one of those innocuous pictures revealing shocking obscenities at certain angles. 'That was a beauty,' she said. 'It could only happen to a white man.'

Grave Digger looked sardonic. 'As long as it's got nothing to do with this caper, let's skip it.'

'It was just between me and him.'

'What we want to know, baby, is what was the set-up of Deke's Back-to-Africa pitch.'

'Where have you been all your life, you don't know that?' she said.

'We know it. We just want you to confirm it.'

Some of her flippancy returned. 'What's in it for me?' she asked.

Coffin Ed stepped forward. 'Try it on, anyway,' he grated. 'Just for size.'

She looked towards his voice but she couldn't see him through the light and that made it sound more frightening.

'Well, you know he was going to take the money and blow,' she began. 'But not until he'd played other cities too. He had the armored car made. The guards were his. Only the agents and other personnel were squares. The detectives were to come in and get him off the hook by confiscating the money until an investigation could be made. Since all the suckers thought he was honest, there was nothing to fear. He borrowed the idea from the Marcus Garvey movement.'

'We know all that,' Grave Digger said. 'We want some names and descriptions.'

She gave him the name and address of Barry Waterfield, alias Baby Jack Johnson, alias Big Papa Domore. She said the two guns who had guarded the truck were known as Four-Four and Freddy; she had never heard them called by their real monickers and she didn't know where they were staying. They were Deke's men, he probably got them from prison; and he kept them out of sight. The dead man who had impersonated the other detective had been called Elmer Sanders. They were all from Chicago.

That was what they wanted and Coffin Ed relaxed.

But Grave Digger asked, 'He wasn't putting the double-cross on his own men by having himself hijacked?'

She thought for a moment, then said, 'No, I don't think so. I'm reckoning on the way he's acted afterwards.'

'Any idea who they were?'

'I keep thinking of the syndicate. Just because I can't think of anyone else, I guess.'

'It wasn't the syndicate,' Grave Digger stated flatly.

'Then I don't know. He never seemed scared of anybody else – Of course he never told me everything.'

Grave Digger smiled sourly at the understatement.

'What you got on Deke?' Coffin Ed asked.

She looked towards the voice behind the lights and felt a tremor run through her body. Why did that mother-raper scare her so? she wondered. Finally she said simply, 'The proof.'

Both detectives froze as though listening for an echo. It didn't come.

'You want us to take him, don't you?' Grave Digger said.

'Take him,' she said.

'Be ready,' he said.

'I'm ready,' she said.

On their way out they stopped again to see Lieutenant Anderson and have him put a tail on Barry Waterfield.

Then Grave Digger said, 'We're going to put our pigeons on Deke. If they get anything they'll phone it to you and you call us in the car.'

'Right,' Anderson said. 'I'll have a couple of cars on alert for an emergency.'

'There ain't going to be any emergency,' Coffin Ed said and they left.

They began contacting all the stool pigeons they could reach. They got many tips on unsolved crimes and wanted criminals but nothing on Deke O'Hara. They filed away the information for later use, but for all of their stool pigeons they had only one instruction: 'Find Deke O'Hara. He's loose on the town. Telephone

Lieutenant Anderson at the precinct station, drop the message and hang up. And disappear.'

It was a slow, tedious process, but they had no other. There were five hundred thousand colored people in Harlem and so many holes in which to hide that sewer rats have been known to get lost.

Barry telephoned Deke at Mabel's from Bowman's Bar at the corner of St Nicholas Place and 155th Street on the dot of 10 p.m. as he had been instructed. The phone rang once, twice, three times. Abruptly a warning sounded in his head; his sixth sense told him the police were there and were tracing the call. He hung up as though letting go a snake and headed towards the exit. The bar girl looked at him as he passed, eyebrows raised, wondering what had spurred him so suddenly. He tossed fifty cents on the bar to pay for his thirty-five-cent beer and went out fast, looking for a taxi.

He caught one headed downtown and said, 'Drop me at 145th and Broadway.' When they turned west on 145th he heard the faint whine of a siren headed towards Bowman's and sweat filmed his upper lip.

Broadway is a fringe street. Black Harlem has moved solidly to its east side but its west side is still mixed with Puerto Ricans and leftover whites. He got out on the north-east corner, crossed the street, walked rapidly up to 149th and went down towards the Hudson River. He turned into a small neat apartment house halfway down the block and climbed three flights of stairs.

The light-bright-damn-near-white woman who had been naked in his bed when Iris had called opened the door for him. She was talking before she closed it: 'Iris killed Mabel Hill right after she left us. Ain't that something? They got her in jail. It just came over the radio.' Her voice was strident with excitement.

'Deke?' he asked tensely.

'Oh, he got away. They're looking for him. Let me fix you a drink.'

His gaze swept the three-room apartment, reading every sign. It was a nice place but he didn't see it. He was thinking that Deke must have tried to contact him while he was out.

'Drive me home,' he said.

She began to pout but one look at his face cooled her.

Five minutes later, the young colored detective Paul Robinson, assigned with his partner Ernie Fisher to tail Barry, saw him get out of the closed convertible in front of the apartment where he lived and run quickly up the stairs. Paul was sitting in a black Ford sedan with regular Manhattan plates, parked across the street, pointed uptown. He got Lieutenant Anderson on the radio-telephone and said, 'He just came in.'

'Keep on him,' Anderson said.

When Barry got off at the fourth floor there was a young man standing in the hall waiting to go down. He was Ernie Fisher. For two hours he had been standing there, waiting to descend every time the elevator stopped. But this time he went. When he came out on the street he got into a two-toned Chevrolet sedan parked in front of the entrance, pointed downtown.

Paul got out of the Ford sedan, crossed the street and entered the apartment without glancing at his partner. He took the stand on the fourth floor, waiting to descend.

The deacon-looking landlord told Barry he had had several urgent calls from a Mr Bloomfield who had left a message saying if he didn't want the car he had found another buyer. Barry went immediately to the telephone and called Mr Bloomfield.

'Bloomfield,' replied a voice having no affinity to such a name.

'Mr Bloomfield, I want the car,' Barry said. 'I'm ready right now to close the deal. I've been out raising the money.'

'Come to my office right away,' Mr Bloomfield said and hung up.

'Right away, Mr Bloomfield,' Barry said into the dead phone for the landlord's ears.

He stopped in his room on his way out, strapped on a shoulder holster with a .45 Colt automatic, and changed into a loose black silk sport jacket made to accommodate the gun.

When he came out into the hall he saw a young man standing by the elevator, jabbing the button impatiently. There was nothing about the young man to incur suspicion or jog his memory. He stood beside him and they rode down together. The young man walked rapidly ahead of him and ran down the stairs and across the street without looking back. Barry didn't give him another thought.

A Chevrolet sedan parked at the curb was just moving off and Barry hailed a taxi that drew up in the place vacated. The taxi went downtown, through City College, past the convent from which the street derives its name, and down the hill towards 125th Street. The Chevrolet stayed ahead. The Ford had made a U-turn and was following the taxi a block to the rear.

Convent came to an end at 125th Street. Taking a chance, Ernie turned his Chevrolet left, towards Eighth Avenue. The taxi turned sharply right. The Ford closed in behind it.

Barry had seen the Ford through the rear window. He had his driver stop suddenly in front of a bar. The Ford whizzed past, the driver looking the other way, and turned left where the street splits.

Barry had his driver make a U-turn and head back towards the east side. He didn't see anything unusual about the Chevrolet pulling out from the curb near Eighth Avenue; it looked just like any other hundreds of Chevrolets in Harlem – a poor man's Cadillac. He had the taxi turn right at the Theresa Hotel on

Seventh Avenue and pull to the curb. The Chevrolet kept on down 125th Street.

Barry dismissed his taxi and entered the hotel lobby, then suddenly turned about and went outside and had the doorman hail another taxi. He didn't even notice the black Ford sedan parked near the entrance to Sugar Ray's bar. This street was always lined with parked cars. The taxi kept straight on down to 116th Street and turned sharp right. The Ford kept straight ahead. There were a number of cars coming cross town from Lenox on 116th Street, among which were several Chevrolet sedans.

The red light caught the taxi at Eighth Avenue and among the stream of cars going north was a black Ford sedan. Harlem was full of Ford sedans – the poor man's Lincoln – and Barry didn't give it a look. When the light changed he had the taxi turn right and stop in the middle of the block. The black Ford sedan was nowhere in sight. The Chevrolet sedan kept on across Eighth Avenue.

Paul double-parked the Ford around the corner on 117th Street and quickly walked back to Eighth Avenue. He saw Barry enter a poolroom down the street. He crossed Eighth Avenue, keeping the poolroom in sight, and stood on the opposite sidewalk. Hundreds of Saturday-night drunks and hopheads were standing about, weaving in and out the joints, putting forth their voices. There was nothing to set him apart other than he was better dressed than most and the whores started buzzing around him.

Within a minute a Chevrolet sedan turned south on Eighth from 119th Street and double-parked near 116th Street behind two other double-parked cars.

Paul crossed the street and made as though to enter the poolroom, then seemed to think better of it and turned aimlessly towards 117th Street, collecting whores from all directions.

The Chevrolet sedan moved off, turned the corner on 116th

Street and double-parked out of sight. Ernie called Lieutenant Anderson and reported, 'He went into a poolroom on Eighth Avenue,' and gave the name of the poolroom and number.

'Stay with him,' Anderson said, and got Grave Digger and Coffin Ed on the radio-telephone.

13

They were talking to a blind man when they got the call.

The blind man was saying, 'There were five white men in this tank. That in itself was enough to make me suspicious. Then when it stopped, the white man with the goatee who was sitting in the front seat leaned across the driver and beckoned to this colored boy who had been loitering around the station. I turned like I was alarmed when I heard the door click and took a picture. I think I got a clear shot.'

Coffin Ed answered the radio-phone and heard Anderson say, 'They got him stationed for the time being in a pool hall on Eighth Avenue,' and gave the name and number.

'We're on the way,' Coffin Ed said. 'Just play it easy.'

'It's your baby,' Anderson said. 'Holler if you need help.'

Grave Digger said to the blind man, 'Keep it until later, Henry.'

'Nothing ever spoils,' Henry said and got out, putting on his dark glasses at the same time.

It was five minutes by right from where they were parked on Third Avenue, but Grave Digger made it in three and one half without using the horn.

They found Paul in the Ford across the street from the pool-room. He said Barry was inside and Ernie was bottling up the back.

'You go and help him,' Grave Digger said. 'We'll take care of this end.'

They pulled into the spot he had vacated and settled down to wait.

'You think he's contacting Deke in there?' Coffin Ed said.

'I ain't thinking,' Grave Digger said.

Time passed.

'If I had a dollar an hour for all the time I've spent waiting for criminals to come and get themselves caught, I'd take some time off and go fishing,' Coffin Ed said.

Grave Digger chuckled. 'You're a glutton for punishment, man. That's the only thing I don't like about fishing, the waiting.'

'Yeah, but there ain't any danger at the end of that kind of waiting.'

'Hell, Ed, if you were scared of danger you'd have been a bill collector.'

It was Coffin Ed's turn to chuckle. 'Naw I wouldn't,' he said. 'Not in Harlem, Digger, not in Harlem. There ain't any more dangerous a job in Harlem than collecting bills.'

They lapsed into silence, thinking of all the reasons folks in Harlem didn't pay bills. And they thought about the eighty-seven thousand dollars taken from those people who were already so poor they dreamed hungry. 'If I had the mother-raper who got it I'd work his ass at fifty cents an hour shoveling shit until he paid it off,' Coffin Ed said.

'There ain't that much shit,' Grave Digger said drily. 'What with all this newfangled shitless food.'

Men came from the poolroom and others entered. Some they knew, others they didn't, but none they wanted.

An hour passed.

'Think they've lammed?' Coffin Ed ventured.

'How the hell would I know?' Grave Digger said. 'Maybe they're waiting like us.'

A car pulled up before the poolroom and double-parked. Suddenly they sat up. It was a black, chauffeur-driven Lincoln Mark IV, as out of place in that neighborhood as the Holy Virgin.

A uniformed colored chauffeur got out and hastened into the poolroom. Within a matter of seconds he came back and got behind the wheel and started the motor. Suddenly Barry came out. For a moment he stood on the sidewalk, looking up and down, casing the street. He looked across the street. Coffin Ed had ducked out of sight and Grave Digger was studiously searching for an acquaintance among the bums lounging in the doorways on their side of the street, and all Barry saw of him was the back of his head. It looked like the back of any other big black man's head. Satisfied, Barry turned and rapped on the door and another man came out and went straight to the limousine and got in beside the driver. Then Deke came out and went fast between two parked cars and got into the back of the limousine and Barry followed. The limousine took off like a streak, but had to slow for the lights at 125th Street.

Grave Digger had to make a U-turn and by the time he got straightened out, the limousine was out of sight.

'We ought to have got some help,' Coffin Ed said.

'Too late now,' Grave Digger said, gunning the hopped-up car past the slow-moving traffic. 'We ought to've had second sight, too.'

He went straight north on Eighth Avenue without pausing to reconnoiter.

'Where the hell are we going?' Coffin Ed asked.

'Damned if I know,' Grave Digger confessed.

'Hell,' Coffin Ed said disgustedly. 'One day we lose our car and the next day we lose our man.'

'Just let's don't lose our lives,' Grave Digger shouted above the roar of the traffic they were passing.

'Pull down,' Coffin Ed shouted back. 'At this rate we'll be in Albany.'

Grave Digger pulled up to the curb at 145th Street. 'All right, let's give this some thought,' he said.

'What kind of mother-raping thought?' Coffin Ed said.

He was near enough to the scene where the acid had been thrown into his face to evoke the memory. The tic started in his face and his nerves got on edge.

Grave Digger looked at him and looked away. He knew how he was feeling but this wasn't the time for it, he thought. 'Listen,' he said. 'They were driving a stolen car. What does that mean?'

Coffin Ed came back. 'A rendezvous or a getaway.'

'Getaway for what? If they had the money they'd already be gone.'

'Well, where the hell would you rendezvous, if you weren't scared?' Coffin Ed said.

'That's right,' Grave Digger said. 'Underneath the bridge.'

'Anyway, we ain't scared,' Coffin Ed said.

The two guns who had handled Deke's armored car were on the front seat, the same one driving. He was also a car thief specialist, and had stolen this one. He doused the lights when they came to the end of Bradhurst Avenue and eased the big car off the road that led to the Polo Grounds, stopping between two stanchions underneath the 155th Street bridge.

'You two guys spot the car,' Deke ordered. 'We'll wait here.'

The gunmen got out, careful of the rifles on the floor, and split in the darkness.

Deke took a large manila envelope from his inside coat pocket and handed it to Barry. 'Here's the list,' he said. He had had it made weeks before from the telephone directories of Manhattan, the Bronx and Brooklyn by a public stenographer in the Theresa Hotel. 'You let him do the talking. We're going to have you covered every second.'

'I don't like this,' Barry confessed. He was scared and nervous and he couldn't see the Colonel giving any clues away. 'He ain't going to pay no fifty grand for this,' he said, taking it gingerly and sticking it into his inside pocket above his pistol.

'Naturally not,' Deke said. 'But don't argue with him. Answer his questions and take whatever he gives you.'

'Hell, Deke, I don't dig this,' Barry protested. 'What's this cracker outfit got to do with our eighty-seven grand?'

'Let me do the thinking,' Deke said coldly. 'And give me that rod.'

'Hell, you want me to go with my bare ass to see that nut? You're asking me a lot.'

'What the hell can happen to you? We're all going to have you covered. Man, goddammit, you're going to be as safe as in the arms of Jesus Christ.'

As Barry was handing over the gun he remembered, 'That's what the Colonel said.'

'He was right,' Deke said, taking the pistol from the holster and sticking it into his right coat-pocket. 'Just his reasons are wrong.'

They were silent with their thoughts until the gunmen materialized out of the darkness and took their places on the front seat. 'They're over by the El,' the driver said, easing the big car soundlessly through the dark as though he had eyes of infra-red.

The trucks and cars manned by the workers cleaning the stadium were moving about in the black dark area beneath the subway extensions and the bridge, which was used by day as a parking space, their bright lights lancing the darkness. Once the black limousine of the Colonel was picked up in a beam of light, but it didn't look out of place in that area where architects and bankers came at night to plan the construction of new buildings when the old stadium was razed. The Lincoln kept to the edge of the area, avoiding the lights, and stopped behind a big trailer truck parked for the night.

The gunmen picked their rifles from the floor and got out on each side and took stations at opposite ends of the truck. They had .303 automatic Savage rifles loaded with .190-point brass-nosed shells, equipped with telescopic sights.

'All right,' Deke said. 'Play it cool.'

Barry shook his head once like shaking off a premonition. 'My mama taught me more sense than this,' he said and got out. Deke got out on the other side. Barry walked around the front of the truck and kept on ahead. His black coat and dark gray trousers were swallowed by the darkness. Deke stopped beside one of his gunmen.

'How does it look?' he asked.

In the telescopic sight Barry looked like the silhouette of half a man neatly quartered, the sight lines crossing in the center of his back as the gunman tracked him through the dark.

'All right,' the gunman said. 'Black on black, but it'll do.'

'Don't let him get hurt,' Deke said.

'He ain't gonna get hurt,' the gunman said.

When Barry stopped walking, two other silhouettes came into the sights, close together like three wise monkeys.

The gunmen widened their sights to take in the limousine and its occupants. Their eyes had become accustomed to the dark. In the faint glow of reflected light, the scene was clearly visible. The Colonel sat in the front seat beside the blond young man in the driver's seat. A white man stood on each side of Barry and a third, standing in front of him, shook him down and took the envelope from his inside pocket and passed it to the Colonel. The Colonel put it into his pocket without looking at it. Suddenly the two men flanking Barry seized his arms and twisted them behind him.

The third man moved up close in front of him.

Grave Digger cut off his lights when they approached the dark sinister area underneath the bridge. In the faint light reflected from the lights of the trucks and filtering down from above, the area looked like a jungle of iron stanchions, standing like giant sentinels in the eerie dark. The skin on Coffin Ed's face was jumping with a life of its own and Grave Digger felt his collar choking as his neck swelled.

He pulled the car over into the darkness and let the engine idle soundlessly. 'Let's load some light,' he said.

'I got light,' Coffin Ed said.

Grave Digger nodded in the dark and took out his long-barreled, nickelplated .38-caliber revolver and replaced the first three shells with tracer bullets. Coffin Ed drew his revolver, identical to the special made job of Grave Digger's, and spun the cylinder once. Then he held it in his lap. Grave Digger slipped his into his side coat pocket. Then they sat in the dark, listening for the sound that might never come.

'Where's the cotton?' the Colonel asked Barry so abruptly it hit him like a slap.

'Cotton!' he echoed with astonishment.

Then something clicked in his brain. He remembered the small sign advertising for a bale of cotton in the window of the Back-to-the-Southland office. His eyes stretched. *Good God!* he thought. Then he felt the danger of the instant squeeze him like an iron vise. His body turned ice cold as though the blood had been squeezed out; his head exploded with terror. His mind sought an answer that would save his life, but he could only think of one that might satisfy the Colonel. 'Deke's got it!' he blurted out.

Everything happened at once. The Colonel made a gesture. The white men tightened their grips on Barry's arms. The third man in front of Barry drew a hunting knife from his belt. Barry lunged to one side, throwing the man holding his right arm around behind him. And the big hard unmistakable sound of a high-powered rifle shot exploded in the night, followed so quickly by another it sounded like an echo.

The gunman beside Deke had shot the white man behind Barry dead through the heart. But the high-powered big-game bullet had gone through the white man's body and penetrated Barry just above the heart and lodged in his breastbone. The gunman at the other end of the truck had taken the white man holding Barry's left arm, the bullet going through one lung, ricocheting off a rib and ending up in his hip. All three fell together.

The third man with the knife wheeled and ran blindly. The big limousine sprang forward like a big cat, knocked him down, and ran over his body as though it were a bump in the road.

'Take the car!' Deke yelled, meaning, 'Take out the car.'

His gunmen thought he meant take their car and they wheeled and ran towards the Lincoln.

'Mother-rapers,' Deke mouthed and followed them.

Grave Digger was coming from three hundred yards' distance, his bright lights stabbing the darkness from where he'd heard the shots. Coffin Ed was shouting into the radio-telephone: 'All cars! The Polo Grounds. Seal it!'

The Lincoln was turning past the head of the trailer truck on two wheels when Grave Digger caught it in his lights. Coffin Ed leaned out the window and snapped a tracer bullet. It made a long incandescent streak, missing the rear of the disappearing Lincoln and sloping off towards the innocent earth. Then the truck was between them.

'Stop for Barry!' Deke yelled to his driver.

The driver tamped the brakes and the car skidded straight to a stop. Deke leaped out and rushed towards the grotesque pile of bodies. The white man who'd been run over was writhing in agony and Deke hit him with the .45 in passing and crushed his brain. Then he tried to pull Barry from beneath the other bodies.

'No!' Barry screamed in pain.

'For God's sake, the key!' Deke cried.

'Cotton . . .' Barry whispered, blood coming from his mouth and nose as his big body relaxed in death.

Grave Digger came around the truck so fast the little car slewed sideways and Coffin Ed's tracer bullet intended for the gasoline tank shattered the rear window of the Lincoln Mark IV and set fire to the lining of the roof. The Lincoln went off in a hard straight line like a missile being fired and began zigzagging perilously in the dark. He threw another tracer and punctured the back door. Then he was shooting at the dark and the Lincoln kept going faster.

Grave Digger dragged the little car down and was out and running towards Deke, gun leveled, before it stopped moving. Coffin Ed hit the ground flat-footed on the other side, prepared to add his one remaining bullet. But it wasn't necessary. Deke saw them coming towards him. He had seen the Lincoln drive away. He dropped the pistol and raised his hands. He wanted to live.

'Well, well, look who's here,' Grave Digger said as he went forward to snap on the handcuffs.

'Ain't this a pleasant surprise?' Coffin Ed echoed.

'I want to phone my lawyer,' Deke said.

'All in good time, lover boy, all in good time,' Grave Digger said.

14

Now it was 1 a.m. Homicide had been there and gone. The medical examiner had pronounced all four bodies 'Dead On Arrival'. The bodies were on their way to the morgue. Both the Colonel's limousine and the Lincoln had gotten away. A search was being made. The seventeen police cruisers that had bottled up the area to keep them from escaping had been returned to regular duty. The workmen cleaning the Polo Grounds had returned to their work. The city lived and breathed and slept as usual. People were lying, stealing, cheating, murdering; people were praying, singing, laughing, loving and being loved; and people were being born and people were dying. Its pulse remained the same. New York City. The Big Town.

But the heads, the mothers and fathers, of those eighty-seven families who had sunk their savings on a dream of going back to Africa lay awake, worrying, wondering if they'd ever get their money back.

Deke was in the 'Pigeons' Nest' in the precinct station, sitting on the wooden stool bolted to the floor, facing the barrage of spotlights. He looked fragile and translucent in the bright light; his smooth black face was more the purplish-orange color of an overpowdered whore than the normal gray of a black man terrified.

'I want to see my lawyer,' he was saying for the hundredth time.

'Your lawyer is asleep at this time of night,' Coffin Ed said with a straight face.

'He'd be mad if we woke him,' Grave Digger added.

Lieutenant Anderson had let them have him first. They were in a jovial mood. They had Deke where they wanted him.

It wasn't funny to Deke. 'Don't get your britches torn,' he warned. 'All you got against me is suspicion of homicide; and I have a perfect right to see my lawyer.'

Coffin Ed slapped him with his cupped palm. It was a light slap but it sounded like a firecracker and rocked Deke's head.

'Who's talking about homicide?' Grave Digger said as though he hadn't noticed it.

'Hell, all we want to know is who's got the money,' Coffin Ed said.

Deke straightened up and took a deep breath.

'So we can go and get it and give it back to those poor people you swindled,' Grave Digger added.

'Swindled my ass,' Deke said. 'It was all legitimate.'

Grave Digger slapped him so hard his body bent one-sided like a rubber man, and Coffin Ed slapped him back. They slapped him back and forth until his brains were addled, but left no bruises.

They let him get his breath back and gave him time for his brains to settle. Then Grave Digger said, 'Let's start over.'

Deke's eyes had turned bright orange in the glaring light. He closed his lids. A trickle of blood flowed from the corner of his mouth. He licked his lips and wiped his hand across his mouth.

'You're hurting me,' he said. His voice sounded as though his tongue had thickened. 'But you ain't killing me. And that's all that counts.'

Coffin Ed drew back to hit him but Grave Digger caught his arm. 'Easy, Ed,' he said.

'Easy on this mother-raping scum?' Coffin Ed raved. 'Easy on this incestuous sister-raping thief?'

'We're cops,' Grave Digger reminded him. 'Not judges.'

Coffin Ed restrained himself. 'The law was made to protect the innocent,' he said.

Grave Digger chuckled. 'You heard the man,' he said to Deke.

Deke looked as though he might reply to that but thought better of it. 'You're wasting your time on me,' he said instead. 'My Back-to-Africa movement was on the square and all I know about this shooting caper is what I saw in passing. I saw the man was dying and tried to save his life.'

Coffin Ed turned and walked into the shadow. He slapped the wall with the palm of his hand so hard it sounded like a shot. It was all Grave Digger could do to keep from breaking Deke's jaw. His neck swelled and veins sprouted like ropes along his temples.

'Deke, don't try us,' he said. His voice had turned light and cotton dry. 'We'll take you out of here and pistol-whip you slowly to death – and take the charge.'

It showed on Deke's face he believed him. He didn't speak.

'We know the set-up of the Back-to-Africa movement. We got the FBI records on Four-Four and Freddy. We got the Cook County Bertillon report on Barry and Elmer. We got your prison record too. We know you haven't got the money or you wouldn't still have been around. But you got the key.'

'Got what key?' Deke asked.

'The key to the door that leads to the money.'

Deke shook his head. 'I'm clean,' he said.

'Punk, listen,' Grave Digger said. 'You're going up any way. We got the proof.'

'Got it from where?' Deke asked.

'We got it from Iris,' Grave Digger said.

'If she said the Back-to-Africa movement was crooked she's a lying bitch, and I'll tell her to her teeth.'

'All right,' Grave Digger said.

Three minutes later they had Iris in the room. Lieutenant Anderson and two white detectives had come with her.

She stood in front of Deke and looked him dead in the eyes. 'He killed Mabel Hill,' she said.

Deke's face distorted with rage and he tried to leap at her but the white detectives held him.

'Mabel found out that the Back-to-Africa movement was crooked and she was going to the police. Her husband had been killed and she had lost her money and she was going to get him.' She sounded as if it was good to her.

'You lying whore!' Deke screamed.

'When I stood up for him, she attacked me,' Iris continued. 'I was struggling to defend myself. He grabbed me from behind and put the pistol in my hand and shot her. When I tried to wrestle the pistol away from him, he knocked me down and took it.'

Deke looked sick. He knew it was a good story. He knew if she took it to court, dressed in black, her eyes downcast in sorrow, and spoke in a halting manner – with his record – she could make it stick. She didn't have any kind of a criminal record. He could see the chair in Sing Sing and himself sitting in it.

He stared at her with resignation. 'How much are they paying you?' he asked.

She ignored the question. 'The forged documents which prove the Back-to-Africa movement is crooked are hidden in our apartment in the binding of a book called *Sex and Race*.' She smiled sweetly at Deke. 'Good-bye, big shit,' she said and turned towards the door.

The white detectives looked at one another, then looked at Deke. Anderson was embarrassed.

'How does that feel?' Coffin Ed asked Deke in a grating voice.

Grave Digger walked with Iris to the door. When he turned her over to the jailer he winked at her. She looked surprised for an instant, then winked back, and the jailer took her away.

Deke had wilted. He didn't look hurt, or even frightened; he looked beat, like a condemned man waiting for the electric chair. All he needed was the priest.

Anderson and the two white detectives left without looking at him again.

When the three of them were again alone, Grave Digger said. 'Give us the key and we'll strike off the murder.'

Deke looked up at him as though from a great distance. He looked as though he didn't care about anything any more. 'Frig you,' he said.

'Then give us the eighty-seven grand and we'll drop the whole thing,' Grave Digger persisted.

'Frig you twice,' Deke said.

They turned him over to the jailer to be taken back to his cell.

'I got a feeling we're overlooking something,' Grave Digger said.

'That is for sure,' Coffin Ed agreed. 'But what?'

They were in Anderson's office, talking about Iris. As usual, Grave Digger sat with a ham perched on the edge of the desk and Coffin Ed was backed against the wall in the shadow.

'She'll never get away with it,' Lieutenant Anderson said.

'Maybe not,' Grave Digger conceded. 'But she sure scared the hell out of him.'

'How much did it help?'

Grave Digger looked chagrined.

'None,' Coffin Ed admitted ruefully. 'She put it on too thick. We didn't expect her to accuse him of the murder.'

Grave Digger chuckled at that. 'She didn't hold anything back. I thought for a moment she was going to accuse him of rape.'

Anderson colored slightly. 'Then how far have you got?'

'Nowhere,' Grave Digger confessed.

Anderson sighed. 'I hate to see people tearing at one another like rapacious animals.'

'Hell, what do you expect?' Grave Digger said. 'As long as there are jungles there'll be rapacious animals.'

'Remember the colored taxi driver who picked up the three white men and the colored woman in front of Small's, right after the trucks were wrecked?' Anderson asked, changing the conversation.

'Took them to Brooklyn. Maybe we ought to talk to him.'

'No use now. Homicide took him down to the morgue. On a hunch. And he identified the bodies of the three white men as the same ones.'

Grave Digger shifted his weight and Coffin Ed leaned forward. For a moment they were silent, lost in thought, then Grave Digger said, 'That ought to tell me something,' adding, 'but it don't.'

'It tells me they ain't got the money either,' Coffin Ed said.

'What they?'

'How the hell do I know? I didn't see the ones who got away,' Coffin Ed said.

Anderson thumbed through the report sheets on his desk. 'The Lincoln was found abandoned on Broadway, where the subway trestle passes over 125th Street, with the two rifles still inside,' he noted. 'It showed where you hit it.'

'So what?'

'The gunmen haven't been found but Homicide has got leaders out. Anyway, we know who they are and they won't get far.'

'Don't worry about those birds, they'll never fly,' Coffin Ed said.

'Those are not the flying kind,' Grave Digger added. 'Those are jailbirds, headed for home.'

'And we're headed for food,' Coffin Ed said. 'My stomach is sending up emergency calls.'

'Damn right,' Grave Digger agreed. 'As Napoleon said, "A woman thinks with her heart but a man with his stomach." And we've got some heavy thinking to do.'

Anderson laughed. 'What Napoleon was that?'

'Napoleon Jones,' Grave Digger said.

'All right, Napoleon Jones, don't forget crime,' Anderson said.

'Crime is what pays us,' Coffin Ed said.

They went to Mammy Louise's. She had changed her pork store with the tiny restaurant in back into a fancy all-night barbecue joint. Mr Louise was dead and a slick young black man with shiny straightened hair and fancy clothes had taken his place. The English bulldog who used to keep Mr Louise at home was still there, but his usefulness was gone and he looked lonely for the short fat figure of Mr Louise, whom he delighted in scaring. The new young man didn't look like the type anything could keep home, bulldog or whatnot.

They sat at a rear table facing the front. The barbecue grill was to their right, presided over by a white-clad chef. To their left was the jukebox, blaring out a Ray Charles number.

Mammy Louise's slick young man came personally to take their orders, playing the role of Patron with mincing arrogance.

'Good evening, gentlemen, what will you gentlemen have tonight?'

Grave Digger looked up. 'What have you got?'

'Barbecued ribs, barbecued feet, barbecued chicken, and we got some chitterlings and hog maws and some collard greens with ears and tails –'

'You'd go out of business if hogs had only loins,' Coffin Ed interrupted.

The young man flashed his teeth. 'We got some ham and succotash and some hog head and black-eyed peas –'

'What do you do with the bristles?' Grave Digger asked.

The young man was becoming irritated. 'Anything you want, gentlemen,' he said with a strained smile.

'Don't brag,' Coffin Ed muttered.

The smile went out.

'Just bring us two double orders of ribs,' Grave Digger said quickly. 'With side dishes of black-eyed peas, rice, okra, collard greens with fresh tomatoes and onions, and top it off with some deep-dish apple pie and vanilla ice cream. Okay?'

The young man smiled again. 'Just a light snack.'

'Yeah, we want to think,' Coffin Ed said.

They watched the young man walk away with a switch.

'Mr Louise must be turning over in his grave,' Coffin Ed said.

'Hell, he's more likely running after some chippy angel, now that he's got away from that bulldog.'

'If he went in that direction.'

'All chippies were angels to Mr Louise,' Grave Digger said.

The place was filled mostly with young people who peeped at them through the corners of their eyes when they came back to play the jukebox. Everyone knew them. They looked at these young people, thinking they didn't know what it was all about yet.

Suddenly they were listening.

'Pres,' Grave Digger recognized, cocking his ear. 'And Sweets.'

'Roy Eldridge too,' Coffin Ed added. 'Who's on the bass?'

'I don't know him or the guitar either,' Grave Digger confessed. 'I guess I'm an old pappy.'

'What's that platter?' Coffin Ed asked the youth standing by the jukebox who had played the number.

His girl looked at them through wide dark eyes, as though they'd escaped from the zoo, but the boy replied self-consciously, '"Laughing to Keep from Crying." It's foreign.'

'No, it ain't,' Coffin Ed said.

No one contradicted him. They were silent with their thoughts until a waiter brought the food. The table was loaded. Grave Digger chuckled. 'Looks like a famine is coming on.'

'We're going to head it off,' Coffin Ed said.

The waiter brought three kinds of hot sauce – Red Devil, Little Sister's Big Brother, West Virginia Coke Oven – vinegar, a plate of yellow corn bread and a dish of country butter.

'Bone apperteet,' he said.

'*Merci, m'sieu*,' Coffin Ed replied.

'Black Frenchman,' Grave Digger commented when the waiter had left.

'Good old war,' Coffin Ed said. 'It got us out of the South.'

'Yeah, now the white folks want to start another war to get us back.'

That was the last of that conversation. The food claimed their attention. They sloshed the succulent pork barbecue with Coke Oven hot sauce and gnawed it from the bones with noisy relish. It made the chef feel good all over to watch them eat.

When they had finished, Mammy Louise came from the kitchen. She was shaped like a weather balloon on two feet, with a pilot balloon serving as a head. The round black face beneath the bandanna which encased her head was shiny with sweat, but still she wore a heavy sweater over a black woollen dress. She claimed she had never been warm since coming north. Her ancestors were runaway slaves who had joined a tribe of southern Indians and formed a new race known as 'Geechies'. Her native language was a series of screeches punctuated by grunts, but she spoke American with an accent. She smelled like stewed goat.

'How's y'all, nasty 'licemen?' she greeted them jovially.

'Fine, Mammy Louise, how's yourself?'

'Cold,' she confessed.

'Don't your new love keep you warm?' Coffin Ed asked.

She cast a look at the mincing dandy flashing his teeth at two women at a front table. ''Oman lak me tikes w'ut de good Lawd send 'thout question, I'se 'fied.'

'If you are satisfied, who're we to complain?' Grave Digger said.

A man poked his head in the door and said something to her fine young man and he hurried back to their table and said, 'Your car's calling.'

They jumped up and hurried out without paying.

15

Lieutenant Anderson said, 'A man was found dead in a junkyard underneath the 125th Street approach to the Triborough Bridge.'

'What about it?' Coffin Ed replied.

'*What about it?*' Anderson flared. 'Have you guys quit the force? Go over and look at it. You might learn that killing is a crime. Just the same as robbery.'

Coffin Ed felt his ears burning. 'Right away,' he said respectfully.

'What about it?' he heard Anderson muttering as he switched off.

Grave Digger was chuckling as he wheeled the car into the traffic. 'Got your ass torn, eh, buddy?'

'Yeah, the boss man got salty.'

'Let that be a lesson to you. Don't play murder cheap.'

'All right, I'm outnumbered,' Coffin Ed said.

They found Sergeant Wiley in charge of the crew from Homicide. His men were casting footprints, dusting for fingerprints, and taking photographs. A young pink-faced assistant medical examiner was tagging the body DOA and whistling cheerfully.

'My old friends, the lion tamers,' Sergeant Wiley greeted them. 'Have no fear, the dog is dead.'

They looked at the dead dog, then glanced casually about.

'What've you got here?' Grave Digger asked.

'Just another corpse,' Wiley said. 'My fifth for the night.'

'So you covered the caper at the Polo Grounds?'

'Caper! Hell, when I arrived there were only four stiffs. You men got the live one.'

'You can have him.'

'For what? If he wasn't any good for you what the hell I want him for?'

'Who knows? Maybe he'll like you better.'

Wiley smiled. He looked more like a professor of political science at the New School than a homicide detective-sergeant but Grave Digger and Coffin Ed knew him for a cool clever cop. 'Let's look around,' he said, leading the way into the shed where the body was found. 'Here's the score. We got a social security card from his wallet which gives his name as Joshua Peavine and an address on West 121st Street. He was stabbed once in the heart. That's all we know.'

The detectives looked carefully over the junk-filled shed. Three aisles, flanked by junk stacked to the corrugated-iron ceiling branched off from the main aisle that led in from the door. All available space was filled except an empty spot at the end of the main aisle beside the back wall.

'Somebody got something,' Coffin Ed remarked.

'What the hell would anybody want from here?' Wiley asked, gesturing towards the stacks of flattened cardboard, old books and magazines, rags, radios, sewing-machines, rusty tools, battered mannequins and unidentifiable scraps of metal.

'The man got killed for something, much less the dog,' Coffin Ed maintained.

'Might have been a sex crime,' Grave Digger ventured. 'Suppose he came here with a white man. It's happened before.'

'I thought of that,' Wiley said. 'But the dead dog contradicts it.'

'He'd kill the dog if it was worth it,' Coffin Ed said.

Wiley raised his eyebrows. 'All that secrecy in Harlem?'

'He'd do what was necessary if the pay was right.'

'Maybe,' Wiley conceded. 'But here's the twist. We found a ball of meat that looks as though it might be poisoned in his pocket – we'll have it analysed of course. So the dog was already poisoned by someone else. Unless he had two balls of poisoned meat – which wouldn't seem necessary.'

'This empty space bothers me,' Grave Digger confessed. 'This empty space in all this conglomeration of junk. Was there anything knocked off the hijack truck the other night that might identify it? Something that might wind up in a junkyard. A spare wheel?'

Wiley shook his head. 'Maybe a gun could have been lost, but nothing I can think of that would be sold here. Nothing at least to fill this empty space. I think we're on the wrong track there.'

'There's only one way to find out,' Grave Digger said.

Wiley nodded. The door to the office had been forced by Wiley's men but nothing had been found to draw attention. The three of them went in and Wiley telephoned Mr Goodman at his home in Brooklyn.

Mr Goodman was horrified. 'Everything happens to me,' he cried. 'Such a good boy, so honest. He wouldn't hurt a fly yet.'

'We want you to come over and tell us what is missing.'

'Missing!' Mr Goodman screamed. 'You're not thinking Josh was killed protecting my place? He wasn't a nitwit.'

'We're not thinking anything. We just want you to tell us what's missing.'

'You think thieves have stolen something from my junkyard? Diamonds, maybe. Bricks of gold. Necklaces of rubies. Have you seen my junk? Only another junk man would want anything from my junkyard and he'd need a truck to take away ten dollars' worth.'

'We just want you to come over and take a look, Mr Good-man,' Wiley said patiently.

'*Mein Gott*, at this hour of the morning! You say Josh is dead. Poor boy. My heart bleeds. But can I bring him back to life, at two o'clock in the morning? Can I raise the dead? If there is junk missing you can see it for yourself. Do you think I can identify my junk? How can anyone identify junk? Junk is junk; that's what makes it junk. If someone has taken some of my junk he is welcome. There will be signs where he has taken truck-loads, unless he is a lunatic. Look you for a lunatic, there is your man. And my Reba is awake and worrying should I go over in that place full of lunatic murderers at this time of night. She is a lunatic too. You just put Josh in the morgue and I will come Monday morning and identify his body.'

'This is important, Mr Goodman –' The line went dead. Wiley jiggled the hook. 'Mr Goodman, Mr Goodman –' The voice of the operator came on. Wiley looked about and said, 'He hung up,' and hung up himself.

'Send for him,' Coffin Ed said.

Wiley looked at him. 'On what charge? I'd have to get a court order to get him out of Brooklyn.'

'There's more ways than one to skin a cat,' Grave Digger said.

'Don't tell me,' Wiley said, leading the way back to the yard. 'Let me stay ignorant.'

They stood for a moment looking at the carcass of the dead dog. The ruddy-faced assistant medical examiner passed them, singing cheerfully, '*I'll be glad when you're dead, you rascal you; I'll be standing at Broad and High when they bring your dead ass by, I'll be glad when you're dead . . .*'

Grave Digger and Coffin Ed exchanged looks.

Wiley noticed and said, 'It's a living.'

'More bodies, more babies,' Grave Digger agreed.

The morgue wagon came and took away the body of the man and the carcass of the dog. Wiley called his men and prepared to leave. 'I'm going to let you have it,' he said.

'We got it,' Coffin Ed said. 'Sleep tight.'

Left to themselves they went back over the ground in detail. 'Anywhere else it would figure something was stolen,' Coffin Ed said. 'Here it don't make any sense.'

'Let's quit guessing, let's go get Goodman.'

Coffin Ed nodded. 'Right.'

They closed the shed and turned out the lights and went slowly through the yard to the gate. When they started to cross the street to where their car was parked, a dark shape came from beneath the bridge like a juggernaut. They couldn't see what it was but they ran because years of police work had taught them that nothing moves in the dark but danger. When they saw it was a black car moving at incredible speed they dove face downward on the pavement on the other side. A burst of flame lit the night as the silence exploded; machine-gun bullets sprayed over them as the black car passed. It was over. For a brief instant there was the diminishing whine of a high-powered engine, then silence again. The black shape had disappeared as though it had never been.

By now they had their pistols in their hands, but they still lay cautiously flat to the pavement, searching the night for a moving target. Nothing moved. Finally they crawled to the protection of their little car and stood up, still searching the shadows for movement. They eased into the car like wary shadows themselves. Their breathing was audible. They still looked around.

Car lights had slowed in the moving chain on the bridge overhead, but the deserted, off-beat street below remained dark.

'Report it,' Grave Digger said as they sat in the dark.

Coffin Ed called the precinct from the car and got Lieutenant Anderson. He gave it just like it happened.

'Why, for God's sake?' Anderson said.

'I don't figure it,' Coffin Ed confessed. 'We got nothing, no description, no licence number – and no ideas.'

'I don't know what you're on to, but be careful,' Anderson warned.

'How much more careful can a cop be?'

'You could use some help.'

'Help to get killed,' Coffin Ed grumbled and felt a warning pressure from Grave Digger's hand. 'We're going to Brooklyn now to get the owner of this junkyard.'

'Well, if you have to, but for God's sake go easy; you don't have any jurisdiction in Brooklyn and you can get us all in a jam.'

'Easy does it,' Coffin Ed said and cut off.

Grave Digger mashed the starter and they went down the dark street. He was frowning from his thoughts. 'Ed, we're just missing something,' he said.

'Goddamned right,' Coffin Ed agreed. 'Just missing getting killed.'

'I mean, doesn't this tell you something?'

'Tells me to get the hell off the Force while I'm still alive.'

'What I mean is, so much nonsense must make sense,' Grave Digger persisted as he entered the approach to the East Side throughway.

'Do you believe that shit?' Coffin Ed said.

'I was thinking why would anyone want to rub us out because a junkyard laborer was murdered?'

'You tell me.'

'What's so important about this killing? It smells like some kind of double-cross.'

'I don't see it. Unless you're trying to tie this to the hijack caper. And that sure don't make any sense. People are getting killed in Harlem all the time. Why not you and me?'

'I got to think something,' Grave Digger said and entered the stream of traffic on the throughway without stopping.

Mr Goodman was still awake when they arrived. The news of Josh's murder had upset him. He was clad in bathrobe and night-gown and looked as though he'd been raiding the kitchen. But he still protested against going back to Harlem just to look over his junkyard.

'What good can it do? How can it help you? No one steals junk. I only kept the dog to keep bums from sleeping in the yard, and cart pushers like Uncle Bud from filling his cart with my junk to sell to another junk man.'

'Listen, Mr Goodman, the other night eighty-seven poor colored families lost their life savings in a robbery –'

'Yes, yes, I read in the papers. They wanted to go back to Africa. I want to get back to Israel where I've never been either. It comes to no good, this looking for bigger apples on foreign trees. Here every man is free –'

'Yes, Mr Goodman,' Grave Digger interrupted with feigned patience. 'But we're cops, not philosophers. And we just want to find out what is missing from your junkyard and we can't wait until Monday morning because by then someone else might be killed. Even us. Even you.'

'If I must, I must, to keep some other poor colored man from being killed, about some junk,' Mr Goodman said resignedly, adding bitterly: 'What this world is coming to nobody knows, when people are killed about some junk – not to speak of a poor innocent dog.'

He led them into the parlor to wait while he dressed. When he returned ready to go, he said, 'My Reba don't like it.'

The detectives didn't comment on his Reba's dislikes.

At first Mr Goodman did not see where anything was missing. It looked exactly as he had left it.

'All this trouble, getting up and dressing and coming all this distance in the dark hours of morning, for nothing,' he complained.

'But there must have been something in this empty space,' Coffin Ed insisted. 'What are you keeping this space for?'

'Is that a crime? Always I keep space for what might come in. Did poor Josh get killed for this empty space? Just who is the lunatic, I ask you?' Then he remembered. 'A bale of cotton,' he said.

Grave Digger and Coffin Ed froze. Their nostrils quivered like hound dogs on a scent. Thoughts churned through their heads like sheets of lightning.

'Uncle Bud brought in a bale of cotton this morning,' Mr Goodman went on. 'I had it put out here. I haven't thought of it since. With income taxes and hydrogen bombs and black revolutions, who thinks of a bale of cotton? Uncle Bud is one of the cart men –'

'We know Uncle Bud,' Coffin Ed said.

'Then you know he must have found this bale of cotton on his nightly rounds.' Mr Goodman shrugged and spread his hands. 'I can't ask every cart man for a bill of sale.'

'Mr Goodman, that's all we want to know,' Grave Digger said. 'We'll drive you to a taxi and pay for your time.'

'Pay I want none,' Mr Goodman said. 'But curious I am. Who would kill a man about a bale of cotton? *Cotton, mein Gott.*'

'That's what we want to find out,' Grave Digger said and led the way to their car.

Now it was three-thirty in the morning and they were back at the precinct station talking it over with Lieutenant Anderson. Anderson had already alerted all cars to pick up Uncle Bud for questioning and they were trying to fix the picture.

'You're certain this bale of cotton was carried by the meat delivery truck used by the jackers?' Anderson said.

'We found fibers of raw cotton in the truck. Uncle Bud finds a bale of cotton on 137th Street and sells it to the junkyard. The bale of cotton is missing. A junkyard laborer has been killed. We're certain of that much,' Grave Digger said.

'But what could make this bale of cotton that important?'

'Identification. Maybe it points directly to the hijackers,' Grave Digger said.

'Yes, but remember the dog was dead before Josh and his murderer arrived. Maybe the cotton was gone by then too.'

'Maybe. But that doesn't change the fact that somebody wanted the cotton and didn't let him live to tell whether they got it, or somebody got it before.'

'Let's quit guessing and go find the cotton,' Coffin Ed said.

Grave Digger looked at him as though he felt like saying, 'Go find it then.'

During the silence the phone rang and Anderson picked up the receiver and said, 'Yes ... yes ... yes, 119th Street and Lenox ... yes ... well, keep looking.' He hung up.

'They found the junk cart,' Grave Digger said more than asked.

Anderson nodded. 'But Uncle Bud wasn't with it.'

'It figures,' Coffin Ed said. 'He's probably in the river by now.'

'Yeah,' Grave Digger said angrily. 'This mother-raping cotton punished the colored man down south and now it's killing them up north.'

'Which reminds me,' Anderson said. 'Dan Sellers of Car 90 says he saw an old colored junk man who'd found a bale of cotton on 137th Street right after the trucks crashed the night of the hijack. The old man was trying to get it into his cart – probably Uncle Bud – and they stopped to question him. Then he got out and helped him load it and ordered him to bring it to the station. But he never came.'

'Now you tell us,' Grave Digger said bitterly.

Anderson colored. 'I'd forgotten it until now. After all, we hadn't thought of cotton.'

'You hadn't,' Coffin Ed said.

'Speaking of cotton, what do you know about a Colonel Calhoun who's opened a store-front office on Seventh Avenue to recruit people to go south and pick cotton? Calls it the Back-to-the-Southland movement,' Grave Digger asked.

Anderson looked at him curiously. 'Lay off him,' he warned, 'I admit it's a stupid pitch, but it's strictly on the legitimate. The captain has questioned him and checked his licence and credentials; they're all in order. And he's got influential friends.'

'I don't doubt it,' Grave Digger said drily. 'All southern crackers got influential friends up north.'

Anderson looked down.

'The Back-to-Africa members are picketing him,' Coffin Ed said. 'They don't want that crap in Harlem.'

'The Muslims haven't bothered him,' Anderson said defensively.

'Hell, they're just giving him enough rope.'

'Just his timing is bad,' Coffin Ed argued. 'Right after this Back-to-Africa movement is hijacked he opens this go-south-and-pick-cotton pitch. If you ask me, he's looking for trouble.'

Anderson thumbed through the reports on his desk. 'Last

night at ten p.m. he phoned and reported that his car had been stolen from in front of his office on Seventh Avenue. Gave his home address as Hotel Dixie on 42nd Street. A cruiser stopped by but the office was closed for the night. We gave it a routine check at midnight. The desk said he had come home at ten-thirty-five p.m. and hadn't left his suite. His nephew was with him.'

'What kind of car?' Grave Digger asked.

'Black limousine. Special body. Ferrari chassis. Birmingham, Alabama, plates. And just lay off of him. We got enough trouble as it is.'

'I'm just thinking that cotton grows in the South,' Grave Digger said.

'And tobacco grows in Cuba,' Anderson said. 'Go home and get some sleep. Whatever's going to happen has happened by now.'

'We're going, boss,' Grave Digger said. 'No more we can do tonight anyway. But don't hand us that crap. This caper has just begun.'

16

Everything happens in Harlem six days a week, but Sunday morning, people worship God. Those who are not religious stay in bed. The whores, pimps, gamblers, criminals and racketeers catch up on their sleep or their love. But the religious get up and put on their best clothes and go to church. The bars are closed. The stores are closed. The streets are deserted save for the families on their way to church. A drunk better not be caught molesting them; he'll get all the black beat off him.

All of the Sunday newspapers had carried the story of the arrest of Reverend D. O'Malley, leader of the Back-to-Africa movement, on suspicion of fraud and homicide. The accounts of the hijacking had been rehashed and pictures of O'Malley and his wife, Iris, and Mabel Hill added to the sensationalism.

As a consequence Reverend O'Malley's interdenominational church, 'The Star of Ham', on 121st Street between Seventh and Lenox Avenues, was crowded with the Back-to-Africa followers and the curious. A scattering of Irish people who had read the story in *The New York Times*, which didn't carry pictures, had made their way uptown, thinking Reverend O'Malley was one of them.

Reverend T. Booker Washington (no relation to the great Negro educator), the assistant minister, led the services. At first he led the congregation in prayer. He prayed for the Back-to-Africa followers, and he prayed that their money be returned;

and he prayed for sinners and for good people who had been falsely accused, and for all black people who had suffered the wages of injustice.

Then he began his sermon, speaking quietly and with dignity and understanding of the unfortunate robbery, and of the tragic deaths of young Mr and Mrs Hill, members of the church and active participants in the Back-to-Africa movment. The congregation sat in hushed silence. Then Reverend Washington spoke openly and frankly of the inexplicable tragedy which seemed to haunt the life of that saintly man, Reverend O'Malley, as though God were trying him.

'It is as though God was testing this man with the trials of Job to ascertain the strength of his faith and his endurance and courage for some great task ahead.'

'Amen,' a sister said tentatively.

Reverend Washington moved carefully, sampling the reaction of his audience before proceeding to controversial ground.

'All of his life this noble and selfless man has been subjected to the cruel and biased judgement of the white people whom he defies for you.'

'Amen,' the sister cried louder and with more confidence. A few timid 'amens' echoed.

'I know Reverend O'Malley is innocent of any crime,' Reverend Washington said loudly, letting passion creep into the solemnity of his voice. 'I would trust him with my money and I would trust him with my life.'

'Amen!' the sister shouted, rising from her seat. 'He's a good man.'

The congregation warmed up. Ripples of confirmation ran through all the women.

'He will conquer this calumny of false accusation; he will be vindicated!' Reverend Washington thundered.

'Set him free!' a woman screamed.

'Justice will set him free!' Reverend Washington roared. 'And he will get back our money and lead us out of this land of oppression back to our beloved homeland in Africa.'

'*Amens*' and '*hallelujas*' filled the air as the congregation was swept off its feet. In the grip of emotionalism, O'Malley appeared in their imaginations as a martyr to the injustice of whites, and a brave and noble leader.

'His chains will be broken by the Almighty God and he will come and set us free,' Reverend Washington concluded in a thundering voice.

The Back-to-Africa followers believed. They wanted to believe. They didn't have any other choice.

'Now we will take up a collection to help pay for Reverend O'Malley's defence,' Reverend Washington said in a quiet voice. 'And we will delegate Brother Sumners to take it to him in his hour of Gethsemane.'

Five hundred and ninety-seven dollars was collected and Brother Sumners was charged to go forthwith and present it to Reverend O'Malley. The precinct station where O'Malley was being held for the magistrate's court was only a few blocks distant. Brother Sumners returned with word from O'Malley before the service had adjourned. He could scarcely contain his sense of importance as he mounted the rostrum and brought them word from their beloved minister.

'Reverend O'Malley is spending the day in his cell praying for you, his beloved followers – for all of us – and for the speedy return of your money, and for our safe departure for Africa. He says he will be taken to court Monday morning at ten o'clock when he will be freed to return to you and continue his work.'

'Lord, protect him and deliver him,' a sister cried, and others echoed: 'Amen, amen.'

The congregation filed out, filled with faith in Reverend O'Malley, blended with compassion and a sense of satisfaction for their own good deed of sending him the big collection.

On many a table there was chicken and dumplings or roast pork and sweet potatoes, and crime took a rest.

Grave Digger and Coffin Ed always slept late on Sundays, rarely stirring from bed before six o'clock in the evening. Sunday and Monday were their days off unless they were working on a case, and they had decided to let the hijacking case rest until Monday.

But Grave Digger had dreamed that a blind man had told him he had seen a bale of cotton run down Seventh Avenue and turn into a doorway, but he awakened before the blind man told him what doorway. There was a memory knocking at his mind, trying to get in. He knew it was important but it had not seemed so at the time. He lay for a time going over in detail all that they had done. He didn't find it; it didn't come. But he had a strong feeling that if he could remember this one thing he would have all the answers.

He got up and slipped on a bathrobe and went to the kitchen and got two cans of beer from the refrigerator.

'Stella,' he called his wife, but she had gone out.

He drank one can of beer and prowled about the house, holding the other in his hand. He was looking inward, searching his memory. A cop without a memory is like meat without potatoes, he was thinking.

His two daughters were away at camp. The house felt like a tomb. He sat in the living-room and leafed through the Saturday edition of the *Sentinel*, Harlem's twice-weekly newspaper devoted to the local news. The hijacking story took up most of the front page. There were pictures of O'Malley and Iris, and of John and Mabel Hill. O'Malley's racketeer days and prison record were hammered on and the claim he had been marked for death by the syndicate. There were stories about his Back-to-Africa movement, bordering on libel, and stories of the Back-to-Africa movement of L.H. Michaux, handled with discretion; and stories of the original Back-to-Africa movement of Marcus Garvey, containing some bits of information that Garvey hadn't known himself. He turned the pages and his gaze lit on an advertisement for the Cotton Club, showing a picture of Billie Belle doing her exotic cotton dance. *I've got cotton on the brain*, he thought disgustedly and threw the paper aside.

He went to the telephone extension in the hall, from where he could look outdoors, and called the precinct station in Harlem and talked to Lieutenant Bailey, who was on Sunday duty. Bailey said, no, Colonel Calhoun's car had not been found, no, there was no trace of Uncle Bud, no, there was no trace of the two gunmen of Deke's who had escaped.

'The *noes* have it,' Bailey said.

'Well, as long as the head's gone they can't bite,' Grave Digger said.

Coffin Ed phoned and said his wife, Molly, had gone out with Stella, and he was coming over.

'Just don't let's talk about crime,' Grave Digger said.

'Let's go down to the pistol range at headquarters and practise shooting,' Coffin Ed suggested. 'I've just got through cleaning the old lady.'

'Hell, let's drink some highballs and get gay and take the ladies out on the town,' Grave Digger said.

'Right. I won't mind being gay for a change.'

The phone rang right after Coffin Ed hung up. Lieutenant Bailey said the Back-to-the-Southland people were assembling a group of colored people in front of their office for a parade down Seventh Avenue and there might be trouble.

'You and Ed better come over,' he said. 'The people know you.'

Grave Digger called back Coffin Ed and told him to bring the car as Stella had taken his. Coffin Ed arrived before he had finished dressing, and they got into his gray Plymouth sedan and took off for Harlem. Forty-five minutes later they were rapidly threading through the Sunday afternoon traffic, heading north on Seventh Avenue.

A self-ordained preacher was standing on the sidewalk outside the Chock Full o' Nuts at 125th Street and Seventh Avenue, exhorting the passersby to take Jesus to their hearts. 'Ain't no two ways about it,' he was shouting. 'The right one is with God and Jesus and the wrong one with the devil.'

A few pious people had stopped to listen. Most of the Sunday afternoon strollers took the devil's way and passed without looking.

Diagonally across the intersection the Harlem branch of the Black Muslims was staging a mass meeting in front of the National Memorial Bookstore, headquarters of Michaux's Back-to-Africa movement. The store front was plastered with slogans: GODDAMN WHITE MAN ... WHITE PEOPLE EAT DOG ... ALLAH IS GOD ... BLACK MEN UNITE ... At one side a platform had been erected with a public-address hook-up for the speakers. Below to one side was an open black coffin with a legend: *The Remains of Lumumba*. The coffin contained pictures of Lumumba in life and in death; a black suit said to have been worn by him when he was killed; and other mementoes said to have belonged to him in life. Bordering the sidewalk on removable flagstaffs were the flags of all the nations of black Africa.

Hundreds of people were lined up on the sidewalk in a packed mass. Three police cruisers were parked along the kerb and white harness cops patrolled up and down in the street. Muslims wearing the red fezzes they had adopted as their symbol were lined in front of the bookstore, side by side, keeping a clear path on the sidewalk demanded by the police. The shouting voice of a speaker came from the amplifiers: 'White Man, you worked us for nothing for four hundred years. Now pay for it . . .'

Grave Digger and Coffin Ed didn't stop. As they neared 130th Street they saw the parade heading in their direction on the other side of the street. They knew that within five blocks it would run head-on into the Black Muslims and there'd be hell to pay. Already some of O'Malley's Back-to-Africa group were collecting at 129th Street for an attack.

Police cruisers were parked along the avenue and cops were standing by.

The detectives noted immediately that the parade was made up of mercenary hoodlums, paid for the occasion. They were laughing belligerently and looking for trouble. They carried knives and walked tough. Colonel Calhoun led them, clad in his black frock coat and a black wide-brimmed hat. His silvery hair and white moustache and goatee shone in the rays of the afternoon sun. He was calmly smoking a cheroot. His tall thin figure was ramrod-straight and he walked with the indifference of a benevolent master. His attitude seemed that of a man dealing with children who might be unruly but never dangerous. The blond young man brought up the rear.

Coffin Ed double-parked and he and Grave Digger walked over to the raised park in the center of Seventh Avenue and assessed the situation.

'You go down to 129th Street and hold those brothers and I'll turn these soul-brothers here,' Grave Digger said.

'I got you, partner,' Coffin Ed said.

Grave Digger lined himself opposite a wooden telephone

post and Coffin Ed crossed to the sidewalk and stood facing the concrete wall enclosing the park.

When the parade reached the intersection at 130th Street, Grave Digger drew his long-barreled .38 revolver and put two bullets into the wooden post. The nickelplated pistol shone in the sun like a silver jet.

'Straighten up!' he shouted at the top of his voice.

The parading hoodlums hesitated.

From down the street came the booming blast of two shots as Coffin Ed fired into the concrete wall, followed by his voice, like an echo, 'Count off!'

The mob preparing for the attack on the parade fell back. People in Harlem believed Coffin Ed and Grave Digger would shoot a man stone cold dead for crossing an imaginary line. Those who didn't believe it didn't try it.

But Colonel Calhoun kept right ahead across 130th Street without looking about. When he came to the invisible line, Grave Digger shot off his hat. The Colonel slowly took the cheroot from his mouth and looked at Grave Digger coldly, then turned with slow deliberation to pick up his hat. Grave Digger shot it out of his hand. It flew on to the sidewalk and with slow deliberation, without another glance in Grave Digger's direction, the Colonel walked after it. Grave Digger shot it out into 130th Street as the Colonel was reaching for it.

The hoodlums in the parade were shuffling about, afraid to advance but taking no chances on breaking and running with those bullets flying about. The young blond man was keeping out of sight at the rear.

'Squads right!' Grave Digger shouted. Everyone turned but no one left. 'March!' he added.

The hoodlums turned right on 130th Street and shuffled towards Eighth Avenue. They went straight past the Colonel, who stood in the center of the street looking at the holes in his hat before putting it on his head. Midway down the block they broke and ran. The first thing a hoodlum learns in Harlem is never run too soon.

The mob at 129th Street turned towards Eighth Avenue to head them off, but Coffin Ed drew a line with two bullets ahead of them. 'As you were!' he shouted.

The Colonel stood there for a moment with three bullet holes in his hat, and residents who had come out to see the excitement began to laugh at him. The blond young man caught up with him and they turned back to Seventh Avenue and began walking towards their office, the jeers and laughter of the colored people following them. The Black Muslims had looked but hadn't moved.

Then the mob herded by Coffin Ed relaxed and started laughing too.

'Man, them mothers,' a cat said admiringly in a loud jubilant voice. 'Them mothers! They'll shoot off a man's ass for crossing a line can't nobody see.'

'Baby, you see that old white mother-raper tryna git his hat? I bet the Digger would have taken his head off if he'da crossed that line.'

'I seen old Coffin Filler shoot the fat offen a cat's stomach for stickin' his belly 'cross that line.'

They slapped one another on the shouders and fell out, laughing at their own lies.

The white cops looked at Grave Digger and Coffin Ed with the envious awe usually reserved for a lion tamer with a cage of big cats.

Coffin Ed joined Grave Digger and they walked to a call box and phoned Lieutenant Bailey.

'All over for today,' Grave Digger reported.

Bailey gave a sigh of relief. 'Thank God! I don't want any riots up here on my tour.'

'All you got to worry about now are some killings and robberies,' Grave Digger said. 'Nothing to worry the commissioner.'

Bailey hung up without commenting. He knew of their feud with the commissioner. Both of them had been suspended at different times for what the commissioner considered unnecessary violence and brutality. He knew also that colored cops had to be tough in Harlem to get the respect of colored hoodlums. Secretly he agreed with them. But he wasn't taking any sides.

'Well, now we're back to cotton,' Coffin Ed said as they walked back towards their car.

'Maybe you are; I ain't,' Grave Digger said. 'All I want to do is go out and break some laws. Other people have all the fun.'

'Damn right. Let's put five bucks on a horse.'

'Hell, man, you call that breaking the law? Let's take the ladies to some unlicensed joint run by some wanted criminal and drink some stolen whisky.'

Coffin Ed chuckled. 'You're on,' he said.

17

The telephone rang at 10.25 a.m. Grave Digger hid his head beneath the pillow. Stella answered it sleepily. A brisk, wideawake and urgent voice said, 'This is Captain Brice. Let me speak to Jones, please.'

She pulled the pillow from over his head. 'The captain,' she said.

He groped for the receiver, experimentally opening his eyes. 'Jones,' he mumbled.

He listened to the rapid staccato voice for three minutes. 'Right,' he said, tense and wide-awake, and was getting out of the bed before he hung up the receiver.

'What is it?' she asked in a tiny voice, frightened and alarmed as she always was when these morning summonses came.

'Deke's escaped. Two officers killed.' He had put on his shorts and undershirt and was pulling up his pants.

She was out of the bed and moving towards the kitchen. 'You want coffee?'

'No time,' he said, putting on a clean shirt.

'Nescafé,' she said disappearing into the kitchen.

With his shirt on he sat on the side of the bed and put on clean socks and his shoes. Then he went into the bathroom and washed his face and brushed his short kinky hair. Without a shave his dark lumpy face looked dangerous. He knew how he looked but it couldn't be helped. He didn't have time for a shave. He put on a black tie, went into the bedroom and took his holstered pistol from a hook in the closet. He laid the pistol on the dresser while he strapped on his shoulder sling and then picked it up and spun the cylinder. It always carried five shells, the hammer resting on an empty chamber. The shades were still drawn, and the long nickelplated revolver glinting in the subdued light from three table lamps looked as dangerous as himself. He slipped it into the greased holster and began stuffing his pockets with the other tools of his trade: a leather-covered buckshot sap with a whalebone handle, a pair of handcuffs, report book, flashlight, stylo, and the leather-bound metal snap case made to hold fifteen extra shells he always carried in his leather-lined side coat-pocket. They also kept an extra box or two of shells in the glove compartment of their official car.

He was standing at the kitchen table, drinking coffee, when Coffin Ed blew for him. Stella tensed. Her smooth brown face grew strained.

'Be careful,' she said.

He stepped around the table and kissed her. 'Ain't I always?' he said.

'Not always,' she murmured.

But he was gone, a big, rough, dangerous man in need of a shave, clad in a rumpled black suit and an old black hat, the bulge of a big pistol clearly visible on the heart side of his broad-shouldered frame.

Coffin Ed looked the same; they could have been cast from the same mold with the exception of Coffin Ed's acid-burned face that was jerking with the tic that came whenever he was tense.

Yesterday, Sunday afternoon, it had taken forty-five minutes to get to Harlem. Today, Monday morning, it took twenty-two.

Coffin Ed said only, 'The fat is in the fire.'

'It's going to burn,' Grave Digger said.

Two white officers had been killed and the precinct station looked like headquarters for the invasion of Harlem. Official cars lined the street. The commissioner's car was there, and cars of the chief inspector, the chief of Homicide, the medical examiner and a D.A.'s assistant. Police cruisers from downtown, from Homicide, from all the Harlem precincts, were scattered about. The street was closed to civilian traffic. There was no place inside for all the army of cops and the overflow stood outside, on the sidewalks, in the street, waiting for their orders.

Coffin Ed parked in the driveway of a private garage and they walked to the station house. The brass was assembled in the captain's office. The lieutenant on the desk said, 'Go on in, they want to see you.'

Heads turned when they entered the office. They were stared at as though they were criminals themselves.

'We want Deke O'Hara and his two gunmen, and we want them alive,' the commissioner said coldly without greeting. 'It's your bailiwick and I'm giving you a free hand.'

They stared back at the commissioner but neither of them spoke.

'Let me give them the picture, sir,' Captain Brice said.

The commissioner nodded. The captain led them into the detectives' room. A white detective got up from his desk in the corner and gave the captain a seat. Other detectives nodded to Grave Digger and Coffin Ed as they passed. No one spoke. They nodded back. They kept the record straight. There was no friendship lost between them and the other precinct detectives; but there was no open animosity. Some resented their position as the aces of the precinct and their close associations with the officers in charge; others were envious; the young colored detectives stood in awe of them. But all took care not to show anything.

Captain Brice sat behind the desk and Grave Digger perched a ham on the edge as usual. Coffin Ed drew up a straight-backed chair and sat opposite the captain.

'Deke was being taken to the magistrate's court,' the captain said. 'There were thirteen others going. The wagon was drawn up in the back court and we were bringing the prisoners from their cells, handcuffed together two by two as customary. Two officers were standing by, supervising the loading – the driver and his helper – and two jailers were bringing the prisoners from the bullpen through the back door and herding them downstairs to the yard and into the wagon. Deke's Back-to-Africa group had collected in the street out front, a thousand or more. They were chanting, "We want O'Malley . . . We want O'Malley," and trying to break through the front door. They were getting unruly and I sent the extra officers out into the street to herd them to one side and keep order. Then they began getting noisy and started rioting. Some began throwing stones through the front windows and others began battering the gate to the driveway with garbage cans. I sent two men from out back to clear the driveway to the street. When they opened the gates to go out they were mobbed and disarmed and the mob streamed into the driveway. Deke had just come from the back door on his way down the stairs, handcuffed to a suspected murderer, one Mack Brothers, when the mob came in sight and saw him. Six prisoners had already been loaded. Then, from what I've been told by a trusty looking out a jail window – all the officers were out front trying to contain the riot – the jailers slammed and locked the door, leaving the two officers alone with the wagon. And at that moment the two gunmen came up from both sides of the high back wall and shot the two officers dead. The gunmen were dressed in officers' uniforms so at first they didn't attract much attention. Then they jumped down inside, put Deke in the wagon and closed the door and got into the front seat – and took the wagon out of the yard.' He stopped and looked at them to see what they would say but they said nothing. So he went on. 'Some of the mob had jumped astride the hood and onto the front bumpers and others were running along beside it. They were shouting, "Make way for O'Malley! Make way for O'Malley!" and they rode the wagon out into the street. The rioters went wild and the officers could only use their saps and billies. They couldn't shoot into those thousand people. The wagon got through. We found it parked a block away around the corner. There must have been a car waiting. They got away. We captured the other prisoners in a matter of minutes.'

'What about the one he was handcuffed to?' Coffin Ed asked.

'Him too. He was wandering in the street. He had been sapped and the cuffs were still on him.'

'It was organized all right, but it needed luck,' Grave Digger said.

'The mob seemed organized too,' the captain said.

'Probably, but I doubt if there was a connection.'

'More likely some planted agitators. They wouldn't have to know an escape was planned. They might have thought of freeing O'Malley by numbers,' Coffin Ed said.

'A holy crusade,' Grave Digger amended.

The captain looked sour. 'We got three hundred of them in the bullpen. You want to talk to them?'

Grave Digger shook his head. 'What are you holding them for?'

Captain Brice reddened with anger. 'Complicity, goddammit. Assisting criminals to escape. Rioting. Accessories to murder. Two officers were killed. And I'll arrest every black son of a bitch in Harlem.'

'Including me and Digger?' Coffin Ed grated, his face jumping like a live snake in a hot fire.

The captain cooled. 'Hell, goddammit, don't be offended,' he threw out the left-handed apology. 'These goddamned lunatics help in a planned escape without knowing what they're doing and cause two officers to get killed. You ought to be mad too.'

'How mad are *you*?' Grave Digger asked. He felt Coffin Ed look at him. He nodded slightly. He knew Coffin Ed read his thoughts and agreed.

'Mad enough for anything,' Captain Brice said. 'Shoot a few of these hoodlums. I'll cover you.'

Grave Digger shook his head. 'The commissioner wants them alive.'

'I'm not talking about them,' the captain raved. 'Shoot any of these goddamn hoodlums.'

'Take it easy, Captain,' Coffin Ed said.

Grave Digger shook his head warningly. The room had become silent. Everyone was listening. Grave Digger leaned forward and said in a voice only for the captain's ears, 'Are you mad enough to let us have Iris, Deke's woman – if she hasn't gone to county?'

The captain sobered instantly. He looked cornered and annoyed. He wouldn't meet Grave Digger's eyes. 'You're asking for too much,' he growled. 'And you know it,' he accused. Finally he said, 'I couldn't if I wanted to. Her case is on the docket. I'm responsible to deliver her. If she doesn't appear it's officially an escape.'

'Is she still here?' Grave Digger persisted.

'Nobody's gone out,' the captain said. 'All the hearings have been postponed, but that makes no difference.'

Still leaning forward, Grave Digger whispered, 'Let her escape.'

The captain banged his fist on the desk. 'No, goddammit! And that's final.'

'The commissioner wants Deke and the two cop killers,' Grave

Digger whispered urgently. 'You had two nights and a day to find those boys – you and the whole Force. And they weren't found. We're only two men. What do you expect us to do that the whole Force couldn't do?'

'Well,' the captain said, expelling his breath. 'Do the best you can.'

'We can find them,' Grave Digger kept on. 'But you got to pay for it.'

'I'll speak to the commissioner,' the captain said, starting to rise.

'No,' Grave Digger said. 'He'll only say *no* and that will be the end of it. You've got to make the decision on your own.'

The captain sat down. He thought for a moment, then looked up into Grave Digger's eyes. 'How bad do you want Deke your-self?' he asked.

'Bad,' Grave Digger said.

'If you can get her out of here without my knowledge, take her,' the captain said. 'I won't know anything about it. If you get caught, take the consequences. I won't cover for you.'

Grave Digger straightened up. Veins stood out on his temples and his neck had swelled like a cobra's. His eyes had turned blood-red. He was so mad the captain's image was blurred in his vision.

'I wouldn't do this for nobody but my own black people,' he said in a voice that was cotton dry.

He wheeled from the desk and Coffin Ed fell in beside him and they walked fast out of the room and softly closed the door behind them.

They got their official car from the garage and drove up to Blumstein's Department Store on 125th Street and went into the women's department. Grave Digger bought a bright red dress, size 14, a pair of dark tan lisle stockings and a white plastic handbag. Coffin Ed bought a pair of gilt sandals, size 7, and a hand mirror. They put their packages into a shopping bag and drove up to Rose Murphy's House of Beauty on 145th Street, near Amsterdam Avenue, and bought some quick-action black skin dye and some make-up for a black woman and a dark-haired wig. They put these into their shopping bag and returned to the precinct station.

All the brass had left but the chief inspector in charge of homicide. They had nothing to say to him. Many of the police cruisers had been assigned to special detail and had gone about their business. But the street was still closed and heavily guarded and no one was permitted to enter the block or leave any of the buildings without police scrutiny.

Grave Digger parked in front of the station house and he and Coffin Ed went inside, carrying their shopping bag. They kept on through the booking room and past the captain's office and the detectives' room until they came to the head jailer's cubicle at the rear.

'Send Iris O'Malley down to the interrogation room and give us the key,' Grave Digger said.

The jailer reached out languidly for the order.

'We haven't got any order,' Grave Digger said. 'The captain's too busy to write orders at this time.'

'Can't have her 'less you got an order,' the jailer insisted.

'She'll keep,' Grave Digger said. 'It just holds up the investigation, that's all.'

'Can't do it,' the jailer said stubbornly.

'Then give us the key to the bullpen,' Coffin Ed said. 'We'll start in the Back-to-Africa group.'

'You know I can't do that either 'less you got an order,' the jailer protested. 'What's the matter with you fellows today?'

'Hell, where have you been, man?' Grave Digger said. 'The captain's busy, can't you understand that?'

The jailer shook his head. He didn't want to be the cause of any escapes.

'Call the captain for goddamn's sake,' Coffin Ed grated. 'We can't just stand here and argue with you.'

The jailer got the captain's office on the intercom, and asked if he should let Jones and Johnson interview the Back-to-Africa group in the bullpen.

'Let them see who they goddamn want,' the captain shouted. 'And don't bother me again.'

The jailer looked crestfallen. Now he was anxious to co-operate to keep in their good graces. 'You want to see Iris O'Malley first or afterwards?' he asked.

'Well, we'll just see her first,' Grave Digger said.

The jailer gave them a key and called his underling on the tier where Iris was celled and instructed him to take her down to the 'Pigeons' Nest'.

They were there waiting when the jailer brought her in and left, and they locked the door behind him. They put her on the stool and turned on the battery of lights. Her scratches were healing and the swelling was almost gone from her face but her skin was still the colors of the rainbow. Without make-up her eyes were sexless and ordinary. She wore a dark blue denim uniform but without a number, since she hadn't been bound over to the grand jury.

'You look good,' Coffin Ed said levelly.

'Tell it to your mother,' she said.

'Deke got away,' Grave Digger said.

'The lucky mother-raper,' she said, squinting into the light.

Grave Digger turned down all the lights except one. It left her starkly visible but didn't blind her.

'How'd you like to escape?' Grave Digger asked.

'I'd like it fine,' she said. 'How'd you like to lay me? Both of you. At the same time.'

'Where?' Coffin Ed asked.

'How is the question,' Grave Digger said.

'Here,' she said. 'And let me worry about *how*.'

'All joking aside–' Grave Digger began again, but she cut him off.

'I'm not joking.'

'All sex aside then. Do you know Deke's hideout?'

'If I knew I wouldn't tell you,' she said. 'Anyway, not for nothing.'

'We'll clear you,' he said.

'Shit,' she said. 'You can't clear your own mother-raping selves, much less me. Anyway, I don't know it,' she added.

'Can you find it?'

A sly look came into her eyes. 'I could find it if I was out.'

'I'm reading your mind,' Grave Digger said.

'And it don't read good,' Coffin Ed said.

The sly look went out of her eyes. 'I can't find him from here, and that's for sure.'

'That's for sure,' Grave Digger agreed.

They stared at one another. 'What's in it for me?' she asked.

'Freedom, maybe,' he said. 'When we get Deke we're going to drop the load on him. His two boys are going to fry for cop killing and we're going to fry him for killing Mabel Hill. And you get the ten per cent reward from the eighty-seven grand if we find it.'

They watched the thoughts reflected in her eyes and Coffin Ed said, 'Steady, girl. If you try to cross us there won't be room enough for you in the world. We'll hunt you down and kill you.'

'And don't think you'll be lucky enough to get shot,' Grave

Digger added. His lumpy unshaven face looked sadistic from behind the stabbing light, like the vague shadow of a monster's. 'Want me to spell it out?'

She shuddered. 'And if I don't find him?'

He chuckled. 'We'll arrest you for escaping.'

She was consumed with sudden rage. 'You dirty mother-rapers,' she mouthed.

'Better to be dirty than dumb,' Coffin Ed said. 'Are you on?'

She blushed beneath her rainbow color. 'If I could only rape you, you dirty bastard.'

'You can't. So are you on?'

'I'm on,' she said. 'You son of a bitch, you knew it all the time.' After a moment she added, 'Maybe if I don't find Deke you'll rape me.'

'You'll have a better chance if you find him,' he said.

'I'll find him,' she promised.

18

'Make yourself into a black woman and don't ask any questions,' Grave Digger said. 'You'll find everything in there you'll need – make-up, clothes and some money. Don't worry about the dye; it'll come off.'

He turned on the bright lights and he and Coffin Ed went out and locked the door behind them. She found the mirror and went to work. Coffin Ed stood outside the door and listened for a time; he didn't think she'd yell and try to draw attention, but he wanted to make sure. Satisfied she was tending to the business, he went upstairs and waited for Grave Digger to come with the keys to the bullpen. They went inside and interrogated the sullen prisoners until they found a young black woman about Iris's size and age, named Lotus Green. They filled out a card on Lotus, then took her down to the Pigeons' Nest for further questioning.

'What you want with me?' she protested. 'I done tole you everything I know.'

'We like you,' Coffin Ed said.

She shocked the hell out of him by blowing coy. 'You got to pay me,' she said. 'I don't do it with strangers for nothing.'

'We ain't strangers by now,' he said.

He stood outside, listening to her explain why he was still a stranger while Grave Digger went inside to get Iris. She was ready, a fly black woman in a cheap red dress.

'These shit-skin sandals are too big,' she complained.

'Watch your language and act dignified,' Grave Digger said. 'You're a churchwoman named Lotus Green and you hope to go back to Africa.'

'My God!' she exclaimed.

He took her out past the real Lotus while Coffin Ed took the real Lotus inside.

'We're going to put you in the bullpen and when the officer comes for Lotus Green you come out with him,' Grave Digger instructed. 'Just act sullen and don't answer any questions.'

'That won't be hard,' she said.

Coffin Ed locked the real Lotus in the place of Iris, assuring her that he was going to get some money, and joined Grave Digger. They went to the captain's office and asked permission to take out Lotus Green, one of the Back-to-Africa group.

'She saw where the woman went who was robbed that night, but she doesn't know the number,' Grave Digger explained. 'And that woman might have seen all the hijackers.'

The captain suspected some kind of trick. Furthermore he wasn't interested in the hijacking, he just wanted Deke. But it put him on the spot.

'All right, all right,' he snapped. 'I'll send for her and you can take her from my office. Just don't forget your assignment.'

'It's all the same thing,' Grave Digger said. 'Here's the report on her,' and gave him the card.

They went back to see the head jailer. 'We're going to try Iris once more and if she doesn't give we're going to leave her in the dark for a spell. We'll fix it so she can't hurt herself and don't get edgy if someone hears her screaming. She won't be hurt.'

'I don't know what you fellers do down there and I don't want to know,' the jailer said.

'Right,' Grave Digger said and they went down and stood

outside the bullpen. When they saw a jailer taking Iris, disguised as Lotus, to the captain's office, they went downstairs and got the real Lotus Green and took her back to the bullpen.

'I waited and I waited,' she complained.

'What else could you do?' Coffin Ed said and they went back upstairs to the captain's office and walked out of the station with Iris between them. They got into their car and drove off.

'We're on our own now,' Coffin Ed said.

'Yeah, we've jumped into the fire,' Grave Digger agreed.

'Well, little sister, where do you want to get out?' Coffin Ed asked the black woman on the back seat.

'Let me out on the corner,' she said.

'What corner?'

'Any corner.'

They pulled to the curb on Seventh Avenue and 125th opposite the Theresa Hotel. They wanted all the stool pigeons in the neighborhood to see her getting out of their car. They knew no one would recognize her, but they were marking her for themselves – just in case.

'This is what you do,' Coffin Ed said, turning about to face her. 'When you contact Deke –'

'*If* I contact Deke,' she cut in.

He looked at her for a moment and said, 'Just don't try getting cute because we sprung you. That ain't going to make any difference if you try a double-cross.'

She didn't answer.

He said, 'When you contact Deke, just say you know where the bale of cotton is.'

'*The what!*' she exclaimed.

'The bale of cotton. And let him take it from there. Then when you get him located, keep him waiting and contact us.'

'Are you sure you mean a bale of *cotton*?' she asked incredulously.

'That's right, a bale of cotton.'

'And how do I contact you?'

'Call either of these two numbers.' He gave her the telephone numbers of their homes. 'If we're not there, leave a number and we'll call back.'

'Shit on that,' she said.

'All right, then call back in half an hour and you'll be given a number where to contact us. Just say you're Abigail.'

Grave Digger muttered, 'Ed, you're giving us a lot of trouble.'

'What do you suggest that's better?'

Grave Digger thought about it for a moment. 'Nothing,' he confessed.

'Bye-bye then,' Iris said, adding under her breath, 'Blackbirds,' and got out. She walked east on 125th.

Grave Digger eased into the traffic on Seventh Avenue and drove north.

Iris stopped in front of a United Tobacco store and watched their car until it passed from sight. The store had five telephone booths ranged along one wall. Iris chose one quickly and dialed a number.

A cautious voice answered: 'Holmes Radio Repair Shop.'

'I want to talk to Mr Holmes,' Iris said.

'Who's calling?'

'His wife. I just got back.'

After a moment another disguised voice said, "Honey, where are you?'

'I'm here,' Iris said.

'How'd you get out?'

Don't you wish you knew? she thought. Aloud she said, 'How would you like to buy a bale of cotton?'

There was a long pregnant silence. 'Tell me where you are and I'll have my chauffeur pick you up.'

'Stay put,' she said. 'I'm dealing in cotton.'

'Just don't deal in death,' the voice sounded a deadly warning. She hung up. When she stepped outside she looked up and down the street. Cars were parked on both sides. Crosstown traffic flowed from the Triborough Bridge headed towards the West Side Highway and the 125th Street ferry and vice versa. There was nothing about the black Ford to set it apart from any other car. It was empty and looked put for some time. She didn't see the two-toned Chevrolet parked down the street. But when she started walking again, she was being tailed.

Grave Digger and Coffin Ed drove their official car, the little black car with the hopped-up engine that was so well known in Harlem, into a garage on 155th Street and left it for a tune-up. Then they walked up the hill to the subway and rode the 'A' train down to Columbus Circle at 59th Street and Broadway.

They walked over to the section of pawnshops and second-hand clothing stores on Columbus Avenue and went into Katz's pawnshop and bought black sunglasses and caps. Grave Digger chose a big checkered cap called the 'Sportsman' while Coffin Ed selected a red, long-billed fatigue cap modelled after those worn by the Seabees during the war. When they emerged, they looked like two Harlem cats, high off pot.

They walked up Broadway to a car rental agency and selected a black panel truck without any markings. The rental agent didn't want to trust them until they put down a large deposit. He took it and grinned, figuring them for Harlem racketeers.

'Will this jalopy run?' Grave Digger asked.

'Run!' the agent exclaimed. 'Cadillacs get out of its way.'

'Damn right,' Coffin Ed said. 'If I owned a Cadillac I'd get out of its way too.'

They got in and drove it back uptown.

'Now I know why the world looks so vague to weedheads,' Grave Digger said from behind the wheel.

'Too bad there isn't any make-up to disguise us as white,' Coffin Ed said.

'Hell, I remember when old Canada Lee was made up as a white man, playing on Broadway in a Shakespearean play; and if Canada Lee could look like a white man, I'm damn sure we could.'

The mechanic at the garage didn't recognize them until Grave Digger flashed his shield.

'I'll be a *mother*,' he said, grinning. 'When I saw you coming I locked the safe.'

'Just as well,' Grave Digger said. 'You never know who's in a panel truck.'

'Ain't it the truth?' the mechanic said.

They had him take their radio-telephone from their official car and install it temporarily in the truck. It took forty-five minutes and Coffin Ed called home. His wife said no one named Abigail had called either her or Stella, but the precinct station had been calling every half-hour trying to get in touch with them.

'Just tell them you don't know where we are,' Coffin Ed said. 'And that's the truth.'

When they left the garage they were able to pick up all the police calls. All cars had been alerted to contact them and order them back to the station. Then the cars were instructed to pick up a slim black woman wearing a red dress, named Lotus Green.

Coffin Ed chuckled. 'By this time that yellow gal has damn sure got that dye off, much as she hates being black.'

'And she ain't wearing that cheap red dress, either,' Grave Digger added.

They drove over to a White Rose bar at the corner of 125th and Park Avenue, across the street from the 125th Street railroad station, and parked behind a two-toned Chevrolet. Ernie was sitting in a shoeshine stand outside the bar, facing Park. The sign on the awning read: AMERICAN LEGION SHOE SHINE. Two elderly white men were shining colored men's shoes. Across the avenue, seen between the stanchions of the railroad trestle, was another shoeshine, its awning proclaiming: FATHER DIVINE SHOE SHINE. Two elderly colored men were shining white men's shoes.

'Democracy at work,' Coffin Ed said.

'Down to the feet.'

'Down *at* the feet,' Coffin Ed corrected.

Ernie saw them go into the bar but gave no sign of recognition. They stood at the bar like two cats having a sip of something cold to dampen their dry jag, and ordered beer. After a while Ernie came in and squeezed to the bar beside them. He ordered a beer. The white barman put down an open bottle and a glass. Ernie wasn't looking when he poured it and some sloshed on to Grave Digger's hand. He turned and said, 'Excuse me, I wasn't looking.'

'That's what's on all them tombstones,' Grave Digger said.

Ernie laughed. 'She's at Billie's, the dancer, on 115th Street,' he said under his breath.

'Don't pay no 'tention to me, son, I was just joking,' Grave Digger said aloud. 'Stay with it.'

The bartender was passing. He looked from one to the other. *Stay with it*, he thought. Stay with what? As long as he'd been working in Harlem, he had never learned these colored folks' language.

Grave Digger and Coffin Ed finished their beers and ordered two more and Ernie finished his and went out. Coffin Ed used the bar phone and telephoned his home. There had been no call from Abigail, but the precinct station had been calling regularly.

The bartender was listening furtively but Coffin Ed hadn't said a word. Then finally he said, 'Stay with it.' The bartender started. Nuts, he thought looking vindicated.

They left their beers half finished and went around the corner and sat in their truck.

'If we could tap the phone,' Coffin Ed said.

'She's not going to phone from there,' Grave Digger said. 'She's too smart for that.'

'I just hope she don't get too mother-raping smart to live,' Coffin Ed said.

Billie was alone when Iris knocked with the brass-hand knocker on the black and yellow lacquered door. She opened the door on the chain. She was wearing yellow chiffon lounging slacks over a pair of black lace pants and a long-sleeved white chiffon blouse fastened at the cuffs with turquoise links. She might as well have been naked. Her slim, bare, dancer's feet had bright red lacquered nails. As always she was made up as though to step before the cameras. She looked like the favourite in a sultan's harem.

Through the crack she saw a woman who looked too black to be real, dressed like a housemaid on her afternoon off. She blinked. 'You've got the wrong door,' she said.

'It's me,' Iris said.

Billie's eyes widened '*Me* who? You sound like somebody I know but you sure don't look like anybody I'd ever know.'

'Me, Iris.'

Billie scrutinized her for a moment, then broke into hysterical laughter. 'My God, you look like the last of the Topsys. Whatever happened to you?'

'Unchain the door and let me in,' Iris snapped. 'I know how I look.'

Billie unchained the door, still laughing hysterically, and locked and chained it behind her. Then suddenly, watching Iris hurry towards the bath, she called, 'Hey, I read you were in jail,' running after her.

Iris was already at the mirror, smearing cleansing cream over her face, when Billie came in. 'I'm out now, as you can see.'

'Well, how 'bout you,' Billie said, sitting on the edge of the bathtub. 'Who sprung you? The paper said you lowered the boom on Deke and now he's escaped.'

Iris snatched a clean towel and began frantically rubbing her face to see if the black would come off. Yellow skin appeared. Reassured, she became less frantic. 'The monsters,' she said. 'They want me to help 'em find Deke.'

Billie looked shocked. 'You wouldn't!' she exclaimed.

Iris was slipping out of the cheap red dress. 'The hell I wouldn't,' she said.

Billie jumped to her feet. 'I certainly won't help you,' she said. 'I always liked Deke.'

'You can have him, sugar,' Iris said sweetly, peeling off the lisle stockings. 'I'll swap him for a dress.'

Billie left the room, looking indignant, while Iris shed to the skin and began removing the black in earnest. After a while Billie returned and threw clothes across the side of the tub. She looked at Iris's nude body critically.

'You sure got beat up, baby. You look like you've been raped by three cannibals.'

'That'd be a kick,' Iris mumbled, smearing her face more thoroughly with the cleansing cream.

'Here, use Ponds,' Billie said, handing her a different jar. 'That's Chanel's you're wasting on that blackening and this is just as good for that.'

Iris exchanged the jar without comment and went on smearing her face, neck, arms and legs.

'Did you really kill her?' Billie asked as though casually.

Iris stopped applying the cream and turned around and looked at her. 'Don't ask me that question. There never was a man I'd kill for.' There was a warning in her voice that frightened Billie.

But she had to know. 'Were you and her –'

'Shut up,' Iris snapped. 'I didn't know the bitch.'

'You can't stay here,' Billie said bitchily, showing her disbelief. 'They'd lock me up too if they found me.'

'Don't be so fucking jealous,' Iris said and began kneading in the cleansing cream again. 'Nobody knows I'm here and not even Deke knows about us.'

Billie smiled with secret pleasure. Mollified, she asked, 'How do you expect to get to Deke after you've ratted on him?'

Iris laughed as at a good joke. 'I'm going to cook up a good story about where to find the money he's lost and see what he'll pay me for it. Deke will forgive anything for money.'

'The Back-to-Africa money? Honey, that money has gone with the wind.'

'Don't think I don't know it. I just want to get something out of that two-timing mother-raper any kind of way.'

Billie had her secret smile again. 'Baby, how you talk,' she said, adding: 'You can wipe it off now,' referring to the cream. 'I'll make you up in tan so you'll look brand-new.'

'You're a darling,' Iris said absently, but in the back of her mind she was thinking furiously why Deke would want a bale of cotton.

Billie was looking at her nude body lustfully. 'Don't tempt me,' she said.

19

The Monday edition of the Harlem *Sentinel* came out around noon. Coffin Ed picked up a copy at the newsstand by the Lexington Avenue Subway Kiosk at one-thirty for them to read with their lunch. There had been no word from Abigail, and Paul had just ridden past giving the high sign that Iris was still put.

They wanted to eat some place where it was unlikely they'd be spotted, and where they wouldn't look out of place in their black weedhead sunglasses. They decided to go to a joint on East 116th Street called Spotty's, run by a big black man with white skin spots and his albino wife.

After years of bemoaning the fact that he looked like an overgrown Dalmatian, Spotty had made a peace with life and opened a restaurant specializing in ham hocks, red beans and rice. It sat between a store-front church and a box factory and had no side windows, and the front was so heavily curtained the light of day never entered. Spotty's prices were too moderate and his helpings too big to afford bright electric lights all day. Therefore it attracted customers such as people in hiding, finicky people who couldn't bear the sight of flies in their food, poor people who wanted as much as they could get for their money, weedheads avoiding bright lights, and blind people who didn't know the difference.

They took a table in the rear across from two laborers. Spotty brought them plates of red beans, rice and ham hocks, and a stack of sliced bread. There wasn't any choice.

Coffin Ed wolfed a mouthful hungrily and gasped for breath. 'This stuff will set your teeth on fire,' he said.

'Take some of this hot sauce and cool it off,' one of the laborers said with a straight face.

'It cools you off these hot days,' the other laborer said. 'Draws all the heat to the belly and leaves the rest of you cool.'

'What about the belly?' Grave Digger asked.

'Hell, man, what kind of old lady you got?' the laborer said.

Grave Digger shouted for two beers. Coffin Ed took out the paper and divided it in two. He could barely see the large print through his smoked glasses. 'What you want, the inside or the outside?'

'You expect to read in here?' Grave Digger said.

'Ask Spotty to give you a candle,' the laborer said with a straight face.

'Never mind,' Grave Digger said. 'I'll read one word and guess two.'

He took the inside of the paper and folded it on the table. The classified ads were up. His gaze was drawn to an ad in a box: *Bale of cotton wanted immediately. Telephone Tompkins 2 – before seven p.m.* He passed the paper to Coffin Ed. Neither of them said anything. The laborers looked curious but Grave Digger turned over the page before they could see anything.

'Looking for a job?' the talkative laborer asked.

'Yeah,' Grave Digger said.

'That ain't the paper for it,' the laborer said.

No one replied. Finally the two laborers got tired of trying to find out their business and got up and left. Grave Digger and Coffin Ed finished eating in silence.

Spotty came to their table. 'Dessert?' he asked.

'What is it?'

'Blackberry pie.'

'Hell, it's too dark in here to eat blackberry pie,' Grave Digger said and paid him and they got up and left.

Coffin Ed called his home from a street booth, but there was still no word from Abigail. Then he called the Tompkins number. A southern voice answered, 'Back-to-the-Southland office, Colonel Calhoun speaking.' He hung up.

'The Colonel,' he told Grave Digger when he got back in the truck.

'Let's don't think about it here,' Grave Digger said. 'They might be tracing our calls home.'

They drove back past the 125th Street railroad station and found the Chevrolet parked near the Fischer Cafeteria. Ernie gave them the sign that Iris was still put. They were driving on when they saw a blind man tapping his way along. They pulled around the corner of Madison Avenue and waited.

Finally the blind man came tapping along Madison. He was selling Biblical calendars. Coffin Ed leaned from the truck and said, 'Hey, let me see one of those.'

The blind man tapped over towards the edge of the sidewalk, feeling his way cautiously. He pulled a calendar from his bag and said, 'It's got all the names of the Saints and the Holy Days, and numbers straight out of the Apocalypse; and it's got the best days for births and deaths.' Lowering his voice he added, 'It's the photograph I told you about night before last.'

Coffin Ed made as though he were leafing through it. 'How'd you make us?' he whispered.

'Ernie,' the blind man whispered back.

Satisfied, Coffin Ed said loudly, 'Got any dream readings in here?'

Passersby hearing the question stopped to listen.

'There's a whole section on dream interpretations,' the blind man said.

'I'll take this one,' Coffin Ed said and gave the blind man a half dollar.

'I'll take one too,' another man said. 'I dreamed last night I was white.'

Grave Digger drove off, turned east on 127th Street and parked. Coffin Ed passed him the photograph. It showed distinctly the front of a big black limousine. A blond young man sat behind the wheel. Colonel Calhoun sat next to him. Three vague white men sat on the rear seat. Approaching the car was Josh, the murdered junkyard laborer, grinning with relief.

'This cooks him,' Grave Digger said.

'It won't fry him,' Coffin Ed said, 'but it'll scorch the hell out of him.'

'Anyway, he didn't get the cotton.'

'What does that prove? He might already have the money and the cotton might just be evidence. He might have killed the boy just to keep from tipping his hand,' Grave Digger argued.

'And advertise for the cotton today? Hell, let's take him anyway, and find the cotton later.'

'Let's get Deke first,' Grave Digger said. 'The Colonel will keep. He's got more than eighty-seven thousand dollars behind him – the whole mother-raping white South – and he's playing a deeper game than just hijacking.'

'We'll see, said the blind man,' Coffin Ed said and they drove back to the White Rose bar at 125th and Park. Paul was waiting at the bar, drinking a Coke. They pushed in beside him. He spoke in a low voice but openly. 'We've been assigned to another case. Captain Brice doesn't know we've been working for you and we won't tell him, but we have to report to the station now. Ernie's waiting for you to take over. She hasn't moved but that doesn't mean she hasn't phoned.'

'Right,' Grave Digger said. 'We're on the lam, you know.'

'I know.'

The bartender approached with a wise, knowing look. These nuts again, he was thinking. But they left without ordering. He nodded his head wisely, as if he'd known it all the time. They drove over to 115th Street and found Ernie parked near the corner watching the entrance of the apartment house through his rear-view mirror while pretending to read a newspaper. Coffin Ed gave him a sign and he drove off.

There was a bar with a public telephone on the corner of Lenox Avenue. So they parked down towards Seventh Avenue, opposite the entrance, so they would be behind Iris if she came out to telephone. Grave Digger got out and began jacking up the right rear wheel, keeping bent over out of sight of Billie's windows. Coffin Ed walked towards the bar, shoulders hunched and red cap pulled low over his black weedhead sunglasses. He looked like one of the real-gone cats with his signifying walk. They figured she had to make her move soon.

But it had turned dark before Iris left the apartment. By now the tenements had emptied of people seeking the cool of evening, and the sidewalks were crowded. But Iris walked fast, looking straight ahead, as though the people on the street didn't exist.

Her skin was a smooth painted tan without a blemish, like the soft velvety leather of an expensive handbag. She wore silk Paisley slacks and a blue silk jersey blouse of Billie's, and one of the red-haired wigs Billie used in her act. Her hips were pitching like a rowboat on a stormy sea, but her cold, aloof face said: Your eyes may shine and your teeth may grit, but none of this fine ass will you git.

This puzzled Grave Digger as he pulled the truck out from

the curb a half block behind her. She wanted to be seen. Coffin Ed had the telephone covered but she didn't look towards the bar. Instead she turned north on Lenox, walking fast but not looking back. Grave Digger picked up Coffin Ed and they followed a block behind, careful but not cute.

She turned east on 121st Street and went directly to O'Malley's church, The Star of Ham. The front door was locked, but she had a key.

Grave Digger parked just around the corner on Lenox and they hit the pavement in a flat-footed lope. But she was already out of sight.

'Cover the back,' he said, and ran up the stairs and tried the front door.

There was no time for finesse. Coffin Ed jumped the iron gate at the side and ran down the walk towards the back.

The front door was locked. Grave Digger studied the windows. Coffin Ed studied the back door and found it locked too. He hoisted himself up on to the brick wall separating the back yard of the apartment next door for a better view.

From the hideout underneath the rostrum, all three distinctly heard her key in the lock, heard the lock click, the door opening and closing, the lock clicking shut, and her footsteps on the wooden floor.

'Here she is now,' Deke said with relief.

'It's a goddamn good thing for you,' the oily-haired gunman said. He had a Colt .45 automatic in his right hand and he kept slapping the barrel in the palm of his left hand as he looked down at Deke.

Deke was tied to one of the two straight-backed tubular chairs and sweat was streaming down his face as though he were crying. He had been tied in that position, with his arms about the chair's back, since Iris had first telephoned, seven hours previous.

The other gunman lay on the couch, his eyes closed, seemingly asleep.

They were silent as they listened over the electronics pick-up to Iris's footsteps tripping across the floor above, but their attention was alerted when they heard another sound at the front door.

'She's tailed,' the gunman on the couch said, sitting up.

He was a stout, light-complexioned man with thinning straight brown hair, slitted brown eyes and a nasty-looking mouth as though he dribbled food. He spat on the floor as they listened.

The footsteps rounded the pulpit and stopped on the other side and there was no more sound from the front door.

'She's on to it,' Deke said, licking the sweat trickling into his mouth, 'She's going out through the wall to lose them.'

The gunman on the couch said, 'She better lose them good, baby.'

They heard the secret door through the wall into an apartment in the building next door being opened and closed and then silence.

The gunman standing slapped the Colt against the palm of his hand as though perplexed. 'How come you trust this bitch when she's ratted on you before?'

The sweat stung Deke's eyes and he blinked. 'I don't trust her, but that bitch likes money; and she's always going to keep this secret for her own safety,' he said.

The gunman on the couch said, 'It's your life, baby.'

The gunman standing said, 'She'd better come back soon or it's gonna be too late. It's getting hotter all the time.'

'It's safe here,' Deke said desperately. 'You're safer here until we get the money than being on the loose. Nobody knows about this hideout.'

The gunman on the couch spat. ''Cept Iris and the people who built it.'

'White men built it,' Deke said. He couldn't keep the smugness out of his voice. 'They didn't suspect a thing. They thought it was to be a crypt.'

'What's that?' asked the standing gunman.

'A vault, for dead saints maybe.'

The gunman looked at him, then looked around as though seeing the room for the first time. It was a small square room with soundproof walls, and access from above through the back of the church organ. There was a niche in one wall with a silver icon flanked by prints of Christ and the Virgin. Deke had furnished it with a couch, two tubular chairs, a small kitchen table and a refrigerator which he kept well stocked with prepared food, beer and whisky. Soiled dishes on the table attested to the fact they had eaten there at least once.

One entire wall was taken up by the electronics system with pickup and amplifier that recorded every sound made in the church above. When turned up full volume even the footsteps of a mouse could be heard. On the opposite wall was a gun rack containing two rifles, two sawed-off shotguns and a submachine gun. Deke was proud of the place. He had had it built when reconditioning the church. He felt completely safe there. But the gunman was unimpressed.

'Let's just hope them white men don't remember,' he said. 'Or that she don't bring a police tail back here. This place ain't no more safe than a coffin.'

'Believe me,' Deke said. 'I know it's safe.'

'We sprang you, baby, to get the money,' the sitting gunman said flatly. 'We figured we'd spring you and then sell your life to you for eighty-seven grand. You get the picture, baby. You going to buy it?'

'Freddy,' Deke appealed to the sitting gunman but got nothing from his eyes but a blank deadly stare. 'Four-Four,' he appealed to the oily-haired one standing with the Colt in his hand and drew another blank stare. 'You've got to trust me,' he pleaded. 'I've never let you down. You've got to give me time . . .'

'You got time,' Freddy said, standing up and going to the icebox for another can of beer. He spat on the floor, slammed shut the box. 'But not all of it.'

From atop the brick wall in back of the church, Coffin Ed got a glimpse of Iris's face peeping from behind the curtains of the back window of a first-floor apartment. It came more from a sixth sense than actual sight. There was only a dim light in back of her, outlining a mere shadow, and the light from outside was filtered from surrounding windows. And she was visible for only a moment. It was the timing more than anything which told him. Who else in the vicinity might be peering furtively from a back window at just that moment.

He knew automatically she had got through the wall. How, he didn't care. He knew she had not only recognized him then, but had made them both from the start. A smart bitch – too smart. He debated whether to burst in on her openly, or take cover and let her make her move. Then he decided to go back and confer with Grave Digger.

'Let her go,' Grave Digger said. 'She can't hide for ever, she ain't invisible. And she's made us now. So let her go, let her go. Maybe she'll contact us.'

They walked back to the truck and drove up to a bar, and Coffin Ed telephoned home. His wife Molly said Abigail hadn't called but Anderson was on duty now and he wanted them to call him.

'Call him,' Grave Digger said.

Anderson said, 'Bring in Iris while I'm on duty and I'll try to cover for you. Otherwise you're certain to be picked up by tomorrow and you'll be finished on the Force – probably face a rap. Captain Brice is furious.'

'He knows about it,' Coffin Ed said. 'He promised to lay off.'

'That's not the way he tells it. He's reported to the commissioner that you've abducted her and he's seeing red.'

'He's mad just because we tricked him; and he's covering himself at our expense.'

'Be that as it may, he's mad enough to break you.'

They sat silent for a moment, tense and worried.

'You figure she might try to take a powder?' Coffin Ed said.

'We got enough to worry about without that,' Grave Digger said. 'And we ain't got time for it.'

'Let's go to Billie's.'

'She's left there for good. Let's go back to the church.'

'That was just to shake us,' Coffin Ed argued. 'She's finished with the church.'

'Maybe, maybe not. Deke wouldn't put in an escape door for nothing. There must be something else there.'

Coffin Ed thought about it. 'Maybe you're right.'

They parked on 122nd Street and cased the back of the church. The backyard was separated by the high brick wall from the garbage-strewn backyards surrounding it. They scaled the wall and examined the back door. It had an ordinary Yale snap lock with an iron grille covering its dirty panes but they didn't touch it. They peered through a window into the vestry back of the choir but it was black dark inside.

Then they went down the narrow walk alongside the church. It was a brick structure and in good condition and on that side two arched stained-glass windows flanked a stained-glass oval high in the wall. The other side of the church was built flush with the apartment house.

'If they got a hideout in there they got some kind of hearing device for protection,' Grave Digger reasoned. 'They can't have a lookout hiding all the time.'

'What do you want to do, wait outside for her?'

'She'll return through the wall, or she might already be in there.'

They looked at one another thinking.

'Listen –' Coffin Ed began and explained.

'Anyway, it beats a blank,' Grave Digger said, as he stopped in the darkness to take off his shoes.

They stood behind the gate and watched the street until it was momentarily empty. Then they scaled the iron gate and hurried up the stairs to the church door, and Coffin Ed began picking the lock. If anyone had passed they would have been taken for two drunks urinating against the church door. When it was open, Grave Digger sat astride Coffin Ed's shoulders and they went inside and closed the door behind them.

The tableau in the hideout was much the same. Deke was still tied to the chair and the oily-haired gunman, Four-Four, was letting him drink from a can of beer. Beer was spilling from his mouth onto his pants and Four-Four said irritably, 'Can't you swallow, goddammit?' slapping his own thigh with the barrel of the Colt. Freddy was lying on the couch again as though he were asleep.

Suddenly they froze at the sound of the front door lock being picked. Four-Four took the beer can from Deke's mouth and put it atop the table and changed the Colt to his left hand, flexing his right. Freddy swung his feet over to the floor and sat up, listening with his mouth open. They heard the door swing open and someone step inside and the door being closed.

'We got a visitor,' Freddy said.

They heard the footsteps come down the centre aisle.

'A dick,' Four-Four said, appraising the walk.

Freddy stepped over to the gun rack and casually took down a sawed-off shotgun. They listened to the steps move around the choir and the pulpit and approach the organ. Freddy looked at the access ladder as though in a trance.

'A big boy,' he said. 'Big as two men. Think I ought go up and cut him down to size?'

'Let him stick his head in, ha-ha,' Four-Four laughed.

'You're not going to leave me tied up!' Deke protested.

'Sure, baby, that or dead,' Freddy said.

The heavy man's footsteps passed the organ, paused for a moment as though he were looking around, then moved on slowly as though he were examining everything. Through the electronics pickup they could hear his heavy breathing.

'A fat baby with a heart,' Four-Four said.

'Guts too,' Deke said. 'Coming here alone.'

'I got something for his guts,' Freddy said, swinging the sawed-off shotgun.

The footsteps circled the pulpit, stopped for a moment, then went down into the auditorium and moved along the walls. They could hear knuckles sounding the walls. The footsteps moved slowly as the man encircled the walls, sounding for a false door. Ear-shattering bangs suddenly shook the small hideout as the man began sounding the wooden floor with his pistol butt.

'Cut that damn thing down,' Four-Four shouted. 'The mother-raper will hear himself upstairs.'

Freddy turned it down until the tapping on the floor became muted. It went on and on until seemingly every inch of the floor was covered. There was silence for a long time as though the man was listening. Then they heard the faint click of his pocket torch being turned on. Finally they heard his footsteps moving towards the door. Half-way they heard him stop and put what sounded like the palms of his hands on the floor.

'What the hell's he doing now?' Four-Four asked.

'Damn if I know,' Freddy said, 'Probably planting a time bomb.' He laughed at his own humor.

'It wouldn't be so damn funny if you got your ass blown off,' Four-Four said sourly.

They heard the imagined dick open the snap lock on the front door and pass out, closing the door behind him.

'It's time for that bitch of yours to be showing,' Four-Four said disagreeably.

'She's coming,' Deke said.

'She'd better come ready,' Freddy said. 'If she don't know where the money is, you can preach both of youse funerals.' He chuckled.

'Dry up,' Four-Four said.

20

Iris came in with perfect assurance. She knew she hadn't been tailed. She had shaken Grave Digger and Coffin Ed and she wasn't afraid. She knew where the cotton was and how they could get it. She knew with this information she could handle Deke. And she had confidence that Deke could handle his gorillas.

Deke and his gunmen heard her when she entered.

'That's her now,' Deke said, sighing with relief.

Freddy got up from the couch and took down the shotgun again. Four-Four jacked a shell into the chamber of his .45 automatic and slid back the safety. Both were tense but neither spoke.

Deke was listening to her walk. He could tell from the rhythm of her steps she was walking with assurance.

'She got it,' he said with a confident look.

'She'd better have it,' Freddy said dangerously.

'I mean the information,' Deke said hurriedly for fear they might mistake his meaning.

Neither answered.

Grave Digger lay face down between two benches, breathing into a black cotton handkerchief, his hand on his pistol underneath his body. His black suit blended with the darkness and she didn't see a thing as she passed. He waited until he heard her footsteps ascending the rostrum, then scuttled down the center aisle on hands and knees to open the front door for Coffin Ed, hoping the sound of her footsteps would cover whatever sound he made.

But they heard it anyway.

'What the hell's she got with her?' Four-Four said.

'Sounds like her dog,' Freddy said and started to laugh, but the look from Four-Four cut it off.

They heard the soft tap on the organ pipe that was the signal for entrance. Four-Four pushed a button and a panel in the back of the organ raised, revealing a small square space beneath the pipes. He pushed the second button and a heavy steel trapdoor opened upward. He raised the ladder and her gilt high-heeled sandals and legs encased in Paisley silk slacks came into view as she descended. He pushed the buttons closing the door behind her when her enticing buttocks showed. Then he raised the cocked .45 automatic and levelled it towards her back.

Her feet touched the floor and she turned around. She looked into the muzzle of the .45 and it looked like the head of a Gorgon. Her body turned to stone. Only the lids of her eyes moved as they continued to stretch as though her eyeballs were squeezed from her head. Slowly, without breathing, her eyes sought the face of Freddy and saw no pity; they slid off and she saw Deke tied to the chair, looking at her with raw anxiety, sweat streaming from a face contorted with terror; next they took in the shotgun in Freddy's hands and finally his nasty-mouthed sadistic face.

Nausea came up in her like the waves of the ocean and she gritted her teeth to keep from fainting. Her terror was so intense it became sexual – and she had an orgasm. All her life she had searched for kicks, but this was the kick she never wanted.

'Who was with you?' Four-Four asked.

She swallowed twice before she could find the handle to her voice, then it came in a husky whisper: 'No one, I swear.'

'We heard something strange.'

'I wasn't tailed, I know,' she whispered. Sweat beaded on her upper lip and her eyes were limpid pools of terror. 'I'm clean, please listen to me,' she begged. 'Don't just kill me for nothing.'

'Tell them, baby, tell them quick,' Deke babbled in terror.

'It's in the cotton,' she said.

'We know that,' Four-Four said. 'Where's the cotton?'

She kept swallowing as though choking. 'I'm not going to tell you just to get killed,' she whispered.

With a sudden movement that made her start, Freddy whipped the second straight-backed chair around behind Deke and said, 'Sit down.'

Four-Four stuck his pistol in his belt and took a coil of nylon clothesline from the floor beneath the gun rack. 'Put your hands behind you, in back of the chair.' She was slow in obeying and he slapped her across the face with the rope. She did as ordered and he began tying her methodically.

'Tell them,' Deke begged piteously.

'She'll tell us,' Freddy said.

Four-Four was tying her chair back to back with Deke's when they heard someone whistling in the street. They froze, listening, but the whistling stopped and there was silence. Four-Four finished tying them together on the two chairs back to back, then they all started nervously as they heard the front door of the church being opened. There was a soft sound like the padded feet of an animal and the door closed softly.

'We better look,' Four-Four said. His voice stuttered slightly and his eyelids blinked rapidly as with a tic.

Freddy's nasty-looking mouth seemed breaking apart and his lips trembled. He got another .45 automatic from beneath the couch, jacked a shell in the chamber and slid off the safety. His motions were jerky but his hands were steady. He stuck the pistol in his belt and held the shotgun in his right hand. 'Let's go,' he said.

Grave Digger and Coffin Ed were deploying along opposite walls when Freddy came from behind the organ, searching quickly with the muzzle of the shotgun like a rabbit shooter. Coffin Ed went down out of sight but Freddy saw the moving shadow. The church exploded with the heavy thumping boom of a twelve-gauge shell of buckshot firing and the heavy charge took a section out of the back of the bench beneath which Coffin Ed had flopped. Grave Digger threw a tracer bullet and in the lightning flash from the trajectory saw the bullet burn through Freddy's sport-shirt collar as he dove towards the floor, and the outline of Four-Four coming from in back of him full speed with the .45 searching.

Grave Digger went down himself, scuttling like a crab, as bursts from the .45 splintered benches above his head. For a moment there was stealthy movement in the dark with no one visible. Then the side of the organ began to burn where the tracer bullet had punctured it.

When Coffin Ed peeped up five rows away from where the shotgun charge had knocked a hole in the back of a bench, the rostrum was deserted and no one was in sight. But he saw the top of a head coming around the front bench on the center aisle and threw a tracer bullet at the round mop. He saw the bullet go through the bushy hair and penetrate the front of the platform supporting the rostrum and the choir. The scream was commencing as he ducked.

A figure with burning hair loomed in the flickering red light from the burning organ with a .45 searching the gloom and Grave Digger peeped. The shotgun went off and splintered the back of the bench in front of him and the church quivered from the blast. Grave Digger fell belly down and began crawling fast, shaken by his narrow escape. Forty-five bullets were breaking up the benches all around him and he didn't dare look. He lay on his belly beneath the benches, looking towards the sound, and made out the vague outline of trousered legs limned against the platform that had caught on fire. He took careful aim and shot a leg. He saw the leg break off like a wooden stick where the tracer bullet hit it dead centre, and saw the trouser leg catch fire suddenly. Now the screaming slashed into the pool of silence like needles of flame and seared his nerves.

The burning shape of the body issuing these screams fell atop the broken leg, on the floor between two benches, and Grave Digger pumped two tracer bullets into it and watched the flames spring up. The dying man clawed at the book rack above him, breaking the fragile wood, and a prayer book fell on top of his burning body.

The burning-headed gunman was down beneath a bench, rubbing his oily hair with blistered hands, while Coffin Ed was peeping above the benches, searching for him with his long-barreled .38 in the red glare from the brightly burning organ.

The smoke had penetrated the hideout below, and the prisoners tied back-to-back on the two chairs had gone crazy from terror. They were spitting curses and accusations, and trying desperately to get at each other.

'You're a pimp for your mother and sister, you money-sucking snake,' Iris screamed with face distorted and eyes terrified like the eyes of a burning horse.

'You two-bit stooling whore, I'll kill you,' Deke grated.

Their legs were tied together like their arms but their feet touched the floor. They were straining with arched bodies and gripping feet to push each other into the wall. The chairs slid on the concrete floor, back and forth, rocking precariously. Arteries in their necks were swelled to bursting, muscles stretched like frayed cables, bodies twisting, breasts heaving, mouths gasping and drooling like two people in a maniacal sex act. Her make-up became streaked from sweat and her wig fell off. Deke doubled forward on his feet tied to the chair's legs, trying to bang Iris sideways against the gun rack. Her chair rose from the floor and bloodcurdling screams came wetly from her scar-like mouth as his chair tilted forward from his superhuman effort and they turned slowly over in a grotesque arc. He fell forward, face downward, striking his forehead on the concrete floor, as she came overtop in her chair. The momentum kept them turning until her head and forehead scraped on the concrete in turn and he was lifted from the floor. They landed up against the wall, her feet touching it, his chair on top supported only by the angle of hers on the floor. She kept trying to use her feet to push back from the wall, while he twisted violently, trying to rub her face against the concrete. The motion rocked them from side to side until both chairs fell sideways with a crash and they were left on their sides on the concrete floor between the gun rack and the table, unable to move. The thunder of the gunfight above that had shaken the room had quieted to darkening with smoke. Both were too spent to curse, they remained still, gasping for breath in the slowly suffocating smoke.

Upstairs in the church, light from the burning gunman on the floor lit up the figure of the gunman with his head on fire crouched behind the end of a bench ahead.

On the other side of the church Coffin Ed was standing with his pistol levelled, shouting, 'Come out, mother-raper, and die like a man.'

Grave Digger took careful aim between the legs of the benches at the only part of the gunman that was visible and shot him through the stomach. The gunman emitted an eerie howl of pain, like a mortally wounded beast, and stood up with his .45 spewing slugs in a blind stream. The screaming had risen to an unearthly pitch, filling the mouths of the detectives with the taste of bile. Coffin Ed shot him in the vicinity of the heart and his clothes caught fire. The screaming ceased abruptly as the gunman slumped across the bench in a kneeling posture, as though praying in fire.

Now the entire platform holding the pulpit and the choir and the organ was burning brightly, lighting up the stained-glass pictures of the saints looking down from the windows. From outside came a banshee wail as the first of the cruisers came tearing into the street.

Grave Digger and Coffin Ed ran barefooted through the flame and kicked in the back of the organ with scorched feet. But they couldn't budge the steel trapdoor.

When the first of the police arrived they had reloaded and were shooting into the floor, trying to find the lock. Screams were heard coming from below and a dark cloud of smoke enveloped them. More police arrived and all worked frantically to open the door, but it wasn't until eight minutes later, when the first firemen arrived with axes and crowbars, it got opened.

Grave Digger pushed everyone aside and went down first with Coffin Ed following. He grabbed the chairs with the two figures and righted them. Iris was facing them and she was strangling in the smoke and tears were streaming down her face. Before moving to release her, he leaned down and looked into her face.

'And now, little sister, where's the cotton?'

Firemen and policemen were crowding around, coughing and crying in the dense smoke.

'Let them loose, take them out of here,' a uniformed sergeant ordered. 'They'll suffocate.'

Iris looked down, thinking furiously, trying to figure an angle for herself.

'What cotton?' she said, to give herself time.

Grave Digger leaned forward until his face almost touched hers. His eyes were bright red and veins stood out in his temples.

His neck swelled and his lumpy unshaven face contorted with rage.

'Baby, you'd have never come here if you didn't know,' he said in a cotton-dry voice, gasping and coughing for breath. He raised his long-barreled .38 and aimed it at one of her eyes.

Coffin Ed drew his pistol and held back the policemen and firemen. His acid-burned face was jumping as though cooking in the heat and his eyes looked insane.

'And you'll never leave here alive unless you tell,' Grave Digger finished.

Silence fell. No one moved. No one believed he would kill her, but no one dared interfere because of Coffin Ed; he looked capable of anything.

Iris looked down at Grave Digger's burned stockinged feet. Fearfully her gaze lifted to his burning red eyes. She believed it.

'Billie's doing a dance with it,' she whispered.

'Take them,' Grave Digger said, as he and Coffin Ed turned, hurrying off

21

The dance floor of the Cotton Club stood on a platform level with the tops of the tables and also served as a stage for the big floor-shows presented. At the back were curtained exits into the wings which contained the dressing-rooms.

When Grave Digger and Coffin Ed peered from behind the curtains to one of the wings, they saw the club was filled with well-dressed people, white and colored, sitting about small tables with cotton-white covers, their eyes shining like liquid crystals in faces made exotic by candlelight.

A piano was playing frenetically, a saxophone wailing aphrodisiacally, the bass patting suggestively, the horn demanding and the guitar begging. A blue-tinted spotlight from over the heads of the diners bathed the almost naked tan body of Billie in blue mist as she danced slowly about a bale of cotton, her body writhing and her hips grinding as though making easy-riding love. Spasms caught her from time to time and she flung herself against the bale convulsively. She rubbed her belly against it and she turned and rubbed her buttocks against it, her bare breasts shaking ecstatically. Her wet red lips were parted as though she were gasping, her pearly teeth glistened in the blue light. Her nostrils quivered. She was creating the illusion of being seduced by a bale of cotton.

Dead silence reigned in the audience. Women stared at her

greedily, enviously, with glittering eyes. Men stared lustfully, lids lowered to hide their thoughts. The dance quickened and people squirmed. Billie threw her body against the cotton with mad desire. Bodies of women in the audience shook uncontrollably from compulsive motivation. Lust rose in the room like miasma.

The act was working to a climax. Billie was twisting her body and rolling her hips with shocking rapidity. She worked completely around the bale of cotton, then, facing the audience, flung her arms wide apart and gave her hips a final shake. 'Ohhh, daddy cotton!' she cried.

Abruptly the lights came on and the audience went wild with applause. Billie's smooth voluptuous body was wet with sweat. It gleamed like a lecher's dream of hot flesh. Her breasts were heaving, the nipples pointing like selecting fingers.

'And now,' she said, slightly panting when the applause died down, 'I shall auction this bale of cotton for the actors' benefit fund.' She smiled, panting, and looked down at a nervous young white man with his girl at a ringside table. 'If you're scared, go home,' she challenged, taunting him with a movement of her body. He reddened. A titter arose. 'Who'll bid a thousand dollars?' she said.

Silence fell.

From two tables back someone said in a level southern drawl, 'One thousand.'

Eyes pivoted.

A lean-faced white man with long silvery hair, a white moustache and goatee, wearing a black frock coat and black string bow, sat at a table with a young blond white man wearing a white tuxedo jacket and a Dubonnet-coloured bow.

'The mother-raper,' Coffin Ed said.

Grave Digger gestured for silence.

'A gentleman from the Old South!' Billie cried. 'I'll bet you're a Kentucky Colonel.'

The man stood up, tall and stately, and bowed. 'Colonel Calhoun, at your service, from Alabama,' he drawled.

Someone in the audience clapped. 'A brother of yours, Colonel,' Billie cried delightedly. 'He's attracted by this cotton too. Stand up, brother.'

A big black man stood up. The colored people in the audience roared with laughter.

'What you bid, brother rat?' Billie asked.

'He bids fifteen hundred,' a voice cried jubilantly.

'Let him bid for himself,' Billie snapped.

'I don't bid nothing,' the man said. 'You just asted me to stand up, is all.'

'Well, sit down then,' Billie said.

The man sat down self-consciously.

'Going,' Billie said. 'Going. This fine bale of natural-grown Alabama field cotton going for one thousand – and maybe I'll go with it. Any other bids?'

Only silence came.

'Cheapskates,' Billie sneered. 'You're going to close your eyes and imagine it's me, but it ain't going to be the same. Last chance. Going, going, gone. And look how many actors will benefit.' She winked brazenly, then said, 'Colonel Calhoun, suh, come forward and take possession of it.'

'Of what?' some wit cracked.

'Guess, you idiot,' Billie sneered.

The Colonel arose and went forward to the platform, a tall, straight, confident white man, and handed Billie ten one-hundred-dollar bank notes. 'I deem it an honor, Miss Billie, to purchase this cotton from a beautiful nigra girl who might also be from those happy lands –'

'Not me, Colonel,' Billie interrupted.

'– and in so doing benefit many deserving nigra actors,' the Colonel finished.

There was a scattering of applause.

Billie ran and pulled handfuls of cotton from the bale and the Colonel tensed momentarily, but as quickly relaxed when she came running back and showered the strands of cotton on to his silvery head.

'I hereby ordain you as King of Cotton, Colonel,' she said. 'And may this cotton bring you wealth and fame.'

'Thank you,' the Colonel said gallantly. 'I'm sure it will,' and then signalled to the stage door opposite Grave Digger and Coffin Ed.

Two ordinary-looking colored workmen came forward with a hand truck and took the bale of cotton away.

Grave Digger and Cotton Ed hurried towards the street, limping like soul-brothers with duck feet. The truckmen brought out the bale of cotton and put it in back of an open delivery truck, and the Colonel followed leisurely and spoke to them and got into his black limousine.

Grave Digger and Coffin Ed were already in their panel truck parked a half-block back.

'So he found his car,' Coffin Ed remarked.

'One gets you two it was never lost.'

'That's a sucker's bet.'

When the truck drove off they followed it openly. It went up Seventh Avenue and drew to the curb in front of the Back-to-the-Southland office. Grave Digger drove past and turned into the driveway of a repair garage, closed for the night, and Coffin Ed got out and began picking the lock of the roll-up door as though he worked there. He was working at the lock when the Colonel's limousine pulled up behind the truck across the street and the Colonel got out and looked about. He got the lock open and was rolling up the door by the time the Colonel had unlocked the door to his own office and the truckmen began easing the bale of cotton down onto the sidewalk. Grave Digger drove the panel truck into the strange garage and cut the lights and got out beside Coffin Ed. They stood in the dark doorway, checking their pistols, and watched the truckmen wheel the bale of cotton into the brightly lighted office and drop it in the center of the floor. They saw the Colonel pay them and speak to the blond young man, and when the truckmen left, the two of them spoke briefly again and the blond young man returned to the limousine while the Colonel turned out the lights and locked the door and followed him.

When they drove off, Grave Digger and Coffin Ed hurried across the street, and Coffin Ed began picking the lock to the Back-to-the-Southland office while Grave Digger shielded him.

'How long is it going to take?' Grave Digger asked.

'Not long. It's an ordinary store lock but I got to get the right tumbler.'

'Don't take too long.'

The next moment the lock clicked. Coffin Ed turned the knob and the door came open. They went inside and locked the door behind them and moved quickly through the darkness to a small broom closet at the rear. It was hot in the closet and they began to sweat. They kept their pistols in their hands and their palms became wet. They wanted to talk but were afraid to risk it. They had to let the Colonel get the money from the bale of cotton himself.

They didn't have long to wait. In less than fifteen minutes there was the sound of a key in the lock. The door opened and two pairs of footsteps entered and the door closed.

They heard the Colonel say, 'Pull down the shades.'

They heard the sounds of the shades covering the front

windows and the door being pulled to the bottom and latched. Then there was the click of the light switch and the keyhole in the closet had sudden dimensions.

'Do you think that'll be enough?' a voice questioned. 'Anyone can see there's a light on inside.'

'There's no risk, son, everything is covered,' the Colonel said. 'Let's don't be too secretive. We pay the rent here.'

There was the sound of the bale of cotton being shifted, probably being turned over, Grave Digger thought.

'Just give me that knife and keep the bag ready,' the Colonel said.

Grave Digger felt in the darkness of the closet for the doorknob, and squeezed it hard and pulled it. But he waited until he heard the sound of the knife cut into the bale of cotton before turning it. Soundlessly he opened the door a crack and released the knob with the same caution.

Now through the crack they could see the Colonel engrossed in his work. He was cutting through the cotton with a sharp hunting knife and pulling out the fibers with a double-pronged hook. The blond young man stood to one side, watching intently, holding open a Gladstone bag. Neither looked around.

Grave Digger and Coffin Ed breathed silently through their mouths as they watched the hole grow larger and deeper. Loose cotton began piling up on the floor. The Colonel's face began sweating. The blond young man looked increasingly anxious. A frown appeared between his eyes.

'Have you got the right side?' he asked.

'Certainly, it shows where we opened it,' the Colonel said in a controlled voice, but his expression and his haste expressed his own growing anxiety.

The blond young man's breathing had become labored. 'You should be down to the money,' he said finally.

The Colonel stopped digging. He put his arm into the hole to measure its depth. He straightened up and looked at the blond young man as though he didn't see him. For a long moment he seemed lost in thought.

'Incredible!' he said.

'What?' the blond young man blurted.

'There isn't any money.'

The blond young man's mouth flew open. Shock stretched his eyes and he grunted as though someone had hit him in the solar plexus.

'Impossible,' he gasped.

Suddenly the Colonel went berserk. He began stabbing the bale of cotton with the hunting knife as though it were human and he was trying to kill it. He slashed it and raked it with the hook. His face had turned bright red and foam collected in the corners of his mouth. His blue eyes looked stone crazy.

'Gawdammit, I tell you there isn't any money!' he shouted accusingly, as though it were the young man's fault.

Grave Digger pushed open the closet door and stepped into the room, his long-barreled, nickelplated .38 revolver leveled on the Colonel's heart and glinting deadly in the bright light.

'That's just too mother-raping bad,' he said and Coffin Ed followed him.

The Colonel and the young man froze, suspended in motion. Their eyes mirrored shock. The Colonel was the first to regain his composure. 'What does this mean?' he asked in a controlled voice.

'It means you're under arrest,' Grave Digger said.

'Arrest? For preparing a bale of cotton to exhibit during our rally tomorrow?'

'When you hijacked the Back-to-Africa meeting you hid the money in this bale of cotton during your getaway, then lost it.

We wondered what made this bale of cotton so important.'

'Nonsense,' the Colonel said. 'You're having a pipe dream. If you think I had anything to do with that robbery, you go ahead and arrest me and I'll sue you and the city for false arrest.'

'Who said for robbery?' Coffin Ed said. 'We're arresting you for murder.'

'Murder! What murder?'

'The murder of a junkyard laborer named Joshua Peavine,' Grave Digger said. 'That's where the cotton fits in. He took you to Goodman's junkyard looking for this cotton and you had him murdered.'

'I suppose you're going to have this Goodman identify this cotton,' the Colonel said sarcastically. 'Don't you know there are seven hundred million acres of cotton just like this?'

'Cotton is graded,' Grave Digger said. 'It can be identified. There were fibers from this bale of cotton left in Goodman's junkyard where the boy was murdered.'

'Fibers? What fibers?' the Colonel challenged.

Grave Digger stepped to the pile of cotton on the floor and picked up a handful and held it out to the Colonel. 'These fibers.'

The Colonel paled. He still held the knife and hook in his hands but his body was controlled with great effort. The blond young man was sweating and trembling all over.

'Drop the gadgets, Colonel,' Coffin Ed said, motioning with his gun.

The Colonel tossed the knife and hook into the hole in the bale of cotton.

'Turn around and walk over and put your hands to the wall,' Coffin Ed went on.

The Colonel looked at him scornfully. 'Don't be afraid, my boy, we're unarmed.'

The tic came into Coffin Ed's face. 'And just don't be too mother-raping cute,' he warned.

The white men read the danger in his face and obeyed. Grave Digger frisked them. 'They're clean.'

'All right, turn around,' Coffin Ed ordered.

They turned around impassively.

'Just remember who're the *men* here,' Coffin Ed said.

No one replied.

'You were seen picking up the laborer, Joshua, by the side of the 125th Street railroad station just before he was murdered,' Grave Digger continued from before.

'Impossible! There was only a blind man there!' the blond young man blurted involuntarily.

With a quick violent motion the Colonel turned and slapped him.

Coffin Ed chuckled. He drew a photograph from his inside pocket and passed it to the Colonel. 'The blind man saw you – and took this picture.'

The Colonel studied it for a long moment, then handed it back. His hand was steady but his nostrils were white along the edges. 'Do you believe a jury would convict me on this evidence?' he said.

'This ain't Alabama,' Coffin Ed said. 'This is New York, and this colored man has been murdered by a white man in Harlem. We have the evidence. We'll give it to the Negro press and all the Negro political groups. When we get through, no jury would dare acquit you; and no governor would dare pardon you. Get the picture, Colonel?'

The Colonel had turned white as a sheet and his face looked pinched. Finally he said, 'Every man's got his price, what's yours?'

'You're lucky to have any teeth left by now, or even dentures,' Grave Digger said. 'But you asked me a straight question, and

I'll give you a straight answer. Eighty-seven thousand dollars.'

The blond young man's mouth popped wide open again and he flushed bright red. But the Colonel only stared at Grave Digger to see if he was joking. Then disbelief came to his face, and finally astonishment.

'Incredible! You're going to give them back their money?'

'That's right, the families.'

'Incredible! Is it because they are nigras and you're nigras too?'

'That's right.'

'Incredible!' The Colonel looked as though he had got the shock of his life. 'If that's true, you win,' he conceded. 'What will it buy me?'

'Twenty-four hours,' Grave Digger said.

The Colonel kept staring at him as though he were a four-headed baby. 'And will you really keep your bargain?'

'That's right. A gentleman's agreement.'

A flicker of a smile showed at the corners of the Colonel's mouth.

'A gentleman's agreement,' he echoed, 'I'll give you a cheque drawn on the committee.'

'We're going to wait right here behind drawn shades until the banks open in the morning and you send and get the cash,' Grave Digger said.

'I'll have to send my assistant here,' the Colonel said. 'Will you trust him?'

'That ain't the question,' Grave Digger said. 'Will *you* trust him? It's *your* mother-raping life.'

22

Tuesday passed. Colonel Calhoun and his nephew had disappeared. So had Grave Digger and Coffin Ed. The entire police force was searching for them. The panel truck had been found abandoned beside the cemetery at 155th Street and Broadway, but no trace of their whereabouts. Their wives were frantic. Lieutenant Anderson had personally joined in the search.

But they had simply ditched the panel truck and limped over to the Lincoln Hotel on St Nicholas Avenue, operated by their old friend, took adjoining rooms and went to bed. They had slept around the clock.

Now it was Wednesday morning, and they had come down to the precinct station in a taxi, wearing bedroom slippers on bandaged feet, to turn in their report.

At sight of them the captain turned purple. He looked on the verge of an apoplectic stroke. He wouldn't speak to them, wouldn't look at them again. He gave orders for them to wait in the detectives' room and telephoned the commissioner. The other detectives looked at them and grinned sympathetically, but no one spoke; no one dared speak, they were hotter than a pussy with the pox.

The commissioner arrived and they were called into the captain's office. The commissioner was distinctly cool, but he had himself well under control, like a man just keeping from biting his nails. He let them stand while he read their report. He leafed through the eighty-seven thousand dollars in cash they had turned in.

'Now, men, I just want the facts,' he said, looking about as though searching for the facts he wanted. 'How was it possible that Colonel Calhoun escaped while you were guarding him?' he asked finally.

'You haven't read our report correctly, sir,' Grave Digger said with great control. 'We said we were waiting for him to come back so we could catch him red-handed taking the money from the bale of cotton. But when he started to unlock the door his nephew said something and they rushed back to their limousine and took off. That was the last we saw of them. We tried to chase them but their car was too fast. They must have had some gadget on the lock to tell them if it had been tampered with.'

'What kind of gadget?'

'We don't know, sir.'

The commissioner frowned. 'Why didn't you report his escape and let the force catch him? Obviously, we have departments better equipped for it – or don't you think so?' he added sarcastically.

'That's right, sir,' Grave Digger said. 'But they didn't catch the two gunmen of Deke's and they had two full days before these same gunmen show up here, in the precinct station, and kill two officers and spring Deke.'

'We figured we'd have a better chance of getting him by ourselves. We figured he'd come back for the money sooner or later, so we just hid there waiting for him,' Coffin Ed added with a straight face.

'For one whole day?' the commissioner asked.

'Yes, sir. Time didn't matter,' Grave Digger said.

The captain cleared his throat angrily but said nothing.

But the commissioner reddened with anger. 'There is no place on this Force for grandstanding,' he said hotly.

Coffin Ed blew up. 'We found Deke and his two killers, didn't we? We gave back Iris, didn't we? We found the money, didn't we? We've got the evidence against the Colonel, haven't we? That's what we're paid for, isn't it? You call that grandstanding?'

'And how did you do it?' the commissioner flared.

Grave Digger spoke quickly, heading Coffin Ed off. 'We did what we thought best, sir,' Grave Digger said amenably. 'You said you'd give us a free hand.'

'Umph,' the commissioner growled, scanning the report in front of him. 'How did this girl, this dancer, Billie Belle, get hold of the cotton?'

'We don't know, sir, we haven't asked her,' Grave Digger said. 'We thought they'd get it out of Iris, they had her all yesterday.'

The captain reddened. 'Iris wouldn't talk,' he said defensively. 'And we didn't know about Billie Belle.'

'Where does she live?' the commissioner asked.

'On 115th Street, not far,' Grave Digger said.

'Get her in here now,' the commissioner ordered.

The captain sent two white detectives for her, glad to get off so easily.

Billie didn't have time for her elaborate onstage make-up and she looked young and demure, almost innocent, without it, like all lesbian sexpots. Her full soft lips were a natural rose color, and without mascara her eyes looked brighter, smaller and rounder. She wore black linen slacks and a white cotton blouse and she looked like anything but a sophisticated belly dancer. She was relaxed and slightly on the flip side.

'It was just a whim,' she said. 'I saw Uncle Bud sleeping in his empty cart when I was driving down beneath the bridge to see about my yawt, and somehow his nappy white head made me think of cotton. I stopped and asked him if he could get me a bale of cotton for my cotton dance; I don't know why, just 'cause if he cut his hair it'd make a bale, I suppose, and he said, "Gimme fifty dollars and I'll git you a bale of cotton, Miss Billie," and I gave him the fifty right then and there, knowing I'd get it back from the club. And sure enough, that same night, he delivered it.'

'Where?' the commissioner asked.

'At the club,' she said, lifting her eyebrows. 'What could I do with a bale of cotton in my home?'

'When?' Grave Digger asked.

'I don't know,' she said, becoming impatient with these senseless questions. 'Before I came at ten. He had left it in the stage entrance where it was in the way and I had it moved to my dressing-room until I wanted it on the stage.'

'When did you see Uncle Bud again?' Grave Digger asked.

'I had already paid him,' she said. 'There wasn't any need of seeing him again.'

'Have you ever seen him again?' Grave Digger persisted.

'Why ever should I see him again?' she snapped.

'Think,' Grave Digger said. 'It's important.'

She thought for a moment, then said, 'No, that was the last time I saw him.'

'Did the bale of cotton look as though it had been tampered with?' Coffin Ed asked.

'How the hell would she know?' Grave Digger said.

'I'd never seen a bale of cotton before in my life,' she confessed.

'How did Iris find out about it?' the commissioner asked.

'I don't really know,' she said musingly. 'She must have heard me telephoning. I saw a want ad in the *Sentinel* for a bale of cotton and called the number. Some man with a southern accent answered and said he was Colonel Calhoun of the Back-to-the-

Southland movement and he needed a bale of cotton for a rally he was planning to have. I thought he was some smart alec making a joke and I asked him where this rally was taking place. When he said on Seventh Avenue, I was sure he was joking then. I said I was having a cotton rally on Seventh Avenue myself, at the Cotton Club, and he could come to see it, and he said he would. Anyway, I know I was joking when I asked him for a thousand dollars for my bale of cotton.'

'Where was Iris when you were talking on the telephone?' the commissioner persisted.

'I thought she was still in the bathroom, soaking, but she must have come into the dining-room in her bare feet. I was in the sitting-room lying on the divan with my back to the dining-room door and I didn't hear her. She could have just stood there and eavesdropped and I wouldn't have known it.' She had her little secret smile on again. 'That would be just like Iris. Anyway, I would have told her all about it if she had asked, but she would rather eavesdrop.'

'Didn't you know she had escaped from prison?' the commissioner asked softly.

There was silence for a moment and Billie's eyes stretched. 'She told me that detectives Jones and Johnson had let her out to look for Deke. I didn't approve of it but it wasn't my business.'

Dead silence reigned. The commissioner looked hard at the captain, but the captain wouldn't meet his gaze. Coffin Ed grunted, but Grave Digger kept a straight and solemn face.

Billie noticed the strange looks on everyone and asked innocently, 'What was so important about the bale of cotton?'

Coffin Ed said jubilantly, 'It had the eighty-seven thousand dollars hijacked from Deke's Back-to-Africa pitch hidden inside of it.'

'Ohhhh,' Billie gasped. Her eyes rolled back. Grave Digger caught her as she fell.

Now a week had passed. Harlem had lived notoriously on the front pages of the tabloids. Saucy brown chicks and insane killers were integrated with southern colonels and two mad Harlem detectives for the entertainment of the public. Lurid accounts of robberies and killings pictured Harlem as a criminal inferno. Deke O'Hara and Iris were dished up with the breakfast cereal; both had been indicted for conspiracy to defraud and second-degree murder. Iris screamed in bold black print that she had been double-crossed by the police. The Back-to-Africa movement vied with the Back-to-the-Southland movement for space and sympathy.

Everyone considered the dead gunmen as good gunmen and Grave Digger and Coffin Ed were congratulated for being alive.

Colonel Calhoun and his nephew, Ronald Compton, had been indicted for the murder of Joshua Peavine, a Harlem Negro laborer. But the State of Alabama refused to exradite them on the grounds that killing a Negro did not constitute murder under Alabama law.

The families of the Back-to-Africa group of O'Malley's who had gotten their money back staged an outdoor testimonial for Grave Digger and Coffin Ed in the same lot where they had lost it. Six hogs were barbecued whole and the detectives were presented with souvenir maps of Africa. Grave Digger was called upon to speak. He stood up and looked at his map and said, 'Brothers, this map is older than me. If you go back to this Africa you got to go by way of the grave.' No one understood what he meant, but they applauded anyway.

The next day Harlem's ace detectives were cited by the commissioner for bravery beyond the call of duty, but no raise came forth.

Undertaker H. Exodus Clay was kept busy all week burying

the dead, which turned out to be so profitable he gave his chauffeur and handyman, Jackson, a bonus which enabled Jackson to marry his fiancée, Imabelle, with whom he had been living off and on for six years.

It was a quiet Wednesday midnight a week later and Grave Digger, Coffin Ed and Lieutenant Anderson were gathered in the captain's office, drinking beer and shooting the breeze.

'I don't dig Colonel Calhoun,' Anderson said. 'Was his object to break up the Back-to-Africa movement or just to rob them? Was he a man with a cause or just a thief?'

'He's a dedicated man,' Grave Digger said. 'Dedicated to the idea of keeping the black man picking cotton in the South.'

'Yeah, the Colonel thought the Back-to-Africa movement was as sinful and un-American as bolshevism and should be stamped out at any cost,' Coffin Ed added.

'I suppose he thought it was the American thing to do to rob those colored people out of their money,' Anderson said sarcastically.

'Well, ain't it?' Coffin Ed said.

Anderson reddened.

'Hell, you don't know the Colonel,' Grave Digger said pacifyingly. 'He intended to give them back the money if they went south and picked cotton for a year or so. He's a benevolent man.'

Anderson nodded knowingly. 'It figures,' he said. "That's why he hid the money in a bale of cotton. It was a symbol.'

Grave Digger stared at Anderson and then looked over at Coffin Ed. Coffin Ed didn't get it either.

But Grave Digger replied with a straight face, 'I know just what you mean.'

'Anyway it made it easier for me and Digger to find,' Coffin Ed said.

'How?' Anderson asked.

'How?' Coffin Ed echoed. The question threw him.

'Because it was still there,' Grave Digger said, coming to his rescue.

Anderson blinked uncomprehendingly.

Coffin Ed chuckled. 'Damn right,' he said, adding under his breath, 'That throws you too.'

Grave Digger said, 'I'm hungry,' breaking it up.

Mammy Louise had barbecued an opossum especially for them and with the fat yellow meat she served candied yams, collard greens and okra, and left them to themselves to enjoy it.

'It's a damn good thing those southern crackers gave Colonel Calhoun enough money to spend to get us back south or we'd still be looking for the Back-to-Africa loot,' Coffin Ed remarked.

'Be a lot of trouble, anyway,' Grave Digger agreed.

'How you reckon he figured it out?' Coffin Ed asked.

'Hell, man, how you think he was going to miss seeing the bale had been tampered with?' Grave Digger said. 'As much cotton as he's handled in his lifetime.'

'You think we should go after him?'

'Man, we've already recovered the stolen money. How're we going to explain another eighty-seven grand?'

'Anyway, let's find out where he's gone.'

Two days later they got a verification from *Air France* that they had flown a very old colored man with a passport issued to Cotton Bud of New York City by way of Paris to Dakar.

They wired the prefecture in Dakar:

WHAT DO YOU HAVE ON OLD COTTON HEADED U.S. NEGRO . . . NEW YORK TO DAKAR BY AIR FRANCE . . . Jones, Harlem Precinct, New York City.

SENSATIONAL STUPENDOUS INCROYABLE . . . M. COTTON

HEADED BUD BUYS 500 CATTLE HIRES 6 HERDSMEN 2 GUIDES 1 WITCH DOCTEUR . . . TOOK TO THE BRUSH . . . WOMEN FAINTED . . . THREW SELVES INTO SEA . . . M. le Prefect, Dakar.

FOR MILK OR MEAT . . . Jones, Harlem.

MONSIEUR QUELLE QUESTION . . . FOR WIVES WHAT ELSE . . . Prefect, Dakar.

HOW MANY WIVES WILL 500 CATTLE BUY . . . Jones, Harlem.

M. COTTON HEADED BUD ALSO HAS MUCH MONEY . . . M. BUD HAS BOUGHT 100 WIVES OF MOYEN QUALITE . . . NOW SHOPPING FOR BEST . . . WANTS LA MEME NUMERO AS SOLOMAN . . . Prefect, Dakar.

STOP HIM QUICK . . . HE WILL DROP DEAD BEFORE SAMPLING . . . Jones, Harlem.

SHOULD HUSBAND DIE WIVES MAKE BEST MOURNERS . . . Prefect, Dakar.

'Well, at least Uncle Bud got to Africa,' Coffin Ed said.

'Hell, the way that old mother-raper is behaving, he might have come from Africa,' Grave Digger said.

PENGUIN MODERN CLASSICS

ALL SHOT UP
CHESTER HIMES

'Outrageous, shocking, wonderful' *The New York Times*

A golden Cadillac big enough to cross the ocean has been seen sailing along the streets of Harlem. A hit-and-run victim's been hit so hard she got embedded in the wall of a convent. A shootout with three heistmen dressed as cops has left an important politician in a coma – and a lot of money missing. And Grave Digger Jones and Coffin Ed Johnson are the ones who have to piece it all together.

All Shot Up is chaotic, bloody – and completely unforgettable. Chester Himes wrote detective fiction darker, dirtier and more extreme than anyone else dared.

'The greatest find in American crime fiction since Raymond Chandler' *Sunday Times*

PENGUIN MODERN CLASSICS

THE HEAT'S ON
CHESTER HIMES

'The best writer of mayhem yarns since Raymond Chandler' *San Francisco Chronicle*

Detectives Coffin Ed and Grave Digger Jones have lost two criminals. Pinky ran off – but it shouldn't be hard to track down a giant albino in Harlem. Jake the dwarf drug dealer, though, isn't coming back – he died after Grave Digger punched him in the stomach. And the dwarf's death might cost them both their badges. Unless they can track down the cause of all this mayhem – like the African with his throat slit and the dog the size of a lion with an open head wound.

Chester Himes's hardboiled tales of Harlem have a barely contained chaos and a visceral, macabre edge all their own.

With a new Introduction by Noel 'Razor' Smith

'A fantasia with a hard brilliant core' *Evening Standard*

PENGUIN MODERN CLASSICS

A RAGE IN HARLEM
CHESTER HIMES

'The greatest find in American crime fiction since Raymond Chandler' *Sunday Times*

Jackson's woman has found him a foolproof way to make money – a technique for turning ten dollar bills into hundreds. But when the scheme somehow fails, Jackson is left broke, wanted by the police and desperately racing to get back both his money and his loving Imabelle.

The first of Chester Himes's novels featuring the hardboiled Harlem detectives Coffin Ed Johnson and Grave Digger Jones, *A Rage in Harlem* has swagger, brutal humour, lurid violence, a hearse loaded with gold and a conman dressed as a Sister of Mercy.

With a new Introduction by Luc Sante

'He belongs with those great demented realists . . . whose writing pitilessly exposes the ridiculousness of the human condition' Will Self

*Contemporary ... Provocative ... Outrageous ...
Prophetic ... Groundbreaking ... Funny ... Disturbing ...
Different ... Moving ... Revolutionary ... Inspiring ...
Subversive ... Life-changing ...*

What makes a modern classic?

At Penguin Classics our mission has always been to make the best
books ever written available to everyone. And that also means
constantly redefining and refreshing exactly what makes a 'classic'.
That's where Modern Classics come in. Since 1961 they have been an
organic, ever-growing and ever-evolving list of books from the last
hundred (or so) years that we believe will continue to be read over and
over again.

They could be books that have inspired political dissent, such as
Animal Farm. Some, like *Lolita* or *A Clockwork Orange*, may have
caused shock and outrage. Many have led to great films, from *In Cold
Blood* to *One Flew Over the Cuckoo's Nest*. They have broken down
barriers – whether social, sexual, or, in the case of *Ulysses*, the
boundaries of language itself. And they might – like *Goldfinger* or
Scoop – just be pure classic escapism. Whatever the reason, Penguin
Modern Classics continue to inspire, entertain and enlighten millions
of readers everywhere.

'No publisher has had more influence on reading habits than Penguin'
Independent

'Penguins provided a crash course in world literature'
Guardian

The best books ever written

PENGUIN CLASSICS

SINCE 1946

Find out more at www.penguinclassics.com